BEWARE THE HELLHOUND!

This time the scream was the pitch and timbre of a man with both hands caught in a meat grinder: still alive but not, definitely *not* wanting to be. The gaping wound in Bruce's throat opened wider, like a second mouth, to let out the scream.

And the body, somehow still animate despite its near decapitation, convulsed then relaxed, convulsed then relaxed. Something... *something* that was less than solid and more than a gas, was squeezed up from the bloody hole where Bruce's head used to be.

Something...

**St. Martin's Press Mass Market
Titles by John Stchur**

DOWN ON THE FARM
PADDYWHACK

JOHN STCHUR

ST. MARTIN'S PRESS/NEW YORK

St. Martin's Press titles are available at quantity discounts for sales promotions, premiums or fund raising. Special books or book excerpts can also be created to fit specific needs. For information write to special sales manager, St. Martin's Press, 175 Fifth Avenue, New York, N.Y. 10010.

*To Mom and Dad,
For love, sacrifice, and life itself...
And for all those Tarzan books the Christmas of 1960.*

Grateful acknowledgment is extended to Dean Pitchford and Jim Steinman for permission to quote the song "Holding Out for a Hero," copyright © 1984 Ensign Music Corporation. All rights reserved.

PADDYWHACK

Copyright © 1989 by John Stchur.

All rights reserved. No part of this book may be used or reproduced in any manner whatsoever without written permission except in the case of brief quotations embodied in critical articles or reviews. For information address St. Martin's Press, 175 Fifth Avenue, New York, N.Y. 10010.

ISBN: 0-312-91535-7   Can. ISBN: 0-312-91536-5

Printed in the United States of America

First St. Martin's Press mass market edition/May 1989

10 9 8 7 6 5 4 3 2 1

This old man, he played seven,
He played knick knack up to heaven.
Knickknack, paddywhack, give your dog a bone,
This old man came rolling home.

—Old American Folk Song

Prologue

THE GIRL, BAHITTA, WOUND HER TREMULOUS WAY BEtween the mud huts and occasional brick building on the northwest edge of Delhi. Each time she approached a shadowed area she seemed to shrink in on herself. True, she was only twelve, small for her age, and twilight would soon give way to darkness... but the fear that gripped her, that drew her concave belly upward till it cramped against her ribs and caused the skin beneath her white cotton sari to tighten and crawl as if it were alive, was a fear disproportionate to her circumstance. It was a premonitory fear, the fear that something terrible beyond measure was about to happen. She'd felt it all evening.

Then, as her course came parallel with the low, ancient wall whose massive stones prevented the higher ground beyond from spilling over onto this, the lowest level of the city, it became more than that, more than a premonition; her fears were given substance in the form of soft footfalls and a repetitious snuffling sound, as of a large animal breathing. She was being followed.

She increased her speed, wishing, oh *wishing* she'd not stayed so late at her uncle's house, and the sounds, unmistakable now in the otherwise preternatural silence that had descended in the narrow alley—cutting it off from the rest of the world as if it were in a time, a dimension all its own—kept pace with her.

Just her own footsteps and the sounds. And the beating of her heart.

Then they were at head level and on her right, and she knew that whatever manner of beast it was that pursued her must have leaped to the wall. Without looking around to see if it were true, she veered to the opposite side of the narrow alleyway, and immediately the sounds became less distinct.

She breathed easier, but the respite was short-lived.

Up ahead a cart blocked her way, taking the whole of the alley's width save a narrow passage right next to the wall. And no space between the buildings at her left to exit the closed lane, nothing left but to go forward!

Grimly Bahitta did just that, almost as if she were in a trance. Her body moved slowly, ever more slowly, yet her mind raced like the chariot of Rama. It flew from thought to thought, a whirling kaleidoscope of memories, bits of knowledge, desperate plans... and settled on something inane, something her grandmother had said several times in the weeks before she'd died: "When the tiger comes for you, look him in the eye so that he may see if your soul is truly to his liking."

Inane.

She turned and looked toward the wall...

And saw nothing.

For a moment it seemed all her strength had left her, and she sagged against the building, feeling as if her shoulders and backside might actually press through the hard clay of this, some family's dwelling, toward the warmth, security, and companionship that lay beyond. It was a good feeling, one she longed to give herself over to entirely, but the premonition snatched her back and she was again a small girl in a darkening alley. Relieved but still frightened.

She forced herself to move on, toward the narrow

aperture between the cart and the stone wall, because this was the way home, keeping Vishnu the Preserver foremost in her mind. She moved so slowly, it took her close to a minute to cover the fifty feet, and during all that time her eyes never left the wall from whence the sounds had last issued. And that is why she knew, when they began again, that it was Shiva rather than Vishnu whose name should have been a steady cant inside her head. Shiva the Destroyer, god of the darker side. Because there was nothing there. Nothing. The wall supported no living creature, and the bare earth beyond, which was level with its top, offered not the slightest cover.

The sounds grew louder, a scrabbling of claws on stone replacing the softer footfalls of before, the snuffling, blowing sound more urgent now. She stretched out an arm in front of her to ward off the noise. It was all she could do; she could not scream nor run nor even fall back; terror froze all but that single arm.

Her reach extended over the wall and *into* the sound.

For a moment there was silence, nothing happened, and she sucked in a single, hiccuping gulp of air.

Then the invisible, needle-sharp teeth of "nothing" sank into and almost met within the fleshy part of her left palm.

Her father speculated it had been a bat, which, had Bahitta been thinking rationally and objectively, would have made some kind of sense—such a creature could have swooped down from the darkening sky (for what purpose?), bitten and flown away with a speed that to a distraught person might make it seem as if their attacker were invisible. But Bahitta was not rational; she was in a state of panic, terrified beyond her distressed parents' powers to soothe her. And her eyes, her father noted, held the same glazed, staring expression as one already dead. When he looked into them, listened to her pitiful moans, even he doubted it had been a bat. Or any other creature of his experience. He shuddered.

It was her mother's words, spoken on the side and not meant for her ears, that finally pulled her back from the dark, inner cave to which her conscious mind had retreated in an effort to shield her from her own hysteria:

"It is her *left* hand."

Her left hand... that which was unclean according to the beliefs of her caste. And she was left-handed. How often had she forgotten and partaken of food with it?

Which was only natural.

Which was forbidden and a blasphemy.

How many times had she touched herself in her sleep with that hand, especially in the last several months? A number beyond even Parvati, beloved goddess of motherhood's forbearance?

How many times had her rebellious nature grown angry and questioned this, her karma, railed privately at the unfairness of her proclivity for the unclean hand, which made the acts of corruption as difficult to avoid as it would be to keep from blinking?

And now she was being punished, both for her transgressions and for the effrontery of questioning the divine wisdom of which they were part. Even in terror and in suffering there must be order, cause and effect, and so Bahitta clung to this tenuous thread of logic as her only comfort: it was with her left hand that she offended. It was that same hand that made her question her faith. Was it not both just and fitting that Shiva, whom many believed consorted with demons, had sent one of those consorts, invisible perhaps, because he was too terrible to look upon, to punish that same hand? In her desperate need for assurance and comfort she even saw significance and some hope in the fact that he had not forced her to gaze upon her attacker, made him invisible. He was an angry but merciful god. Her wound cleansed and dressed, she gradually drifted into a natural, if fitful, sleep, no longer hysterical, sure the ordeal was over now that she understood and would mend her ways.

Which made the second attack, centered on her right shoulder and neck, enough to permanently damage her twelve-year-old psyche.

It began with the same persistent snuffling sound as before. Close, powerful, like a miniature bellows. A disturbing, evil sound that pulled her struggling, protesting, from her dreams.

She awoke with the glacial breath of something cold, something with a frigidity whole dimensions beyond the mere absence of heat blowing against her neck. Her bladder instantly voided itself.

Before she could scream or cry out, it began. Needle-sharp teeth seized her neck, causing her to bury her chin against her chest reflexively. Whereupon her right shoulder and her cheek were each bitten several times.

Then the back of her neck was seized, and by now she *was* crying out, screaming, gurgling, whimpering all at once as she rolled first to one side and off her sleeping mat, then to the other.

In a matter of seconds the single kerosene lamp was lit and Raveen, Bahitta's father, stared in horror at his only child as she thrashed about on the dirt floor of their one-room dwelling. Her eyes, already beginning to glaze from the inside, as they had before, turned toward him, caught his own for a moment. She reached out her arm in supplication, and even as he watched, invisible jaws closed around it, just below the elbow. In terror and agony he saw the skin indent in a dozen places, the arm compress, then puncture wounds appear and well blood.

Then he was at her side, seeking to grab and pull off her invisible assailant. His hands encountered nothing, though they swept and brushed repeatedly at each new spot where bite marks appeared.

And when the invisible fiend shifted its attack, when it became clear it had somehow worked its way *beneath* her robes, and she felt its icy breath, then its teeth at her inner thigh, Bahitta's mind retreated for a final time to an inner cave, away from herself, away from reality, and closed, then locked the door.

The attacks continued intermittently throughout the night. Bahitta was beyond much further reaction as new bite marks, each about the size one might expect from a monkey or a small dog, would appear on yet another part of her body. An occasional moan, a shudder... but for the most part quiet.

Living meat.

Her mother, a superstitious woman, was terrified of her, of what was happening, and finally withdrew within herself, though not so perfectly as Bahitta.

Her father was also terrified... terrified *for* her, and he did what he could.

He held her, and the thing that was evil beyond his beliefs within the Hindu religion continued to bite even those parts of the girl his body, his arms shielded.

He took her to the personage he believed most holy in that part of Delhi, and that man both prayed for and bathed Bahitta with water drawn from the Ganges, most sacred of rivers. When the biting continued, he sat back down and prayed and would not further acknowledge their presence.

And finally he took her to the home of a British doctor known to treat the occasional patient not of

British blood, if their case were an unusual one or of sufficient interest. He was able to do no more than the holy man to stop the attacks, though he did much to stem the flow of blood, which by now had so completely soaked her sari that bright red threads of it dripped from the hem.

When the nightmare finally ended, it ended on its own. At approximately four in the morning on that mid-June day in 1910, the final bite marks appeared, a particularly nasty set on the girl's left cheek. Their cause, their source, was never explained. For the rest of Bahitta's life, till she died of cholera in her twenty-seventh year, the attacks never resumed. It wouldn't have mattered, though, at least not to her. The real Bahitta ceased feeling, ceased caring, ceased being a person when she was twelve years old.

Eventually the macabre events of that single, seemingly endless night would fade in people's minds. In all minds except those of the people who actually witnessed the attacks. As the tale was told, then retold, the helpless, *hopeless* terror of the supernatural—and therefore *unstoppable*—would begin to fade. It would be another forty years before a second, almost identical incident would occur, this time in post-war Manila, this time much more fully and formally documented, due to the fact that the mayor, the chief of police, and the chief medical examiner of that Philippine city all were witness to the attacks *as they occurred*. The facts surrounding that second incident are duly summarized in Frank Edwards' interesting and somewhat disturbing book, *Stranger Than Science*.*
But they are just that, facts, the bare bones of what happened, and like Bahitta's story, far enough removed in time and distance from the reality of the

---

*Frank Edwards, *Stranger Than Science*, New York, Lyle Stuart, 1959, pp. 169–171

experience that it would be no more possible to grasp their real horror than it would be to imagine what the gut-watering, hell-on-two-legs monstrosity Tyrannosaurus Rex must have been by merely observing its more corporeal bones in a quiet museum.

Until the whole thing happens again.

In this country.

In a small town in Michigan.

Now.

PART I

Among the Living

"Such an animal! Such an indomitable spirit! That little bull terrier had more spunk, more personality, than any four dogs...!"
   —Dolores Mallory, Blanche Lerille's
      next door neighbor

I

"*I NEED A HERO...!*" BONNIE TYLER'S VOICE WAILED in song from the car radio, with enough emotional power to give anybody goose bumps. *"I'm holding out for a hero till the end of the night! He's gotta be strong, and he's gotta be fast, and he's gotta be fresh from the fight!"* The words, the images they evoked, set off a burning halfway between the back of Jack's throat and a spot just beneath his eyes. A burning that could have easily spread to his tear ducts had he let it.

Damn.

He switched off the radio with the same kind of quick, angry decisiveness his wife, who shot him a pained look of empathy from across the seat, might have used to hang up on an obscene phone caller. The song—the theme from a spy show popular a few years back whose intros had featured a rock-muscled Green Beret type doing incredibly "heroic" things while the music washed over the viewer—had never failed to affect him, make him ache with a certain wistful longing... and a sense of personal failure.

A burning in the aforementioned spot.

All his life Jack had wanted to be a hero. Not necessarily in the danger/risk-taking sense of the word, although that would have been fine, too, but in the sense that he wanted to do great things, larger-than-*life* things. Live life dramatically.

Judy had been his wife for eight years, had known

him for fifteen, and thought she understood. Thus the look when the song just happened to come on the air now. Today. And she did understand. At least about the big things, the big disappointments. The smaller ones were not so apparent, could only be truly appreciated by someone with his own gift for seeing (or was the word *creating*?) the worst in things. This was a biggy though; the irony was all too obvious:

The day he'd been given the lead in the off-Broadway play *Video* had been the biggest, most "heroic" in his life. The fact that the management had insisted upon total commitment, which meant leaving his relatively secure, not unpleasant position in the acquisitions department at the mid-Manhattan branch of the New York Public Library, had made it all the more dramatic. But the play had folded after only a week, the critics resting most of the blame with his own and the female lead's performances, and suddenly it had been impossible for him to land even a small part. *Anywhere*. Or to get his job back with the NYPL.

And now here they were, driving along I-94 on their way to minuscule Granger, Michigan, the midwest equivalent of Mayberry RFD, to take up residence

(Free residence. Don't forget rent-FREE. A chance to escape, rethink, regroup...)

with his seventy-year-old, never-been-married aunt, and her dog, a pug-faced, bulgy-eyed bullterrier, whom she talked to—and about—incessantly. So that he, Jack Lerille, could begin his new job, his new *identity*, as librarian of the one-room Granger Public Library.

And "Holding Out For a Hero" comes on the air.

The thought occurred to Jack that the timing was not entirely right, though, not the way it would have been if this were a movie. In the film version the song would play just as they pulled into town. Or maybe as they paused in front of the tiny library, housed in what

PADDYWHACK 13

used to be a Ben Franklin department store. More dramatic that way. Even in his unfulfilled state he failed to reach the intensity of emotion of which more heroic, more meaningful lives were made. Which was par for the course, he thought bitterly.

He mumbled as much, but mostly to himself.

Judy laid a hand on his thigh, squeezed. "What?"

He ignored the question—his mind had already moved on. "He's dead, honey."

"Who? John Eric Hexum?"

For a moment the name made no sense at all. Then he saw the connection. "Whoever. The hero she wants in the song. He's dead. There *are* no more heroes, not in my life."

The hand began a slow kneading motion. Its warmth, a living, healing, soothing thing that could better be measured in degrees of caring than in degrees celsius—a warmth that never ceased to amaze him—seemed to permeate his whole leg.

"There are all kinds of heroes, you know."

It was exactly the kind of thing he would have expected her to say, but rather than prove irritating, it made him regret his words. Because she was right, there were all kinds. Like those whose capacity for kindness and unselfish love were of truly heroic proportions:

The room was painted a drab institutional green. Bleak, sterile, its focal point was a wall clock eighteen inches in diameter—he'd had plenty of time to decide it must be eighteen—that mocked them from the moment they'd wheeled Judy in. The contractions seemed almost continuous now, hitting her like twenty-foot waves of pain. And when they were so bad she could no longer suppress a groan, she'd taken his hand and stroked it—she'd taken his hand, for Christ's sake!—and said, "Oh, honey, I don't want you to see me this way. I don't want you to worry. I'll be okay. Really." He'd wanted to cry.

Or like the product of that labor six years ago, asleep for the moment, in the back seat. Wondrous in her innocence, fearless in her optimism, Rachel would be just like her mother. In everything. The kind of child that had him asking over and over again how anyone so special could be a product of himself. Already she was a *physical* copy, in miniature, of Judy, with her silky blue-black hair and dark eyed, happy-mouthed femininity. . . .

Jack mentally squared his shoulders and resolved to try his hardest to be the kind of husband and father they both deserved. They drove on in silence.

Outside, the drab regularity of the farmlands between Ann Arbor and Jackson spun by beneath a gray, listless sky, and as they turned off at the Granger exit, it began to drizzle one of those slow, off-and-on, November in the Great Lakes State drizzles that smeared and dirtied your windshield but failed to wet it enough for your wipers to work properly. Just as they entered town—as they passed the city-limits sign, in fact—the sky opened up in earnest and, for approximately sixty seconds, pelted everything in a deluge.

The cloudburst's timing did not go unappreciated. "Ah, for the melodramatic, even the portentous!" Jack expounded in a not-so-bad imitation of W. C. Fields.

The fact that a smallish, short-haired mongrel stood stiff-legged just beyond the sign, with its head bowed in patient misery against the rain, and that it seemed to follow them with its stare as they went by, was something he wouldn't remember or place any significance in till later. About two months in hell later.

* * *

The old woman raised the delicate porcelain cup to her lips, grasping its tiny handle between thumb and forefinger, and sipped at her tea. Between the same fingers of her other hand and directly beneath the cup, she held an equally delicate saucer.

"Are you sure you won't have some, Bruce?" she said. "It might help you to relax."

Bruce didn't answer; he just stared at her from across the narrow room, looking urbane, grinning the same half-amused, half-tolerant grin she usually found so irresistibly handsome. But today it held no magic; today she knew that beneath the facade her dear, sweet Bruce was genuinely frightened.

"I could put some—" she started to say, then cut herself short. She'd been about to offer to add some brandy to the drink but thought better of it. Bruce was all male, to be sure, and had the usual masculine fondness for alcohol, but it wouldn't do to even suggest that that was the proper way to deal with one's insecurities. Besides, it wouldn't be proper for him to greet their guests with liquor on his breath.

Bruce licked his lips and swallowed. It was obvious he'd guessed what she'd been about to say, but he was much too proper to suggest it himself. No doubt he knew as well as she that now was not the time. She admired his restraint.

"We could talk about it, you know. Sometimes it helps to vocalize your fears."

The poor dear's eyes filled with reproach, and she was reminded they'd just spent the entire last night and into the wee hours of the morning doing that very thing. It had been hard for Bruce, whose family resided in a taciturn seacoast village in Maine and simply did not open up to each other... hard for him to admit he sometimes regarded himself as something less than a man, and that he feared that her nephew, who was coming to live with them, might recognize this in him and disapprove of the love she and Bruce shared.

They both were silent for a while then, she a woman in her early seventies with her face too heavily made-up, her blue-gray hair, and a body withered from lack of anything more vigorous in the way of exercise than dusting and fixing their meals... and Bruce. Bruce, so sturdy, so quietly strong and marvelously endowed, still in the prime of his years...

"You'll grow to like them. I just know you will," she said by way of broaching the subject again.

Bruce only stared at her, a bit poutily, it seemed.

"The child, you'll like the child..." Her voice drifted off, and she appeared flustered. A blush crept up her neck, making it impossible to discern where the heavy layer of Blossom Pink rouge left off and her natural coloring began. "I, uh—I do believe we'll never have one of our own."

Bruce cocked his head sideways now and feigned a bewildered, puzzled expression. Which was extremely ungallant; she knew he understood perfectly well what the statement had cost her, what with their age difference and... everything else.

In exasperation she said, "Well, say *something*. Let me know you'll at least try to accept them."

Bruce responded in a way so rude and out of character it nearly broke her heart; a method of communicating his dislike he'd promised he would never use again... and hadn't for close to five years. He stood up, circled around several times on the cushion of the davenport where he'd been sitting, then lifted his right hind leg and peed.

To Jack the notion that any locale might truly have "stood still in time" was an appealing one, bringing to mind all sorts of pleasant, even nostalgic associations. Granger was the single exception. It hadn't changed,

PADDYWHACK 17

but it hadn't changed in the same way petrified trees or fossilized beetles frozen in amber don't change. It wasn't a healthy constancy but one imposed upon it by virtue of its abandonment in the hearts of men.

Jesus, he thought as they drove at a snail's pace along Granger's deserted main street, imaginatively dubbed "Main Street," *I've read one too many Dickens novels.*

But it was true. The men's and boy's clothing store on their right featured a single, youth-size mannequin and nothing else in its entire dozen-odd feet of display window. The plastic dummy was dressed in the same flared jeans and lemon-yellow sweatshirt as when Jack had last visited Granger. Five years ago. He remembered the sweatshirt very well. And a little farther up the street, the red, thirty-inch letters above the south side of the local movie theater's marquee still spelled out: AD MS HE TER. From the north, Jack noted as they drove by, it did slightly better, reading: A AMS THEATER.

The only sign of movement along the entire way was a woman in heels just now exiting the Fidelity Trust Building a half block ahead, and there was something about the way she quick-stepped diagonally across the street without looking either way that reminded Jack of an ant scurrying about on the body of a corpse.

Ant. Aunt. Aunt Blanche, and Granger was . . .

But the thing that clinched it, that spoke volumes to Jack about where it was at in Granger and made something inside him coil around itself and pull tight, was a small thing really. Innocuous. There was an IGA grocery on the corner of Main and Romeo (Romeo Road was the northernmost of Granger's three principal cross streets, and the one his aunt lived on), and as they turned, an advertising poster in the bottom-left corner of its window caught his eye.

Faded, incredibly worn-looking even at a distance, it featured a grinning, apple-cheeked caricature of a boy (man? imp? *satyr?*) with red hair and freckles, holding aloft a Hostess cupcake in one hand, a Hostess fruit pie in the other, while a clown named Clarabell and a man named Buffalo Bob beamed their approval in the background.

(What time is it boys and girls?)

Apparently in Granger it was...

II

SOMETHING ABOUT HIS EYES... THEY SHOULD HAVE been able to see more than they were seeing. It made him feel insecure, vulnerable. Something...

But he couldn't quite pin it down.

"We're proud of what we've done here, Jack," the voice boomed.

A hand thumped him between the shoulder blades. It didn't hurt, but he didn't like the hollow-log sound it produced; it made him uneasy.

"Expect you to feel that way too."

The hand suddenly became visible within his limited field of vision, reaching for what seemed an impossible distance in front of him with an enormous key. *(Why couldn't he see the man, then?)* The key fit a lock in a massive double door of some heavy, darkly-polished wood. Mahogany. Yes, it was mahogany, and Jack sensed rather than saw that the doors rose to a towering height.

PADDYWHACK

The key turned. The man was saying something else in his boomy, echoey voice, something like: "...be happy here...Granger Public Library, your new home." And he couldn't see anything of the speaker but his arm. Damnit, why couldn't he see his face? It was like viewing everything through a six-inch piece of stovepipe.

He forced his head, then his whole body to turn—it was like trying to move, to run away in a nightmare—and finally he saw. The man was a prominent critic who'd sat in the front row on opening night. No, it was his father, and he had the face of Jonathan Winters. The face looked down at him with a mixture of puzzlement and disapproval, and suddenly he knew why he couldn't see properly, what had happened to his peripheral vision:

It was his own hands, cupped to the sides of his face and partly covering his eyes, that limited his field of vision. He was hiding behind them, peeking around them like a child viewing a scary movie!

Jack groaned aloud in his sleep, and the sound of his own voice awakened him.

In the room below, a lone voice droned on. It was his aunt's room; somehow, even in the momentary panic and confusion of being snatched from his dream to the unfamiliarity of a strange bed in a strange room, that fact impressed itself upon his consciousness. It was two A.M.

He lay there for a few minutes, allowing the deep and regular breathing of his wife next to him to wash over him and soothe his shaken nerves. God, what a dream! Is that the way it would be with his new job, emotionally if not in point of fact? And what had his subconscious placed beyond those doors? Something bad, something...

The voice continued in the room beneath them, and that part of Jack's mind which had so quickly identified the *where* now tugged on his cerebral coat sleeve and told him this was NOT RIGHT, this was WRONG. It was the middle of the night, Judy lay next to him, and there were no other "house guests," as Aunt Blanche preferred to call them. (It's so nice to have house guests again. Bruce and I are so excited ...) And, though he could not identify the voice, or voices, or catch what was being said, both its unbroken pattern and its purposeful tone made him sure he was not listening to the random mumblings of someone talking in their sleep.

Then who?

His first thought was of Rachel. Could she have awakened in the night and somehow decided to pay a visit to her great-aunt's room? It seemed unlikely; she'd only been eighteen months old the last time they'd been here, and while Rachel wasn't exactly a shy girl, she certainly wouldn't feel she knew the woman well enough to—

(Then who?)

The possibility that some intruder had broken in, accidentally wandered into his aunt's room, and that even now the latter was bargaining for her life, hit him with all the visceral effect of falling off a building. He pulled back the feather comforter, sat up and very quietly swung his feet to the floor, more out of a sense of duty than from an excess of courage. The bare, painted floorboards were cold, and he could feel their individual warps and textures as he made his way to the bedroom doorway, which opened onto a minuscule five-by-five landing at the head of the stairs.

His aunt's was a small house, an old Cape Cod, with room beneath its shingles for only two upstairs rooms—that which he and Judy occupied and another directly across the landing, which was Rachel's. Rather than cross the narrow space and peer in,

PADDYWHACK 21

he reached back for his robe and began to descend the stairs.

The second step from the bottom groaned under his weight in a staccato protest that, in his raw-nerved condition, seemed only slightly less noisy than machine-gun fire.

The voice in the room below grew silent.

It remained that way for a duration very closely matching the maximum amount of time Jack could hold his breath, then resumed. He stood poised in mid-step for at least thirty seconds more, then descended the rest of the way.

The stairs faced the front entrance to the house. To their left was the living room. Another left would bring one to the kitchen, which was the room his aunt's bedroom opened onto. Feeling an inordinately paranoid level of guilt at sneaking around someone else's home in the middle of the night, Jack entered the first of those rooms.

It was bathed in moonlight, a cold, silver-gray luminescence that leeched the color from everything it touched and made the sofa and chairs appear as if they might have just ceased moving the millisecond before your eyes fully rested on them.

Outside it would be even worse, the kind of dead brightness that allowed you to pick out the individual blades (*like miniature stilettos*) of grass on the front lawn. The kind of false light a prepubescent Jack Lerille used to stare at from his bedroom window, convinced that someone (*God? the Devil?*) hoped to trick him into believing it was daytime so he would come out (*all alone*) and play... Some urge, some "calling" pulled at him to cross over to the picture window and see if it were still that way. It carried with it a dread fascination almost equal to that of the nocturnal voice, still conversing (*with whom?*) two rooms away.

Almost.

Careful not to make a sound, he crossed to the doorway between living room and kitchen and listened:

"Of course you're more important to me," his aunt's very precise, very carefully modulated voice said. "I'd ask them to leave in a minute if I believed —" (momentary silence) "What? No, you can't *mean* that."

There was a more lengthy silence, and Jack strained forward, listening for—no, *hoping* for— even the whisper of a second voice. All he could hear was the rustle of his own breathing. That and the voiceless rhetoric of his brain, saying, *She's crazy, Jack. Insane. Too many years alone, no one to talk to*... A frozen scene from *Psycho*, with Tony Perkins dressed as an old woman, knife raised over his head as the music went *skree, skree, SKREE*, flashed in his head. Only it wasn't Perkins, it was an old woman, it was—

"It grieves me to hear you say those things," she went on. "How can you be like that? We have forever; have you forgotten our vows? The ceremony...?"

He breathed a small sigh of relief at hearing her voice again. At least he could be reasonably sure of her location as long as she kept talking.

He waited.

No one answered.

He would have been surprised if someone had. But he had to be sure, had to *know* there was no one there to plan his next step....

He moved quietly into the kitchen. From there he could see the doorway to her room. It stood partway open, and he could see...

Something inside him turned to ice in that instant; the moment itself seemed frozen, as if its not-yet-grasped significance were something too awful and too pivotal in all their lives to be confined within the normal limits of time.

Why should it be so much worse that it was the animal she'd been speaking to? Bruce. Bruce the bug-eyed. Bruce the Boston bull, sitting patiently at the foot of the bed, staring raptly at his aunt, whom Jack could not see from where he stood, as if he actually understood what she said. As if he might answer.

And why did cold sweat trickle from beneath his robe and his balls pull tight in reflex when that *in*human, dog-lecher of a face slowly turned and stared, so knowingly, directly at him? *As if it had been waiting for him to come.*

III

SOMETIMES, WHEN SHE WOULD LOOK AT BRUCE, AT how virile and handsome he was, the years would slip away, and 1946 would seem like yesterday. *Yesterday...*

Blanche Lerille made an effort to tear her eyes from Bruce's magnificent, oh, so masculine form. A feeble effort. Then she gave up even that, because it was happening again, just like it happened every night, and there was really no way to resist it. They would be talking, Bruce and she, and she would start noticing things, little things...like the way the muscles in his shoulders moved beneath the skin each time he shifted positions. Or the clearness of his eyes, the way they focused so unwaveringly on her and her alone. And then his shape, his visage, would shift and change, though his essence would remain the same. And that's what frightened her at times—that even after all these years, beneath the skin he was still the same....

Tonight, the first time he'd humiliated her publicly drifted up from the past, then was here in its entirety. All she had to do was continue to stare at him, and he—no, Bruce *Holmes*—was there, at the foot of her—

No, they were at a dinner, a public dinner in honor of the town's having just completed construction on a new high school. It was forty-odd years ago, and Bruce C. Holmes was sitting across the table from her, smiling in her direction with lips that were sensuous yet thin and cruel. Bruce Holmes. Her lover. Who had stayed on in Belgium, then France, an extra year after the war was ended and had learned things in the back streets and brothels there that she had never dreamed of...

"Do it," he'd urged her earlier, on the way over and then again as they were hanging up their coats. "I need to know you care at least that much. Let them know." And, oh, God, he'd been so handsome, with his jet-black hair combed straight back and his steely-blue eyes. And she had been so naive... And plain. And thirty years old. She couldn't lose him. Couldn't. There would never be another man like Bruce Holmes for a girl like her. It was as unlikely, as impossible, as were she to expect Cary Grant to come walking down the street, see her, and fall in love....

He was nodding at her now, from across the table, in that peculiar stiff-necked way he had. One eyebrow was raised. Was it a signal? Did he want her to do it now?

clink-clink-clink-clink
(No!)

PADDYWHACK

Even as she struck the water glass with her spoon a fourth and final time, she could feel the heat of embarrassment creep from her neck, up past her cheek, and finally into her hairline. She was completely scarlet by now, and yet she rose slowly, reluctantly, to her feet anyway. The hall, with its three long tables lined with townspeople, lapsed into polite but uneasy silence. Or maybe not so polite; the women closest to her—all of them prettier than she could ever hope to be—seemed to be watching her with the same amused, disdainful expression they might also have worn if a vagrant off the street had laid his hat down as they passed by and danced a shuffle step or two in hopes of a coin.

"I...I have an announcement to make," she stammered. The silence, already complete, now intensified in some living, ominous way, so that it was an entity all its own, turning now on soundless feet to stare at her along with the crowd. "I'm in love. I am in love with this man." She pointed to Bruce Holmes. "So ...I'll...no longer be seeing other men s-socially."

She promptly sat down. The silence continued to stare at her, and she could feel both its pity and its amusement. Then someone snickered. No longer see other men? She'd not seen any in the first place! No young man had ever come calling on plain, straight-figured Blanche Lerille, and she could see the dumb, pathetic humor in what she'd just said. She could have died with embarrassment in that moment; and then, before it could be prolonged into something that left scars, someone clapped their hands together. Once. Twice. Three times...They were big hands, solid hands, belonging to Henry Mallory, who, at twenty-one, was as perceptive and kind as he was strong, and she was thankful for them because now everyone was joining in, applauding, and the moment passed.

For them. But not for her. Because Bruce Holmes's smile had turned into a frozen glare. A look of mortification. Then he stood, very stiffly, and strode from the room.

A tiny piece of her did die then. A piece of her self-respect. Or, perhaps more accurately, a "layer." Self-worth, self-respect, is laid down in layers, so that it envelops our entire psyche, and it is sloughed off in exactly the same way. Layer by layer. And each layer gone leaves us more vulnerable, more unbalanced. Blanche felt very vulnerable indeed with this, one of her outer layers, gone. She also felt flustered, confused, humiliated. After suffering the sympathetic (and not so sympathetic) stares of those closest at her table for more than a whole minute, she got up and followed in Holmes's path.

He was waiting for her in the coatroom.

"Where was your head tonight?" He spat the words out, all venom and disgust, through lips that held an unlit cigarette. Then he struck a match, viciously, and just before he touched it to the Lucky's tip, it illuminated his face in such a way that it highlighted his cheekbones, made him look even more like a handsome, petulant prince. "My God, sometimes you're so... provincial!"

Blanche Lerille wasn't even completely sure what the word meant. But she was sure it was something she didn't want to be—and *would* be without Bruce Holmes. And panic set in on top of the humiliation. "But... but you said for me to—"

"To let them know, in subtle ways, that you belong to me now, not stand up and announce it like a... a toastmaster! You made yourself into a fool, and *me* to look like I'd put you up to it!"

"But... but you did! You said, 'Tell them—'"

"Shut up, Blanche! Everytime you open your mouth, your ignorance leaps out at me like bad breath!" He said it loudly. Anyone nearby might have heard, and it filled her with shame that she wasn't even made angry. She just ... could not ... lose him.

"We'll go home now," he continued in a quieter voice, "and do what you do best." He chuckled. "Some people are just not adept at thinking on their feet. You, my dear Blanche, merely go them one better. Your flashes of brilliance—should you have any —will all, without exception, be limited to the horizontal." Then he leaned close and, in a manner that somehow still seemed gallant despite what he'd said, kissed her cheek. "Screw the screw-up," he murmured with his lips still close to her cheek. "I forgive you. Screw the screw-up, screw the people of Granger, and ... screw you. With enthusiasm. When we get home. The whole ... night ... long!"

He took her by the arm then, and guided her from the coatroom and out the front door; and, though she hated herself for it, already she could feel herself becoming wet. Because, *damn* him, the last was no idle boast.

IV

THE FIRST THING JACK FELT UPON AWAKENING THE next morning was amazement that it *was* morning, that it was sunshine and not the cold, dispassionate light of the moon that filtered in through the single, dormer-style window in their bedroom. Last night, after returning upstairs, he'd been sure his being able to fall back to sleep was out of the question.

His next thought, almost immediate upon the first, was a question, the same that had played over and over in his mind last night before sleep had so mercifully claimed him: Had his aunt been aware of his presence just outside her room, and, if so, how might she react?

She knows. Bruce probably told her.

The intended levity fell flat, the way a facetious remark about ghosts or restless spirits has a way of never seeming quite so clever or self-bracing late at night when the wind blows.

(Too close to the truth)
Bullshit.

If she did know, there'd been no indication of it. She'd gone on with her bizarre, one-sided conversation as Jack had backed noiselessly from the kitchen. And Bruce had turned back toward his *(confidant? paramour?)* master. It wasn't until around three in the morning, long after he'd returned to bed, that the talking had ceased altogether.

He arose slowly, marveling, not for the first time, at the way emotional stress had a way of manifesting itself in physical aches and pains, and, like a man twice his thirty-four years, shuffled across the room to where his clothes lay draped over an as yet unpacked suitcase.

It wasn't until he was most of the way dressed and happened to glance at the time, 10:14, that he was reminded he had another reason for feeling like he'd just been used for a tackling dummy by the Detroit Lions. The dream. He had one thing to be thankful for anyway—today was Saturday; he didn't have to face the reality of Granger Public Library for another forty-eight hours.

He tried to leave it at that, not think about any of it

any further. But despite his best efforts, the nagging half-thought that it was all related somehow—the dream and his aunt's nighttime monologue—kept forming, re-forming, then dissolving at the furthest edges of his consciousness.

Judy was just coming in the side entrance from outdoors as he entered the kitchen downstairs. She set a small bag of groceries on the table.

"Hi," she said with affected sunniness. "Got you some milk and some bran flakes."

But he could tell from the way she avoided his eyes that his preference in cereals had been only marginally responsible for the early morning run to the IGA; it was more a matter of her not wanting to be alone in the kitchen, or any other room, with his aunt, who, last time they'd been here, had tended to react to even a momentary lull in conversation with such a distressed, panic-stricken look of personal failure that they'd both had indigestion the entire three days from swallowing their meals half chewed so as not to miss a beat.

(My God, what are we doing here?)

"I have milk. It's on the refrigerator door." His aunt stood at the door to her bedroom; she must have been there when he came in, though he couldn't imagine not noticing.

Judy flushed and looked to him for support.

"We know," he said, "but it's skim and I've never been able to get used to skim milk on cereal. Sorry, I should."

His aunt openly studied him for a moment, then Judy. "Oh."

Oh? Just... *oh*? Things had definitely changed. Five years ago she would have lacked the self-confidence for so noncommittal a reply; everything she'd said back then seemed to require prefacing, explaining... justification. Confidence, yes, that was it. He'd sensed a difference with her last evening when they'd arrived, but hadn't been able to put his finger on it. She *had* been a person whose life, insofar as it related to others, was one continuous apology. Somewhere along the way she'd managed to pick up a little self-worth *(was it self-worth that had her conversing with dogs?)*; he could sense it. It reminded him of another relative, a once-shy cousin, and the change that had taken place once she'd married...

He was pulled back to the moment as she walked to the cupboards, still uncharacteristically silent, and removed three bowls. These she set on the table, along with a box of Life cereal, two spoons, and the skim milk from the refrigerator door.

Judy and he exchanged worried glances as his aunt poured some of *her* cereal, then *her* milk, into one of the bowls, especially when she broke what would have formerly been considered an appallingly long stretch of time with no conversation by saying, "Don't wait for me; I had breakfast earlier, with Rachel."

They both relaxed some when, after a lengthy pause, she added, "This is for Bruce."

But she didn't set it on the floor. Instead she adjusted the chair on that side of the tiny, four-by-four table, pulled it out just enough so that—

"BRUCE?" Her voice rose an octave, quavered there; it was like listening to an inept yodel. "BRUCE DEARRRR... BREAKFASSSTT!"

Jack began to feel nervous.

There was the slide-tap, slide-tap of claws scrabbling on linoleum, and the ugly bullterrier appeared on cue, as if he'd been waiting in the wings. He scrambled up onto the chair, put his front paws on the table, and without

PADDYWHACK

(what? without WHAT? Uttering a word...? Saying grace...? Christ, Jack...)

pause, began lapping up squares of cereal and milk with a pink tongue that seemed impossibly long to fit inside his pinched-together, foreshortened face.

Judy looked as if she were going to be ill.

"I think it's so...so *prejudicial* to make anyone dine on the floor because they're...*short*," his aunt observed breezily. "Don't you?"

Neither of them answered. Judy was still too dumbstruck to speak. And Jack's attention was given wholly to the dog, the beast who, in timing with Blanche's remark, slowly raised his bulged-out eyes even as his head remained bent to the dish and regarded him with the same knowing, *measuring* stare he'd cast Jack's way in the middle of the night.

He was twenty pounds of muscle, sinew, and bone. Though he'd never done anything more strenuous than an occasional mad dash at a squirrel or the neighbor's cat, the rocklike density of his pectorals and deltoids bunched and played beneath the short hairs of his coat with the ultra-lean definition of a Mr. Olympia contestant. He was a natural, a canine super-athlete whose body was a steel spring. And right now all of it quivered with anticipation.

The little girl's hand shot out; the flesh and blood spring was released, and the black and white body streaked across the rug, launching itself three times its own height into the air, ripping the toy from its trajectory rather than catching it. It was in the shape of a rat, solid rubber, and had it been real, the pressure from the bullterrier's jaws would have crushed its spine like an overdone french fry.

Rachel giggled—as much as a result of nervous tension as from delight. Bruce's face, all pinched and growling (playfully?) from around the toy in his jaws looked so much like something from *Gremlins,* the scariest movie Mommy had ever allowed her to see. She considered stopping the game. She didn't want nightmares; *Gremlins* had given her nightmares....

But there was something about the animal, the power in him, in the *game*, that fascinated her. She crossed the room, reached for and took hold of the rat's rubber tail with the same heart-in-throat, will-power-over-fear determination she'd had to muster the time Daddy pushed her forward last year at the circus when the man had said, "Who'd like to touch Mr. Elephant's trunk?"

"Let go," she said when he growled and chomped down tighter. "Let go, Brucey." She said it with the perfect faith her command would be obeyed that only a child, and those unfamiliar with the breed's tenacity once they've clamped onto something, can possess. It never occurred to her that he might choose not to, or that he might not understand.

But Bruce did understand, and because the little girl was the only one of the visitors he did not resent, he let go. The words meant nothing, since he had never been played with in so typically a *doglike* fashion; but their meaning was clear. Had Rachel said "Hide," or "Chase the car," or "Bite," or "Kill him," with equal conviction, with an equally strong projection of her thoughts in what could only be called a "mind picture," he would have understood as well, though any and all of those commands would have been just as unfamiliar. Because Bruce's nonhuman mind sidestepped, or, perhaps, *vaulted beyond* the verbal; his mind grasped *concepts*...if the mind in which the concept was born was able to envision it with the right kind of clarity.

Like many children and few adults—because the latter become too proficient with *words*—Rachel had that kind of ability, all unknowing.

Her great-aunt had it, too, only *she* knew.

Rachel withdrew the toy rat from Bruce's mouth and held it out at shoulder height by its tail. "Jump!" she ordered, enamored, of a sudden, with the power of command.

Bruce launched himself into the air and plucked the toy delicately from her fingers as if it were an hors d'oeuvre.

Her father came into the room. Anxious to impress, she bid Bruce let go again, and this time she held the rubber rat as high as she was able. "Jump!" she commanded again, and Bruce captured the prize with ease.

Jack was impressed, not so much with his daughter's skill as a trainer of animals, as with the fact that said animal had just cleared the floor by a height approximately the equivalent, in terms of explosion and lift, of a human being high jumping ten feet. Forever an awed, an envious admirer of truly superlative physical performance, no matter its source, it made him wonder what the dog's limits were. Last night's and today's secret foreboding concerning the animal were momentarily forgotten in his enthusiasm.

"Here, let me try that," he said. "Let's see how high he can go."

Wordlessly, but not without a flicker of both disappointment and rebellion in her eye, Rachel handed the toy rat over. Jack looped the tail once around his index finger then held the thing about five and a half feet from the floor. Even standing on his hind feet the dog couldn't have been more than thirty inches tall.

"Jump," he commanded.

Bruce didn't even glance in the proffered toy's direction.

"Jump," he repeated.

Nothing.

"Jump, Brucey," Rachel's voice pleaded, and instantly the animal was aquiver with suppressed energy. Like a human athlete, he backed off a few steps, gathered himself, and shot forward, then up. He seemed to hang in the air, just short of the toy. Then he had it somehow, and Jack's arm was yanked downward.

What it was, exactly, that made him fight against that pull, he couldn't even guess, but suddenly it was very important that he not allow the rat to be torn from his grip. He steeled his arm and shoulder, and, despite a straining sensation along his entire deltoid, managed to stop both the toy and the dog's descent just short of the latter's hind feet reaching the floor. Bruce hung suspended by his teeth, bobbing just a bit as the rubber tail stretched then contracted against the pull, threatening to break.

A continuous, low-pitched growl, malevolent, challenging, rumbled from somewhere deep in his throat.

"Let go," Jack commanded, and was surprised at the noticeable degree of shakiness in his voice.

The dog responded by adjusting his hold, gathering more of the toy into his mouth, so that he was practically gagging on it, in one lightning-quick lunge . . . *as he hung still suspended!*

"Let GO!"

Bruce rolled his eyes and snarled some more.

Rachel echoed the command, and still no result. By now the finger around which the rubber tail was wrapped was being cut to the point of breaking through the skin.

And the rat's head had to be partway down Bruce's throat; he had to be choking on it.

Something dark inside Jack's mind took satisfaction in that fact (*little fucker can choke to death*). That same rage/loathing made him want to sling the little troll-in-the-shape-of-a-dog sideways like a pendulum and smash him against the wall. Part of that feeling, he knew, stemmed from the knowledge that even if he'd done that—battered the animal half to death, in fact—Bruce would have hung on; it was in his breeding—they never let go

(of an enemy; it's you or him, Jack; one of you has got to go)

their hold unless they can get a better one. Part of it was something more basic than that, though, the same impulse so many people share, which makes it impossible for them to resist a step sideways to smash a spider or a centipede...or a subtle turning of the steering wheel in order to run over a snake in the road. Because they're alien and ugly and *(evil)* something we don't understand.

If Jack could have killed Bruce at that moment and gotten away with it, he would have done so. The psychic atmosphere in the room fairly crackled with the killing impulse.

Then, from behind him, the single word, not loud, but reproachful beyond measure: *"Bruce!"*

Bruce released the toy instantly and dropped to the floor.

All the anger ebbed from Jack's body in that moment; he was left feeling drained, confused.

The dog trotted from the room quietly, as if nothing had happened.

Jack turned to face his aunt. She was regarding him with the same disappointed, disapproving stare she might have used a generation ago, had she caught him going through his mother's purse for cigarette money. Her eyes shifted to the toy rat still in his hand, and the corners of her mouth turned down even farther, if that were possible.

"How could you bring him something so...so *demeaning*?" she asked in a voice that was softly condemning. "If he were black, would you offer him a loin cloth or...or perhaps a slave collar?" When his mind didn't immediately make the connection, she went on: "He's more than you can see, so...*much* more. Please don't treat him like a...a common *animal*." Then she turned like a drill sergeant and walked stiffly from the room.

V

THEY LAY NEXT TO EACH OTHER—IN BODY—EACH caught up in their own private world of despair. The silences, like this one—once a welcome, shared thing —were frightening to Judy now. They worked at her from the inside, producing a queasy, cramping sensation just below her navel, the result of wondering what *he* was thinking, whether *he* was as depressed as she was.

Why couldn't she make him happy? If he loved her, she should be able to make him happy.

It had been this way even before they left New York. It was as if they had run out of things to say, and the unreasonable fear had grown in her that maybe he was aware of it, too, maybe they were silent so much because he was doing the same as she: questioning the relationship.

Oh, Jack, I couldn't live if—

The *times*, it was just these difficult...*times*. And the day. But whatever it was that was wrong between them, mercilessly turned even that around—somehow the bad times were a result of their relationship

PADDYWHACK 37

rather than vice versa. No. That wasn't true. She replayed the last sixteen hours as a case in point:

They had tried to make light of the incident at breakfast. But when the same thing happened at lunch, and they'd had to watch Bruce work his way through two grilled-cheese sandwiches—cut in dainty, bite-sized pieces—and a bowl of split-pea soup, there'd been no humor in it. The muscles on either side of Jack's jaw had stood out in bold relief, always a reliable barometer of the degree of irritation he felt.

They'd gone out for supper, and probably done a poor job of hiding their relief when his aunt had declined an invitation to accompany them. ("You don't serve dogs here do you?" Jack had asked the waitress in a dry, laconic tone. "Good, because if we ever come in here with someone named Bruce, I want you to make *sure* he doesn't get a menu.") That had broken the mood, and for a little while they were a family again, enjoying being together on a Saturday afternoon. Jack had even agreed with her suggestion that they buy both Blanche and the dog a present at Jowett's hardware/department store on Main.

Then, about an hour after they'd come back, something had happened, and it all turned sour again. She didn't know exactly what; she'd been upstairs at the time, and Jack had refused to discuss it. It was "Nothing, no big deal," but she could tell he was upset again, and she suspected it had to do with the dog.

Bruce... what was it about the terrier that affected them so? Affected *her personally*? It was more than the mixed bag of embarrassment, disgust, and even a little bit of guilt that she, with both a husband and a child to love, felt at observing the way Jack's aunt fussed over him, a mere *animal*. That was normal. It was the other feelings, the *abnormal* ones, the ones that got to her on a deeper level, that had her worried.

Like the fleeting but recurring thought, gone *(or squelched)* each time before it really took shape, that maybe there *was* something to the way the woman acted, maybe Bruce really was more than... other dogs.

Or the way she was so aware of his sexuality. Unlike Jack, who'd been brought up in a suburb of Ann Arbor, she was a country girl, having grown up on the same farm, a single township over, where her parents still lived. She was familiar with animals... yet never had been so constantly, so acutely aware of a creature's maleness. Not even with the stallion her girlfriend used to ride (and there had certainly been a lot there to remind her!). But with Bruce it was a threatening, a *lecherous* sexuality; there was no other word for it. She felt the same way, when he looked at her, as she'd felt as a sixteen-year-old, wading through a sea of grasping, coveting male stares one Saturday night in order to retrieve her father, who had too much to drink, from his bar stool at LaRoy's, the local tavern.

Of course, much of what she felt now might be the result of the way things had been the last time, five years ago. The dog had just been outgrowing his puppy stage then, entering the canine equivalent of puberty, and had had an acute case of satyriasis. He'd tried to have sex with anything and everything in sight. When he wasn't humping—with a machine-gun rapidity that made it even more obscene—against someone's boot or shoe or even a blanket with who-knows-what kind of scent on it, he was dragging himself, belly down, across the living room rug, all moony-eyed and grin-faced, as if he expected people to applaud his efforts. It had disgusted her. It shouldn't have, but it did; and when, on the last day of their visit, he'd suddenly wrapped his forelegs around her ankle, began his convulsive, spastic heaving and looked up at her that way...

She shuddered.

It was at that moment that Jack's hand stole silently beneath her nightgown, rested lovingly on her upper thigh.

(No! Not now! TALK to me! KNOW me! It's—)

She rolled toward him, trapping the hand between his hip and her own. "Hold me?"

He held her without speaking and nuzzled her ear, her cheek. Then he kissed her on the lips, the eyelids, the throat, and with the fingertips of his free hand he traced the hollow of her back, the soft twin mounds of her buttocks... and gradually she relaxed, gradually she was made part of a world where the silences were warm, where there was no such thing as depression, groundless fears, and strained relationships.

And finally, a moment when everything was liquid openness and trust, a desire to sink, to meld into one.

It was good. It would have been perfect had he not paused, just before he entered her, and turned on the tiny bedside lamp.

"I... want to look at you. Just for a minute. You're so... beautiful this way...."

For a moment she'd frozen, vividly clear images of the face—the dog-lecher face as it gaped up at her from around her ankle—flashing on-and-off, on-and-off in her mind's eye with all the intermittent brilliancy of a strobe light. Then she relaxed again, because she understood her man, understood *men,* and opened her legs... to share with him her mystery.

"There's this guy in the movie, see," he'd said to her once, a long time ago. *"He's a high school wrestler—the movie's about wrestling—but that doesn't matter. What matters is that he's eighteen, a virgin, in lust/love with an older girl, and he's studying like*

mad all these books on female... on pelvic anatomy. When his friend asks what for, he proudly announces he's decided to become a gynecologist.

"'Why?' his friend asks.

"'Because I want to understand women. I want to be able to look right up inside them and see what it is, this power they have over me.' All guys feel that way, Judy. It's part of the attraction. Most just won't put it into words...."

After they had made love, the silence was still a warm thing, their friend rather than a soundless lament, and she relished the difference. If only there had been a little more street noise, though—the kind of hustle and bustle that was a constant in New York—they could have ridden the mood the whole way into sleep. But the quiet was very nearly absolute... so they easily heard the muffled tones of her voice when it started up in the bedroom below.

She felt Jack stiffen, and, little by little, she could sense she was losing him again to that other kind of silence.

(It's not just Bruce; it's HER.)

"It's nothing," she said, fighting The Mood. "She's talking in her sleep, that's all."

They both listened for a while, then he answered, and she knew that whatever quiet was to follow would be part of the bad times, the silent brooding: "No, she's not. She's talking to *him*, to *Bruce*. She's crazy, Judy. Fucking, certifiably crazy. And we've got to live with her. With *them*."

"See?" Blanche said with a forced cheeriness. "It wasn't so bad, was it? They left us alone for a little while. Even today. And it'll be better during the week—Jack will be at work, Rachel at school... and July..." She allowed herself a pause—for drama—and turned to smile at Bruce, who lay watching her

PADDYWHACK 41

from where the pillow should have been on his side of the bed. "Judy will be gone too. She's going to substitute teach; she told me today." She positively beamed then, as if this were the most wonderful of surprises.

Bruce regarded her steadily, apparently unaffected by the news. But it had always been so hard to read him; his face was absolutely stoic at times. She was far better off trusting her ... "other" senses. She relaxed and tried to think the way *he* might think.

Ah ...! So that was it?

"The way her certificate reads, she can sub for anything at the secondary and for art and music at the elementary. She'll be called just about every day." She beamed again, pleased, as always, to anticipate his concerns, his misgivings before he was forced to voice them aloud. "And, Bruce, she's going to put her name on the *county* sub list, not just Granger schools...."

This time Bruce crept forward on his belly the necessary few inches to kiss her wetly on the cheek. But it was a kiss of appeasement, his way of apologizing for being less than reassured by the news.

She placed a cupped hand gently, lovingly on either side of his upturned face and kissed him back. "I have another surprise," she breathed softly. "I bought it in Jackson, a week ago." Very slowly, deliberately, she crept from the bed and crossed to her bureau, never allowing her eyes to leave Bruce's own. She felt slightly giddy, her heart racing like a schoolgirl's on prom night. She had planned on waiting with this one —for a time when it would do the most good. But that time was now. He needed to know he was still first in her heart.

"Now ... DON'T LOOK. TURN around."

Instantly Bruce was on his feet, appearing nonplussed. He circled completely around once, then stared aloofly at a point just above the bed's headboard.

Satisfied he would not turn back, Blanche quickly unbuttoned and let fall to the floor the long flannel nightgown that was her usual sleeping attire and, just as quickly, slipped on a pullover lounging robe made from double-layered terry cloth and taken from the bureau's top drawer. It was floor-length, white, and *might* have been attractive by virtue of its very simplicity, but Blanche Lerille was never one to leave well enough alone. Next to the shop where she'd purchased the robe was a sporting-goods store that specialized in team uniforms. And in that store's window was a display of varsity jackets featuring the various sew-on insignias depicting local teams' nicknames. There was an insignia for the Cougars, for the Wildcats, for the Hawks, and for the Bears. And, of course, there was one for the Bulldogs... whose stylized symbol—that of a squashed-in, pugnosed canine face—looked remarkably similar to Bruce's own face, albeit he was, in truth, a *Boston* bull.... She had purchased three of them, one for each oversize pocket and another for the back of the robe, and they looked about as ridiculous and out of place as sweat pants worn with a dinner jacket.

But she didn't know that, or if she did, it didn't matter. All that mattered was that *he* should like it.

"You can turn around now," she said with a tremor in her voice. And perhaps canine aesthetics are different from man's, perhaps more charitable... because when Bruce looked at her, she felt quite lovely.

"Do you like it?"

Bruce assured her that he did by the way his front feet danced a steady tattoo on the bedspread and his pink tongue kept darting out and over his muzzle the way it always did in moments of happy excitement.

Thus encouraged, she decided to go the whole way

toward convincing him that nothing had changed with the arrival of their guests, that her devotion to him was something she took seriously.

"I, uh, know a... 'chaste' relationship like ours is hard, even with*out* other people around to make you jealous. But I do love you, Bruce, and..." She blushed just a little, but made herself look directly into his eyes anyway. "... and I thought tonight might be the perfect time to repeat our vows."

She held her breath, not sure how so "macho" a personality as his might react to the sentimentalism inherent in the suggestion. She needn't have worried; he was touched by it. His eyes alone told her how touched he was, their extra-moist, almost-but-not-quite rheumy appearance more eloquent than any words he might have uttered.

"Come. Let's KNEEL together."

Bruce immediately skittered off the bed and took his place next to her, where she had lowered herself onto the floor near its edge. He sat up doggy-begging style, even placed a paw delicately atop her forearm. The scene *should* have been one to inspire "Awwws" and "Isn't that adorable?" had there been any onlookers. Or at worst, a sense of its ridiculousness. It would have produced neither. What it *would* have produced was a sense of unease, a discomfiting awareness of the unnatural, the very nearly macabre. It had to do with the air of absolute solemnity there, and it would have deepened as they began their vows:

"That we may be one, forever and beyond, we pledge..."

Of course only Blanche spoke them aloud, and, after the first dozen words or so, even her voice shriveled to a whisper barely audible beyond a few feet. But *had* there been any onlookers, any listeners, it would have been the strong feeling, almost a certainty, that Bruce was repeating the vows, too, *inside*

—or at least that he knew full well what was being said—which would have cinched it.

And had they been able to hear all the words, from start to finish, the sense of things not right would have pushed right on through the macabre and entered the realm of the monstrous.

She'd been with him, off and on, for almost a year before he'd caused her to do anything really dirty.

The "off and on" meaning that he left her sometimes. For a day, a week, two weeks...This was 1947, and the really long, really devastating separations wouldn't come till later. But even then it was always her fault. Bruce C. Holmes had a talent for making everything seem as if it were Blanche's fault —and maybe some of it had been; she was never sure. He also had an uncanny talent for coming back just when she needed him most; the very moment between the final collapse of her self-respect and the beginnings of the rebuilding process. Was it planned that way? she often wondered. Because, intentional or not, each time he "came back," he strengthened his hold on her in the same insidious way a boa constrictor uses each gasp for air from its victim to tighten its coils....So that, eventually, she would have done anything for him.

July 14, 1947. Something dirty...

His most recent "departure" had been for ten days and had to do with the inheritance she and her brother had split when both their parents had drowned in a boating accident on Lake St. Clair two months earlier. It was of considerable size, due to the senior Lerille's brilliance as a commodities speculator, and Bruce had claimed she was suggesting, in subtle ways, that he was attempting to get at that fortune through her. She didn't remember saying anything of the kind, but by the time he showed up on her doorstep again, she'd

PADDYWHACK

convinced herself she must have said something; and by the time they were in the bedroom, ten minutes later...and he had her naked and was running his hands over her body at the same time he was telling her how hurt he'd been...she was begging his forgiveness. Through shudders of pure delight.

They were on the bed then, and he was deliciously, achingly inside her. She felt almost whole again, was on the verge of losing herself in another way—and that *would* make her whole—when he said, "Do you ...love me...enough to...share?"

He never broke his rhythm as he said it, and in her near-climactic state, what little portion of her mind still able to reason at all thought he meant the inheritance, sharing the inheritance. "Yes!" she gasped. "Oh, yes!"

"Enough to...share...unques-tioningly?"

"Yes!"

Then he said, in a voice much louder than the soft tones he'd been using, *"Frank,"* and she stiffened.

She stiffened more when she felt the bed sink even lower with the addition of a new and sinister weight ...as she felt somebody else's hand on her thigh.

She might have screamed if she hadn't kept her eyes closed. But she did keep them closed, because if she didn't see, then maybe it wasn't really happening. All she said was, "Oh, Bruce..."

And then she forced herself to shut everything out but the tactile. She was a nonentity, a vessel of flesh, blood, and nerve endings, and she didn't come back within herself until she felt the bed lighten again, and the shameful extra weight was gone. Then, somehow, she found release, with her one true love, and great tears of relief welled behind her lids, that she was only his again, that—

The backlog of tears forced her eyes open. She

screamed. And shoved Frank off of her in a flurry of beating fists and raking claws...

She didn't remember much beyond that point. This strange man, Frank, standing there naked with his hands pressed to his bleeding face. Cursing.

Bruce rushing into the room, dressed in slacks and nothing else, taking in the scene at a glance and then turning on her, face contorted with rage and indignation. "You *slut!*" he boomed in a voice whose richness and depth had always reminded Blanche of what God must sound like. "This was for YOU! It's what you want! If you hadn't been enjoying it so much, I wouldn't have left!" And he'd looked so imposing standing there, so towering—like some sullen but magnificently built, magnificently handsome God-hero off the cover of an Erskine Caldwell novel—that she'd known she could never oppose him.

He was a cruel god at times, but he was *her* god....

The dream again. Part Two of the Welcome to Granger Public Library Your New Home dream. The fun part. The man who is his father with the face of Jonathan Winters pushes open the towering mahogany doors and ushers him inside. Jack can barely suppress a groan of dismay—no, despair; the place is a thousand times worse than he ever could have imagined. It is the lower level, half below ground, of an abandoned barn. Remnants of ancient milking stalls still stand here and there... poking out through what must be a two-foot-deep layer of manure on the floor as old and dry-rotted as the stalls themselves. It is so deep, in fact, that it diminishes the height of the ceiling to the point where walking anywhere in the room is a continuous process of ducking your head to avoid hitting one of the cobwebbed, two-by-twelve joists spaced every eighteen inches. By the light of the single bulb that hangs suspended from a frayed cord in

PADDYWHACK 47

the room's center, he can see that the only concessions made to the room's current use as a library are a desk placed unevenly atop the manure and shelves along the damp stone walls (also slanted at various angles) on which some moldy books, several old sets of encyclopedias, and hundreds of issues of *Farm Journal* rest. As

(oh, Jesus, Dad, all I wanted was to be an actor, be somebody, and—)

he turns to tell the man that this is wrong, that this can't possibly be happening to him, the doors swing shut and he hears the click of a lock, then Jonathan-Winters-Dad's booming voice saying, "I'll come let you out when your workday is over and you've got a better idea of who you are."

He can't talk or

(is that so bad, to want to be *somebody? Huh? Christ, I can't—)*

go to the door to pound on it; he's afraid he'll sink in the manure—all the way—even though a moment ago it was dry, and probably still is.

And it's cold, the dampish cold of an unheated cellar in November. He goes to the desk (not sinking after all) and sits down at it, staring around him in the same way a condemned man must stare at the details, the bare walls inside the gas chamber, and there is an overwhelming sense of sadness and defeat, of a lifetime thrown away for nothing. He is not the man condemned to die, after all, but the man condemned to a life he cannot endure.

Then, finally, another emotion. Fear? Curiosity? *Hope?* His blank-staring eyes gradually make connection again with his numbed mind, and he becomes aware that some of the shelves are much deeper than they originally appeared. And there are other, more meaningful *(treasures? ANSWERS?)* books behind the moldy first row. He gets up and crosses the room, drawn to find out, yet afraid. It is the same mix of expectancy and apprehension with which one might open a buried chest—one large enough to hold either a fortune or a skeleton...

As in a dream within a dream his hand reaches out, reaches into and beyond the shelf, up to his armpit, and he feels

(a face!)

something grab his wrist. Something with teeth. Something powerful and evil. He screams, tries to pull free but cannot, and the thing goes to work on his wrist in earnest now, with all the efficiency of a meat grinder. There is a strange absence of pain, yet he can feel, is aware of his wrist, his hand being mutilated beyond saving. At one point he can specifically feel the thing's fangs hook a large tendon on the underside of his wrist and pluck it from the bone till it twang-snaps like a cut piano wire...

And he continues to scream.

The last thing he remembers before waking up in Judy's comforting arms is trying to reach to the back of the shelf with his other hand to fight the thing off ...and encountering nothing but the ruined flesh of his own hand, even as the attacks continue....

VI

SUNDAY WAS A BEAUTIFUL DAY, ONE OF THOSE DAYS in mid-November when the weather takes a two-month leap backward and almost convinces you the date must be closer to Labor Day than Thanksgiving. Almost. But there is something fraudulent about all that sunshine and warmth; it is a cheap copy, insidious somehow, thin... and it can make one uneasy, like a banker's smile. Bruce sensed it, animal fashion, as he was let out the front door and swagger-trotted across the front yard in that peculiar gait of bullterriers that appears bowlegged but isn't. But it affected him differently than it would a human being; it made him feel defensive, aggressive. Put simply, had the stranger messed with Bruce this day, he would have been much more liable to be bitten.

Bruce quickly made the rounds of his territory, pausing only a fraction of a second at various key rocks, trees, and bushes to lift his leg and leave his calling card—an expertly aimed jet of bright yellow, acidic-smelling urine. He was more than halfway done, coming up the west property line toward the front—where he had begun after having scouted the entire backyard—when he caught the Cat's scent. Instantly he froze, and every muscle in his body quivered as if his paws were nailed to the ground while a thousand volts of electricity surged through his body. Then, after a moment, he followed the trail, nose to the ground, to where it led up against *his* house, across *his* Territory. Panic/rage/hate set off flares of bright violet and orange inside his head, and a mother load of adrenaline was dumped into his system. He felt precisely the way a man, a very physically-oriented man, might feel if he were to come home and find his house broken into and in shambles, his most personal effects violated.

As he sniffed about, cognizant by scent alone of just where and for how long the Cat had rubbed up against *his* house, the first blind rage settled into a seething, gut-eating anger. The Cat. He hated, *despised* the slinky, sneaky nightwalker with a primal hate that went back a million years. It was a loathing, an intolerance peculiar to many of his kind, in the same way that such a large portion of mankind loathes snakes. Till now that loathing had been held in check with regard to this particular Cat only because his man-female willed it so. The very first time it had appeared, late that summer, picking its way so boldly across the neighboring yard, he had gone for it, launched himself at it, post haste... but his man-female had called him back. By her tone alone he'd known that she did not approve, and the powerful thought-pictures that had sprung full-blown in his mind had somehow gotten across the idea that, so long as the Cat kept outside *his* territory, it must be left alone. Now, however, it had violated that condition, and no thought-picture, no kind of instruction, told him what he must do; his hate was his only advisor. So he followed the hours-old scent, and when it finally cut back into the neighbor Territory, he did not turn back.

The trail led to a sheltered spot beneath some bushes and up against the neighboring house, and here, judging by the more intense, wider-spread scent, the Cat must have lain for a while. But this

PADDYWHACK 51

stronger scent, this scent from where *more* than just the animal's feet had touched the ground, told Bruce things more interesting than that, things that made him quiver anew, this time with an eager, pitiless kind of joy. The Cat was female, and it was lactating; and though Bruce did not understand all this precisely, the very glandular combination of smells triggered something frenetic and depraved in his mind, something like a blood lust. He went on, trailing faster now, anxious to

(kill, tear, rend)

catch up with the Cat and sink his teeth into its

(BABIES, helpless, mewling ...)

flesh. The trail led to a smaller building behind the house, a building with wide, wide-open doors.

Bruce entered the building. Inside it smelled of oil and tires and cement. And of Cat. And over in one corner was a box, and from the box issued tiny, plaintive mewling sounds. Helpless sounds...

The mother cat was not in at the moment, and to the three, week-old kittens the head and jaws that suddenly loomed over them must have seemed part of a bug-eyed monster. Which was more or less correct, if pure malevolence and a taste for blood are the measure of that word.

Those jaws shot downward now and seized one of the kittens, a gray-and-white female, by the head. They could have closed completely, crushed the baby skull like an egg; instead they tossed both the head and the body it was attached to skyward. The kitten arched through the air and landed on the cement with a sickening plop. Bruce capered around it in a paroxysm of joy. *(Wonderful, fun, HURTING fun!)* And as the kitten crouched there, in the tottering, not-quite-got-my-legs fashion of all very young animals, stunned beyond crying out but by some miracle still alive, Bruce rushed in and seized it again and again tossed it in the air.

This went on again and again, Bruce working himself into a happy-eyed, tongue-lolling frenzy—toss ...*plop*, toss...*NERVELESS plop*—until finally, in his exuberance, he yanked too hard and the tiny head separated from the body. He stood stock-still in amazement, still mouthing his pathetic trophy, looking down at the headless body as if to say, *Why did you do that? This was so much fun.* Then he bit down on the thing's skull, deciding to see if small Cat tasted better than it played. It did not, and he let it fall from his mouth and went back to the box for a less defective replacement.

The second kitten, a gold-striped little girl, was more fortunate; Bruce savaged her with such a gleeful fury that she was dead within seconds, and he learned that *KILL* was almost as much fun as *HURT*.

A black cat, however, is unlucky, and such was the case with the third, a charcoal male. This one was to keep—the rubber rat he never had, the balm whose own pain would soothe something hideous and cruel within himself—and he would allow it to live. At least for a while. As he grabbed it up between his jaws and caper-trotted from the garage, he caught again the muskier scent of its mother, and his truculent doggy-brain was filled with two emotions: One was a resurgence of the hate/loating for the Cat. The other was the blissful, almost to the point of being erotic, feeling he got whenever he closed his mouth down, just a little, on the kitten's soft underbelly and it mewled/cried for its very life. And the former emotion made the latter all the more delicious.

Wriggle Wriggle Worm Free was fun, too, and, once back in *his*, Bruce experimented with variations of this cat-and-mouse game—letting the kitten squirm free of his slack jaws, allowing it to drag itself a few yards away, then grabbing it up again. But it soon became boring, and so he began killing his enemy's baby a little bit at a time.

First he bit down on its hindquarters, hard, crushing its spine just above the hind legs, savoring the feeling of that portion of the body going so suddenly limp. It felt wonderful, much better than Wriggle Free; it was the canine equivalent of crunching down on a Life-Saver after having sucked on it for a long time while thinking of nothing else.

Then he chewed again, a little further up, and the kitten squalled its baby death squall a second time.

He let the half-paralyzed body fall to the ground and studied it. Now only the top half worked, and its pathetic efforts to drag its dead hindquarters away fascinated him; it was mesmerizing...

Consequently, the footsteps approaching up the front walk then off onto the grass, though he heard them, heard how they quickened, didn't register on his brain the way they should have; otherwise he might have been able to avoid the sneaker-clad foot altogether as it pendulumed through the air, accompanied by the bitterly hateful cry of, *"Youlittleshit, I oughtakill—"*

It was the Man, who now lived at *his*, and despite his lightning reflexes, the kick caught him a glancing blow. And in that moment it was clear, *mind-picture* clear, that the Man felt the same hate-loathing for him as he felt for the Cat.

It was also clear that to grab hold of the Man's leg, sink his teeth deep into the calf and not let go, even if he was beaten senseless, would have been an ecstasything, better even than anything he'd done with the small-Cats. The fact that he didn't, that he postponed that rare treat for a time more opportune, was indica-

tion that perhaps Blanche Lerille was right: *He's more...so...much...more.*
But *what*?

Jack was just coming up the front walk after a brisk, twenty-minute jog through the streets of Granger when he saw the dog. At first he thought someone— maybe Judy—had gotten him another toy, a fur-covered stuffed animal perhaps. But then the stuffed animal cried out, and there was no mistaking what Bruce was up to. He paused, afraid if he came any closer, the bullterrier would bolt and run with the kitten still in his mouth, and during those few moments Bruce, still unaware of his presence, dropped it onto the grass.

He saw the pitiful way it dragged its paralyzed hindquarters in an effort to escape.

He saw the way Bruce watched its progress, totally without pity, ready to pounce again.

And then he saw red.

His anger made him move with a speed he wouldn't have thought possible; he was almost on top of Bruce before the dog even noticed him, and it seemed impossible that he could miss. *"You little shit! I oughta ki"*—But as quick as he was, Bruce was quicker; the kick only caught him a glancing blow. He danced away, crouched down with his forelegs stretched out in front of him, as if all this were just a game. And his eyes looked from Jack to the kitten, and they were laughing. But it was a mirthless laugh, one that said, *If I could manage it, somehow, I'd to that to you, too, ha-ha.*

Grim-faced, Jack advanced on the animal, determined to
(kick, STOMP the stinking-evil guts out of)
teach
(the bug-eyed monster.)

him a lesson. Bruce remained crouched in the same spot till he was very close, then he bolted off to the left in a peculiar humping run that, even in his anger, reminded Jack of a toy he'd had as a child, a dachshund whose hind legs had moved in the same kind of ridiculous conjunction with its front ones simply because their connector, the dog's middle, was a slinky toy. Only with Bruce the motion was speeded up twenty times, and obscene.

Jack went after him again, and again Bruce humped-ran a few yards away as he drew near.

"You bastard! You c—"

Then again. And again. And each time, the look in Bruce's eyes seemed to him a bit more as if the dog were gloating... a malefic kind of gloating.

Finally he gave up, and with Bruce still watching from just out of reach, returned to the mauled kitten to see what, if anything, could be done for that poor creature.

Nothing; it was beyond his or anybody's help. He watched in misery as it continued to drag itself across the grass, mewing in a stricken, plaintive way that cut into his heart. Calling for its mother, his overactive imagination told him, and just for a moment he wished to hell he'd come back from his run just a few minutes later so that

(What, Jack? So that Bruce could have tortured it some more...?)

it might already be out of its misery. But now it was his responsibility, and he felt helpless and so damned guilty.

(Why guilty?)

As gently as possible he picked the kitten up. It quit crying almost immediately, nosed then nuzzled against the inner surfaces of his cupped hands, as if he were its mother and it were trying to nurse. *(Oh great, that makes me feel a LOT better!* Then: *Jesus, how can you worry about how YOU feel?)*

Now what? It occurred to him that he couldn't take it inside; hurt this badly, it was doomed, and both Rachel and Judy were in there. Especially Rachel; this was more than she needed to be exposed to at age six. She'd probably held this very animal only yesterday, when both she and her mother had gone next door, along with his aunt, to...

(Good ol' Aunt Blanche. How would SHE react? Would she really be shocked? REALLY...? Would she stay up late and TALK to Bruce?)

He canned that line of thought immediately and decided the best thing would be to take the kitten next door and inform its owner.

Henry Mallory was sixty-three years old, a member of Jack's dad's generation—that older, tougher, more hard-working generation that all his life Jack had felt he could never measure up to. And, judging from the looks of him, he must have been one of its most exemplary products: tall, square-boned, 220 *hard* pounds... the kind of man whose wife had a problem buying gloves large enough to fit his thick hands; but that was okay, too, because they were so tough they probably didn't *need* any protection in any weather warmer than twenty below zero. Jack had seen the retired farmer/truck driver out in his yard both yesterday and the day before, knew he'd moved into town only recently but had not gone over and introduced himself simply because, even at a distance, he was sure he'd recognized the type. And now he stood on the Mallorys' back steps facing the man, holding out the ruined kitten, feeling the same sense of inequality and apology as when he was ten, or sixteen, or twenty-seven, and had stood before THE MAN, saying "I—I'm really sorry, but I'm afraid my aunt's dog got this ki—"

Henry Mallory's calm, hazel-flecked eyes took in the situation at a glance, and he cut Jack off. "How bad is he?" At the same time his hands, size extra-large, were reaching for the kitten, probing it with blunt fingers that seemed both practiced and gentle. Then: "Jesus, it's bad. Let's step outside so the Missus don't hear. I'll tell her later."

Jack stepped back, surprised by how quickly the man had reached even that small decision and acted on it. He felt he had just relinquished control somehow.

"Its back's broke," Mallory continued. He was already past Jack, so the latter couldn't see the expression on his face, and his tone of voice revealed nothing. Then Mallory was striding purposefully in the direction of the garage and Jack was hurrying to keep up.

"I really am sorry," Jack said again. "If I'd had any idea—"

"I know y'are." This over his shoulder. "It ain't your fault." He broke stride suddenly, turned and really looked at Jack for the first time. There was regret, concern, but no enmity in those eyes. "Helluva way for two neighbors to meet, though. Listen, to my way of thinkin' you did me a favor comin' and tellin' me. Prob-lay saved the Missus from the kind of thing she don't need to see." As he spoke he nodded in the direction of the garage. Jack tried to cover the awkwardness he felt with a puzzled frown.

"There's two others," Mallory continued by way of explanation. "In there. The momma keeps 'em in a box. If that devil got one, he most likely got the others too."

Of course; Jack had known there were others. Rachel had been bubbling over about a gray-and-white one. Suddenly he was sure he didn't want to go into that garage.

He went anyway, and all talk ceased for a while. Extreme violence, or its aftermath, has a way of doing that—stunning most people to silence. It's as if it's so far beyond our comprehension that, for a moment or two, we mistrust our senses. Or maybe by acknowledging its existence we feel guilty by association.

Mallory was the first to find his voice again. "Jesus!" he said. *"JeeeZUS!"* The hand not holding the butchery's sole survivor clenched into a white-knuckled fist as he looked about him. "Pitiful! This is...*pitiful!*"

Jack's eyes were fixed on the severed head of the gray-and-white kitten. The one Rachel had liked. No matter how many times he looked away—and he did try to look someplace else, *anyplace* else—his gaze was always drawn back to its face. It looked so...so normal, so *still intact*...as if it were merely sleeping ...but with its headless body lying elsewhere. He shuddered, and by an act of will managed to fight off the wave of nausea that threatened to envelop him. Just barely.

The thing that finally freed him of its spell was the sound of Mallory shaking open, with one hand, a paper grocery bag he'd taken from a stack of newspapers, magazines, and more bags that sat in one corner. His other hand still held the charcoal male, the kitten that was only half dead. "Gotta get rid of this before Dolores comes upon it," he said grimly.

"Can—Can I help?"

"Naw. No sense both of us gettin' into this."

Jack watched, at a loss as to what to say or do, as the man picked up first the head (by an ear), then the body (by its tail), then the more or less whole, but torn, remains of the other kitten and deposited them in the sack. He then placed the whole thing inside a

PADDYWHACK

larger burlap bag, after first having used it to wipe up the surprisingly small amount of blood *(how much could a week-old, eight-ounce kitten have: less than a river, more than a stream?)* traces from the floor. And while he was doing all this, he began talking, talking in a manner probably meant to divert both their minds from the grisly reality of the task, but which went a long way toward helping Jack shake off some crazy feeling of blame he felt for the incident as well:

"Never cared that much for cats. Always admired them; they're nature's true athletes. Just never thought of them as pets, livin' on a farm with so many of 'em around most my life. It was the Missus' idea to adopt the momma." He paused, glanced around him, down at what was in the bag, then shook his head and continued. "But I'll tell you one thing: cats is better than that insult to the genus 'dog' that lives next door!"

Jack wanted to tell him how much he agreed; instead, he merely nodded, and Mallory continued, after putting the finishing touches on the cleanup process in silence.

"Met your little girl yesterday. She's a sweetheart." He paused again, momentarily, fixed him with a measuring stare. "I know this next ain't my business, but ... I'd keep her play with that dog to a minimum if I was you. This work *here* is his true nature. And don't let that grin he always wears fool you; it's the devil's grin."

Jack met his stare. "I know. Thanks."

Their eyes remained locked a few seconds longer, then the other nodded in a manner suggesting they'd just shared more than the brief exchange of words could account for. "It's more than what he did here" —he gave a disgusted snort—"or the fact that he pisses on everything he comes across, thinkin' it's his ... it's, well ... you see the way it is with your aunt and him; she prit near lives and breathes that animal, can't see him for what he is. And... and my Dolores thinks he's just fine too. Women—*females*—tend to trust him, I think. And mebbe they shouldn't." He clamped his mouth shut then and looked away, almost as if he were embarrassed to have gone on at such length.

Sensing a need for it, Jack changed the subject.

"What you think we should do about *it*?" he asked, indicating the paralyzed kitten lying so quietly now in the other's cupped hand.

Henry Mallory looked down at the damaged piece of fluff with a genuinely pained expression. "When I was little I saw one like this; got stepped on by a cow. My dad told me, 'Look away,' and picked it up and, just like that, smacked its head against the stone foundation of our barn, which o' course, killed it instantly. Then he looked at me and said, 'Don't think me cruel; it hurt me to have to do that, but *it needed doin, it was sufferin'.*'" He glanced back over at Jack, and just for a moment Jack tensed, wondering if those eyes were looking for some sort of sanction to do the same thing. Then he saw their expression: half apology, half... something else, maybe stubbornness, pride... "I could never do that. I'm glad our generation has vets close by and ways of layin' things to rest more tender."

Jack crossed back to his own yard wondering how things might have been different with him had he known Henry Mallory, or someone like him, twenty years ago. He said nothing to his aunt about the incident.

Normally Hank Mallory's whole attention would have been given over to the simple pleasure of driving his new truck as he headed north of town. It was a beaut, a Ford three-quarter-ton pickup with heavy-duty suspension, four-wheel drive, the biggest monster-engine they made, and an interior as fancy and gadget-filled as his brother-in-law's Lincoln...and ten years ago he would have given his left nut for a truck just like it. One of life's little ironies: ten years ago he'd been working every day from light till dark and still wouldn't have been able to afford it. But now that he'd sold the farm he'd worked most of his life to pay off and had retired...

Normally Hank Mallory's whole attention would have been focused on the *feel* of the road and the machine, transmitted up through the steering column to his hands, in the same rapt, appreciative way his eighteen-year-old self would have savored the feel of a pretty girl's waist beneath his hand as he guided her through the intricacies of the box step of a Saturday night at the Grange Dance. But not today; today his mind was on other, less pleasant things.

He glanced down at the burlap bag lying on the floor on the passenger side. The charcoal kitten had gone into the vet's office a living, dependent (on him) creature of God, come out an inanimate lump packaged neatly in a tiny cardboard box hardly big enough to accommodate even its diminutive body. The box was warm on the bottom from its content's residual heat, and he'd wanted to break the seal and open it to make sure the kitten was dead. And now he had some burying to do in a field that used to be his; he was sure the new owners wouldn't mind.

He thought about Jack Lerille, whom he'd just met and who also couldn't be having the most cheerful of mornings. What kind of man was he? First impressions told him he was going to like the guy, which surprised him; Blanche had told Dolores, and Dolores had told him that Lerille was an actor, one who had *almost* made it big...and it seemed like someone would have to have just a little bit of prima donna in them to make it far in that business. Wouldn't they? Yet he'd found himself talking a lot more back in the garage than was really necessary, even admitting to a few sentiments someone insensitive might look upon as weakness, simply because his instincts told him here was a good man, one with empathy. And coming over and telling him what that dog had done, taking responsibility that way, had shown him some stuff too. Hell, even his taking a real shot at being an actor —something quite a few folks probably raised their eyebrows at—took something: balls, mostly, but that was something.

So, Jack Lerille had balls. And he could dream, obviously. And if there was ever a man Hank Mallory should be open-minded about, it was a dreamer. And,

(he's Blanche Lerille's nephew. CONNECTED)

too, there'd been a definite void in his life since his son Andy had moved to Grand Rapids; they'd been friends as well as father and son, and everyone left in Granger he could hang that appellation on was his age (which wasn't old, *damnit!*) and seemed too caught up in mourning the demise of the forties and fifties. . . .

He wasn't surprised when that line of reasoning steered him around to Blanche Lerille. She had her own daft way of clinging to what should be let go, and never mind the rumors. Even before that bastardizing gigolo, Holmes, had got hold of her during that same "golden" era his friends pined for, corrupted her—living off her, off and on, all those years, using her, with nary a word about marriage—there'd been something predatory in the way she'd looked at men, himself included, that was about as charming as the way a starving fox looks at a chicken. And when they'd moved next door last year, and he'd heard her call that gnome of a dog by Holmes's first name, Bruce . . .

He wondered if the small shadow of doubt he still felt at the prospect of getting to know Jack better, despite first impressions, had much to do with the fact that the man's aunt was a woman whose peculiarities had earned her, in her day, every label from strumpet and slut to town witch.

The field Henry chose to bury the three kittens in was about a mile outside town and reached by a side dirt road that was barely more than a country lane. A row of pines bordered it and sifted rather than diminished a cold west wind with a lonely, *swushing* sound that made the place seem more isolated than it really was. A separate world from Granger...

And so when he looked up from where he was digging the hole and saw the victims' mother, whom Dolores and he had simply dubbed "Momma," standing there watching him, he was more than just startled, he was struck by the unlikely coincidence of the fact. Enough so the short hairs at the nape of his neck lifted with a light, prickly sensation.

And Momma, on her part, just sat there, watching.

He went back to work, thinking now that he'd better deepen the hole, in case she tried to recover her babies, feeling sorry for the old girl to a degree that prevented him from even looking in her direction till the job was done, the burlap bag and its contents buried, the soil tamped.

Then he approached her, because she was a good animal, even if she was a cat—gentle and placid in nature—and maybe it would be best, after all, if he gave her a ride back into town. He approached her as he had a hundred times before, with easy deliberation ... and when he got within a yard or two, she metamorphosed. She changed into something else. Something ugly, *demonically* ugly, with its whole face pulled tight against its skull so that what was left was all teeth, blazing, slitty eyes, and pure hate. This other thing, this demon-cat, had its ears laid back and its back hunched up more than any back should hunch, and from somewhere deep within its soulless depths there issued a hissing sound that would have done justice to an animal ten times the size.

Again the hairs on Henry's neck pulled erect. They remained that way as he backed away from the creature toward his truck.

"Easy, Momma. It ain't me," he said. "It's that dog that got your babies." And he wondered if all dogs and cats—the meat eaters, the *biters*—were capable of being possessed, the way his grandpa, dead since 'forty-two, swore they were....

VII

CRRRACK! THE FIRST BLOW SENT BLANCHE REELING backward, and she sat down hard on the coffee table. It collapsed. Then she was sitting on the floor, legs splayed wide. Seeing stars, but feeling surprisingly little pain—yet—she still had the presence of mind to clamp them together, fast.

The last time he'd kicked her. *There*.

Then the pain set in, and she wondered if her jaw was broken. It had been a slap, not a punch, but it had caught her with the heel of his hand.

"See what you made me do? *See?*" Bruce Holmes advanced on her like a giant avenging angel. He looked immense, with his doubled-up fists, his legs planted wide, and his godlike face wearing a thundercloud for an expression, and she skuttled backward on her bottom to escape. She was terrified.

Too late. Rough hands seized her beneath her arms and yanked her to her feet as easily as if she were made of straw. She kept on going up until she was level with his face and her feet dangled ten inches off the floor. "*You* drive me to this! *You* make me crazy this way . . . !" He waltzed her around the room to the accompaniment of some inner sonata whose composers were dementia and rage, finally slamming her against one wall hard enough to make a picture there jump off its hanger. *Huhhh!* went the air that used to reside in the very depths of her lungs. "*You!*" Bruce Holmes bellowed, and he let her go. But during the long, slow slide back onto her butt, he changed his mind, decided to lend additional emphasis to his point by palming her face one-handed—the way a smaller-limbed individual might palm a grapefruit—and slamming the back of her head against the wall three times, in perfect sync with his shouting, "You! You! *YOU!*"

Then he strode into the next room, apparently satisfied that he had said all that he could.

It was the first beating of the new decade. February 14, 1950. She shouldn't have expected a valentine....

He didn't beat her often. It wasn't like it was a regular thing...

Not more than five or six times a year.

And it was always her fault; she made him crazy.

Still slumped against the wall, she consoled herself with that fact—with the idea that if she could manage to be a better person, these things wouldn't happen—and the realization that her jaw must not be broken after all. Then, as a result of a severe concussion, she threw up on the front of her heart-patterned blouse.

VIII

JACK SAT LISTENING TO THE ALTERNATING TICKS AND gurgles of the three cast-iron radiators (circa 1910) spaced evenly along the southern wall on this, his first morning at Granger Public Library, immobilized by depression. The place was empty; not that it mattered.

Earlier he had made the rounds of the long, narrow room, running his hands along the walls, the shelves, the books themselves, as if, through his hands, his sense of touch, he could come to terms with his being there.

Now he just sat, a paperback copy of *Rocky*, pulled from one of the shelves, in his lap. Some masochistic element within him had made him open it to his favorite passage, the one where the always eloquent Mr. Balboa tells Adrian that all he wants from the upcoming fight is for people to know that "... I weren't just another bum from the neighborhood."

Heroes.
Heroic efforts.
Granger Public Library.

It wasn't the facility itself; he'd imagined it a lot worse. There was really very little on the inside, in fact, to indicate it had ever been anything other than a library. And Mrs. Combes, the media specialist at Granger High School to whom the city had paid a consultation fee for overseeing all "outfitting" pur-

PADDYWHACK

chases, had made just about the same choices he would have made, given the pocket-sized budget she'd had to work with.

It was more the feeling of being *buried* . . . buried in a nowhere land of insignificance and futility.

Of course, a little of that was to be expected. After the seemingly unlimited resources and savvy of the intellectual supernova that was the New York Public Library system, he was bound to feel a little like the man demoted from colonel in the Marines to pack leader in the Cub Scouts. But there was something more, something he hadn't been prepared for, that had made the day crash in on him despite his best efforts to remain positive. And that *thing* was named Michaels.

Bob Michaels was the city manager and, despite the fact that Granger had both a mayor and a city council, the real power in town. It was Michaels who did all the hiring and the firing, so far as municipal jobs were concerned. Practically everything that had to do with the expenditure of city funds, as a matter of fact, fell under his jurisdiction. That fact had been alluded to several times during even the two brief, long-distance conversations they'd had regarding Jack's interest in the opening, and he should have been forewarned then as to the type of man he'd be working under. But he hadn't been. Michaels had hired him sight unseen at the end of the second call ("Hell, I've met your ma and dad a number of times. Used to live across from ol' Blanche. That makes you practically a local"), and he hadn't had occasion to meet the man in person till eight o'clock this morning, when the latter had met him at the library's front door.

It hadn't taken Jack long to figure out he was working for an asshole. The worst kind: one who is ignorant, mistakes his ignorance for enlightenment, and has the power to impose it upon others.

"Jack? Jack Lerille?" the man had boomed as if the person he were addressing were across the street instead of the width of the sidewalk away. He was a big, beefy man with a high-blood-pressure-red complexion and a fattish neck bulging from his too-tight collar and tie in a way that made him look as if someone had inflated him with a bicycle pump. "Welcome to Granger Public Library." He laid a hand on Jack's shoulder as he reached forward with his left to insert a rather large key into the lock. "We're real proud of what we've done here...."

At that point Jack felt panic rising like gorge from somewhere north of his stomach, and he had to glance, then glance again, at the library's doors to assure himself they were just ordinary doors. Not towering. Not mahogany. Same beginning, same script... different nightmare.

He was ushered inside.

Michaels finally let go of his shoulder and swept his hand expansively. "Voillah!"

Jack glanced around him, relieved that it was nothing like in his dream of two nights ago, but also acutely aware that what he was viewing was *all* it. No wings, no second or third floors, no annexes. He knew he was supposed to look impressed, but couldn't quite muster it.

Michaels didn't seem to notice. "There's more than four thousand books here. Four thousand three hundred and nine, to be exact. My wife and I counted them. Yesterday." He paused to glance back at Jack. "Not bad, eh?"

Jack swallowed. "Oh, uh... wow!" *The man was serious, wasn't he? He'd actually COUNTED them?!*

A flicker of something, annoyance possibly, passed across Michaels's face and was gone again before it was clearly defined. "Your main job, as I see it, is to make sure that every one of these books gets used." He paused. "A glorified book peddler, you might say." That seemed to strike him as amusing, and he laughed the laugh of someone who shares an inside joke. "Yep, you're a book peddler all right. But don't you worry, I promise not to call you that... same as I promised not to call old Charlie Brooks, who cleans this place, a janitor. He tells me he's a 'city custodian.'" He paused again, and now it was back: something hard and cold in those eyes, watching, reading him. "Same as *he* had to promise *me* not to call me son of a bitch if I ever had to ream his ass for givin' the city less than an honest day's work." He chuckled again and winked at Jack, but this time the laughter was forced.

Things were moving too quickly here; precedents, perhaps, being set. Normally Jack wasn't a "confronter"; it took all his will to call Michaels on his little speech: "Just what is it you're trying to say? Was that a warning?"

Michaels laughed again, his booming, *real* laugh, and he thumped Jack's shoulder. "Oh, *hell* no! I'm a kidder, Jack; you'll have to learn that about me. If anything, I was tryin' to lighten things up; you looked so serious standing there. We want you to be happy here at Granger Public Library"—he looked at Jack peculiarly—"your new home." He continued to stare at him half leering, for long seconds. Then, speaking quietly for the first time, he said, "Tell me, Jack, aren't you just a little bit pleased. And impressed?"

Jack lied to him. "Yeah. Yeah, I guess I am."

"Good. I'm pleased that you're pleased."

During the remainder of his brief visit, City Manager Michaels had expounded on everything from the current crop of kids ("... brains turned to mush from watchin' too much crap on TV... should stick their noses in a book 'stead of each other's crotches!") to his own background in literature (he'd read *Black Beauty*, the whole *Tom Corbett, Space Cadet* series, and everything ever written by Mickey Spillane). Which is to say that he did a pretty good job of convincing Jack that, yes, he probably *was* the kind who would drag his wife over here on a Sunday afternoon to count books....

But he saved the best for last: By the way, had he mentioned to Jack the arrangement he'd made with the three schools in the area? Every other weekday Jack was to close down between one and three and drive out to one of them in an old, decrepit, city-owned van that had been converted to a minuscule bookmobile—the elementary on Monday, the middle school on Wednesday, and the high school on Friday. And while he was there, if he could do something "inspiring" to get the kids to use more books...

Even that might not have broken Jack, cemented the feeling that real life and his worst dreams were melding into one. But just then he'd happened to look at Michaels out of the corner of his eye instead of straight on... and from that perspective, in that split second, the man had borne a striking resemblance to a taller, more overstuffed Jonathan Winters....

IX

JACK DISCOVERED SOMETHING ALARMING ABOUT HIMself the day Blanche had her fall: he was genuinely afraid of Bruce. Had someone, to this point, suggested such a thing, he would have been quick to point out the difference between disgust, even revulsion, and real fear. The difference that allowed you to reach down and brush away the half-dozen or so maggots that had already hatched around the bloodied mouth and eyes of your best friend's dog, killed on the road, before said friend rounded the corner and caught up with you . . . but that would *not* allow you to follow your cousin, whom you idolized, in a mad dash across the tiny field where your uncle's Holstein bull was pastured. Up until Blanche's fall, Jack had thought he had Bruce neatly compartmentalized with the maggots, somewhere in the same rather-not-see-touch-or-think-about drawer with leeches, spiders, and tapeworms. But he was wrong; he was afraid of the bullterrier. And it wasn't a healthy kind of fear; it was more the kind of superstitious, illogical dread one might feel at having been left alone in a closed room with a corpse.

He'd walked home from the library that day because Judy had needed the car to pick up Rachel from school and drive with her to the grand opening of a new shopping center outside Chelsea. It was cold—cold enough, he noticed, that the puddles left over from last night's rain had a skim of ice on them. And this wasn't even December yet.

He didn't sense anything wrong, didn't hear the sounds until he was at the front door trying to get it unlocked with his key. That was because they weren't really that loud, just...frantic. And as he got the door opened and stepped inside, they became more frantic still. A crazed, strangling moan of a growl, more a groan, really—the kind of sound a very old man, tortured and exhausted, might make just before his last breath. It was followed by a sound that had become semi-familiar to him now, the hard, scrabbling tap-skid-tap of claws on linoleum. He bolted for the kitchen, but not before the scrabbling was cut short by a shuddering thud.

Then, a noise like a man both gargling and whimpering at the same time, some more claw taps, another groan, and Jack burst into the room just in time to see Bruce stagger from the side door leading to the driveway. The dog glared up at him from a face that seemed even more mashed-in than usual, with a crazy-wild expression that could have been anything from a plea for help to an accusation...and the inane thought struck Jack that he'd never heard of a dog having a nosebleed before.

He'd never seen or heard of a dog—or any other creature, for that matter—running deliberately, unflinchingly, full steam ahead into a brick wall, either, but in essence that is what he witnessed now. After staring up at him a moment longer, groaning one more time, Bruce wheeled and, with much of the coiled-spring power Jack had witnessed the day in the living room with the toy rat still there—and despite his battered condition—launched himself at the solid oak door.

When he was still a third the long kitchen away, he became airborne, and Jack's eyes were drawn inexo-

PADDYWHACK

rably to the point, impossibly high on the door, where dog and solid-grain, unyielding wood would impact.

No guesswork there; the whole area was dabbed and spotted with blood.

Question: Can an animal, lacking jet engines or a propeller of any kind, continue to accelerate once its feet have left the ground? Answer: only by some preternatural force of will. Bruce hit the spattering of blood dead center, with more force, more speed, it seemed to Jack, than he had left the floor. He had actually *seen*—though his eyes had been focused beyond the flying body, on the door itself—the dog accelerate in the air, like some giant doggy-magnet had suddenly been switched on... *hadn't* he? It was that impression, plus the chillingly insane single-mindedness and the complete absence of fear for self demonstrated by the kamikaze attacks on the door, as much as what happened later outside, that planted the first seeds of a wholly irrational and superstitious dread in Jack's mind.

Beyond the door, of course, lay Blanche; a part of Jack had known she was there from the moment he'd seen Bruce launch himself at the obstacle.

She lay where she had fallen, slipped on the ice as she'd begun to descend the three cement steps leading from the side entrance to the driveway. She lay very, very still—in the same position, no doubt, as when she landed. She lay that way not because the fall had killed her or even knocked her unconscious, but because of the pain. She was pinned there by it, held fast by its agony, and its grip on her had squeezed all the color from her face. All of it; for Jack, the words "deathly pallor" would describe his aunt's face from that point on, forever. Each tiny mole, each blotch and imperfection, stood out as if afloat on something transparent—a clear gelatin, perhaps—rather than skin. And where this alien covering was drawn tight in a frozen grimace of pain, especially around the cheekbones and brow, its foundation, which was the skull itself, seemed clearly visible.

He was bent over her, not remembering how he'd gotten there, not remembering anything from the point at which Bruce hit the door till now. "My God, Aunt Blanche, are you all right? Are you hurt?"

(Dumb... really dumb)

She rolled her eyes toward him, then past him, tried to relax the lines of her face enough to speak. "It's ... all right. Don't... worry... Bruce, dear I..."

(Bruce?)

A wet slurping sound, and something inside him tightened as he slowly shifted his gaze in the direction of the noise. Bruce was there and—

Oh God and sweet Jesus, how could he not have seen it! How could he have shut that out!

The splintered bone end glistened where it poked through the skin. It was a pinkish-gray pearl in color —not the stark white one associates with bone at all —and there were streaks of blood on it. Blood. Not a lot of blood for so gruesome an injury, but he supposed the way the skin around it was so puffy and livid with angry reds, purples and blues, as far down as her ankle, meant that there was considerably more bleeding inside. Her foot, plus half the length of her calf, must have wedged itself between the twisted bars of the steps' wrought-iron railing as she fell, first doubling the leg back on itself then snapping it at the tibia like a stick wrapped in cellophane.

And Bruce was there... *licking* it! Licking her mangled leg! That pink, obscene tongue of his flashing in and out, in and out... And now it flicked over the exposed bone end itself; and rather than screaming out in pain and outrage at the violation, she... she *cooed* something soft and unintelligible through a smile made of pain-compressed lips and, as the positioning of the doubled-up leg had him within easy reach, reached along her side and petted him oh-so-lovingly, so reassuringly...

Even as his tongue still worked, snaked in and out as if it were a creature with a life of its own, Bruce rolled his bulgy eyes upward and stared at Jack. Stared at him with the same knowing, conspiratorial look Jack had seen one other time—when he had stood outside *their* bedroom in the middle of the night, witness to a sharing, to a communing he could not comprehend. This time, however, an urge to vomit—an afternoon lunch of tuna on whole wheat mixed with blueberry yogurt, already on the rise, already at the back of his throat, in fact—forced Jack to yank his gaze away almost immediately... before he could read anything more in those eyes, something that might have been even more disturbing.

X

BLANCHE LERILLE ALWAYS KNEW HE WOULD COME back. When Bruce Holmes died in 1952 during one of his prolonged absences from her, gunned down in Detroit by a man she'd never heard of and for reasons having to do with the man's wife which she didn't want to hear of, she was sure he would come back. Because, after all, he was immortal—he'd told her that many times. And by 'fifty-two she was so much in his power, convinced he was either half god or half devil, that she believed him.

So that when he didn't come back, and the years dragged by... it made her crazy.

The fact that the people of Granger eventually knew all about her on-and-off affair with him didn't help. They shut her out, and with no family save a brother—who was even less charitable than the town—she was as alone as only a soul in an unfriendly, alien sea of souls can be. Ten years... Twenty years ... Thirty years and more for her insanity to refine itself. She was old, life was slipping away, and she was ready to grasp at any straw...

And then salvation came, in the form of a knock at her door.

"Here," Mrs. Amberly from across the street said as Blanche opened the door, no preliminaries. She followed this up with, "He's yours if you want him."

"Him" turned out to be a black and white Boston terrier—what most people call a Boston bull—and Blanche was immediately reminded, in some way having to do with the slope of the dog's forehead and its musculature, of Bruce Holmes.

"My Johnny's deathly allergic to him, come to find out," Bev Amberly went on. "So we can't keep him, and I was thinkin'—"

"What's his name?" Blanche cut in, already feeling the stirrings of something instinctive within her brain, telling her what was happening now was IMPORTANT.

"We called him Bruce."

A wave of vertigo hit her then was gone again so quickly that the only visible sign was a slight rocking back onto her heels. There were also some chest pains—first time, ever—before her heart rate came back down from "dangerous" to just plain "too fast."

"You all right?" Beverly asked. She was staring at

PADDYWHACK 77

Blanche narrowly, no doubt watching the color creep back into her face, and the latter was seized with a sudden panic that Bev might change her mind about *him* if she observed her acting strangely.

"I'm fine. And, yes, I do want him... if I could. Thank you. Thank you for such a beautiful, handsome... 'dog.'" She took him from the outstretched hands. A shiver of happiness and recollection rippled through her body; he had the same hard, muscular feel she remembered so well....

"I'll bring over what food we have for him, his blanket, and his wicker bed, and you're in business, then."

Blanche thanked her again and closed the door.

That night, as she lay in bed considering the irony in the possibility that he had come back as a dog (at least this time *she* would be in control), she heard the tip-tap-tapping of clawed doggy feet on linoleum for the first time. She had made a place for Bruce in one corner of the kitchen, which adjoined her bedroom, and he was obviously up and walking around.

Tip-tap, tip-tap. The way the sound carried, in the dead silence of the house, seemed almost surreal.

Tip-tap, tip-tap. He came around to the left side of the bed, the side *(your heart is on)* where she kept her favorite picture of Bruce Holmes. In the half light from the moon he seemed to be studying the photo, looking first at it then up at her. He repeated the process several times, dwelling, it seemed, longer on the photo each time. Then he exhaled all the air from his puppy lungs rapidly, audibly, in what could only be taken as a doggy-sigh. Then he lay down.

"Bruce?" she breathed, ready to scream or weep if he answered.

He didn't. Not aloud, anyway. But he did stand back up again. Duck his head then raise it, duck-and-raise, in the same peculiarly stiff-necked method of "nodding" she'd grown accustomed to so long ago. And on a deathly quiet night, after three decades of waiting...knowing every moment that she has thrown her life away and is getting old...she is ready to grasp at anything, even if it leads to more madness.

Even if it leads her straight to the Devil.

Or to those who cut his deals for him here on Earth.

"Now...Jack*ie*..." Even over the phone her voice sounded authoritative, the way she raised the pitch of it with the last syllable of his name. Jack-EEE. She sounded like his sixth-grade teacher, Miss Stilwell. And when had she started calling him that, anyway? Before or after the accident?

"*Please*, I know what's best for him."

Part of Jack's mind rebelled at what she was suggesting. The other part remembered how it had been three days ago, after he'd called for the ambulance, and that part was less sure...

By the time he'd come sprinting back from the phone, Bruce must have judged the wound cleansed enough

(That's all it had been, hadn't it? Something instinctive? A perfectly normal animal response...?)

and he moved on to licking her face. Jack hadn't even tried to interfere, and after the animal had thoroughly bathed her cheeks, they had all simply waited, he trying his best to say something positive and reassuring when all that really wanted to come out were goodies like, "Oh *jeez*," and "*Damn*, I hope they hurry and *get* here!"

Bruce and his aunt had their own peculiar way of enduring, and it was decidedly spooky. It consisted of the dog pressing his foreshortened, still-bloodied nose against Blanche's cheek, just below eye level and alongside her own nose, so that their eyes were only inches apart and gazing into each other. They remained that way the entire time it took for the ambulance to arrive, and in some strange fashion it seemed to help; the pain mask that was her face seemed to smooth some. A gray ghost of her former color returned.

But when the ambulance did finally come and the attendants began the delicate task of getting her moved, it looked like there would be real problems. She cried out in pain, and Bruce was instantly transformed into something very, very ugly... something for which Jack's own appreciation of the uncanny, the preternatural, was entirely unnecessary in order to inspire fear. The way the skin around the animal's face seemed to melt backward, leaving nothing but teeth and two bulgy eyes, the way something in the dog's stance, in its growl, managed to say, *not without a fight. Not without some real* hurt *on you, you, and you!* had them all backed away.

"A net. We need a goddamned *net*!" one of the men in white swore.

And then she spoke to the dog—no, she *explained* things to him:

"Bruce, you must *let* them *take* me. They must *take* me to *help*." She spoke quietly, very slowly, but her only real concession to the fact that she was addressing an animal was the way she emphasized certain key words. "It's *okay*. I'll *be back*."

The change, again, was almost immediate. From something demonic, with the light of insanity in its eyes, to something as meek as a lamb whose whole countenance and every movement managed to convey apology and nonaggression in only a second. Bruce backed away then, licking his chops abashedly, and the ambulance attendants moved in.

From that point on he'd remained clear, except to move in close as they were about to close the rear door of the ambulance with Blanche inside. Then he'd hopped up, laid his nose against her right ankle—the uninjured one—licked it once, and groaned the same old-man suffering groan Jack had heard earlier.

"It's *okay*, Bruce. Be *back*."

He hopped back down, and they'd taken Aunt Blanche away.

And now here it was three days later, and here *she* was, calling from her hospital bed in Ann Arbor to demand that he put Bruce on the line because the dog hadn't taken a bite of food since the ambulance pulled away, and with a bullterrier's hopped-up metabolism, that was very bad indeed. Part of him did rebel at the idea. But the other part reminded him that the smell in Blanche's bedroom, where the animal chose to say most of the time now, was the same sickly, burnt-sweet smell he'd smelled once before, in the room of a terminally ill cancer patient—the smell of a body cannibalizing itself.

Hell, what can it hurt besides my dignity, he thought. *It's a big WATELL, Jackie-boy...*

"All right, Aunt Blanche, I'll bring him to the phone, but..." He giggled, which was unlike him. "...he may not want to talk to you." He set the receiver down, shrugged, then mentally squared his shoulders. *It's a big WATELL, all right.*

WATELL. He and a closed circle of high school buddies had coined the word, along with several others, in the early seventies in an effort to be different, to be cool.... It stood for what-the-hell, and it had come to represent any semi-desperate situation (in those days life itself in the "cool" lane was a semi-desperate situation) where you had nothing to lose by trying. That was the *big* WATELL. Said another way, and without the qualifier, it stood for the same three words yet expressed the directly opposite sentiment: Who knows? Who cares? Why try to understand or change things? They had used it only among them-

selves, and never in mixed company or around adults
... which was the difference between then and now;
now a word like that might end up as the name on
some rock group's latest album, everyone would be
using it, and the little girl down the street would try it
on her mother... right after she told Mom that learn-
ing her multiplication tables "sucks."

He went into his aunt's bedroom to get Bruce.

The dog lay in one corner, didn't even shift his eyes
from straight ahead as he entered.

"Up and at 'em, Bruce. You've got a phone call."

Bruce failed to catch the humor in the remark; in
fact, he ignored Jack completely.

"Here boy. *Blanche* wants you."

That, too, failed to elicit a response, and Jack felt
his jaw set involuntarily, the way it used to five and a
half years ago, when Rachel had first gone on to solid
food and it was his turn to change her green-beans-
and-carrot-surprise soiled diapers. He would have to
pick the dog up and carry him to the phone, and the
sense of revulsion he felt went way beyond dirty
diapers. There was simply something about the animal that disgusted and frightened him.

It was bad; he could feel the dog's starvation. Not
only in how light he was and the way the animal's ribs
felt—as if he were lifting a skeleton—but in the lack
of any palpable body heat beneath his hand. Cold
as...

At least he didn't offer any resistance, and Jack
carried him into the kitchen. He set him in a standing
position on a chair, where he immediately sagged onto
his haunches, then his belly.

"Aunt Blanche? He's here. Talk to him." He held
the receiver to the dog's ear.

She spoke loudly enough, and the receiver formed
an imperfect enough seal against the dog's nonhuman-
shaped auricle, that Jack was able to hear her quite

well. She said, "Bruce, you must *eat*. I'm *okay*. I'll *be home. Tomorrow. EAT!*"

For the last day and a half both he and Judy had tried everything they could think of to get the dog to eat. Now the same animal half lay, half sat in front of them, looking like death warmed over, listening to a voice on the phone and blinking stupidly. After the voice was done and Jack had pulled the receiver away, he remained that way a few seconds longer. Then, quite suddenly, Bruce jumped from the chair. He landed badly, his front legs collapsing momentarily on impact so that his chin and upper chest skidded along the floor. Undaunted, he picked himself up, wobbly-walked to his bowl in the corner, and began devouring its contents, dry Gravy Train, as if it were filet mignon.

WATELL.

XI

THERE WAS A COLDNESS IN THE MIDDLE OF Blanche's chest. Along her flanks, her shoulders, her hands and feet too. She shivered, and it made her breathe in more sharply than she should have. The breath rattled in her throat—her lungs were filled with fluid; there was simply no place for the air to go—and that rattle threatened to set off a whole paroxysm of coughing. She fought to control it with everything she had. They must not know; her Jackie and his Judy must not hear how bad she was. They would insist she return to the hospital after just five days at home, and that could not be.

She allowed herself a smile as her mind touched on Jack. On Jackie. Her brother's child... He had surprised her with how caring, how sensitive he was. And he was beginning to understand how it was with Bruce and her...

But no hospital. For Bruce's sake, no hospital. She would have to fight this new affliction, which had settled in her chest and frightened her far more than the damage done her leg, from right here in her own bed. With Bruce at her side.

A slight turn of her head on the pillow, and her eyes rested softly on the object of her devotion. He lay there on a chair that dear, sweet Jack had pushed up next to the bed and placed a cushion upon. He was watching her, chin resting on his outstretched paws, his eyes liquid pools. She could gaze into those eyes forever, but right now, right now...

Even as her eyes dropped closed and the muscles of her face relaxed with sleep, a portion of her brain felt dismay that she should be so tired, that the energy she had expended fighting off a simple fit of coughing should so thoroughly deplete her reserves. For a brief moment her eyes flew open again in an effort to refocus on her love and on the room. The room...

She was in the room again. That awful, terrible room, painted black-on-black by Satan's friends. Her friends now... Or at least the only soulless souls she can turn to. It is like being inside a living organism—a mouth perhaps—and, again, the feeling: What have I done? Who can I turn to? Then the sudden urge to pray, to fall down on her knees and beg His forgiveness, beg Him to save her...from herself. But of course she cannot be forgiven, not for what she is about to do....

The inevitability of it all makes her feel as if she

were falling through the dream, drawn by a gravity grown greedy and malignant and able to suck one through time as well as space. Emotions, impressions, rush by her like the windows of a tall building must to its plummeting victim, lured to its high places by the promise of a final solution:

Bruce being led in, wearing the scarlet, stiff-collared satin robe they'd insisted she fashion for him—and the sudden, dread uncertainty she feels at the sight of him. Who is she doing this for? Bruce, the man, or Bruce, the dog? Are they really one and the same? What if she is wrong?

Oh, God—

But God is definitely not part of it.

Other memories, impressions... So real:

The feel of her own satin robes against her bare skin.

The goat's blood—the taste, the smell of it.

The ceremony, the vow, so that, even in death, they will not be apart.

The vow...

   (What if they're not the same?)

    The vow...

      (What if he is just a dog?)

       (What if she's got them mixed?)

        The vow!

Again her eyes fluttered open. How long had she slept. It was still daylight outside, but just barely. Bruce was still staring at her, unblinkingly. There was no way to tell.

Another chill coursed through her body, and the fluid inside her lungs shifted like a living organism. It had grown while she slept; she was sure of it. She imagined it rolling halfway up her throat the next time she dozed off. And the time after that, it would fill her mouth and nose, a vile, viscous fluid the color of amber, the consistency of oil, but infinitely colder and tasting like something dead...

She imagined herself drowning in it, and the things she'd done, the promises she'd made, filled her with fear.

XII

IT WAS ALMOST AS IF DEATH BENT THE RULES JUST A little to ensure its claim on Blanche Lerille.

Her pneumonia grew worse with a rapidity matched perhaps by only one case in every several thousand. When Jack came in to check on her a final time on the evening of Thursday, December sixth—the same evening which, earlier, had brought her dreams of satin robes, goat's blood, and promises—she had been able to hide her condition, answering his questions in monosyllables and with little wheezing. When he burst into the room again, at seven-forty Friday morning, he was just in time to see her die.

She awoke at 7:37, suddenly, and she knew immediately that she'd been right; whatever was inside her lungs was alive. She'd been dreaming again, and when the terror of that dream made her heart want to go faster, increased her need for air, the thing had squeezed down on her, writhed, then squeezed again with a savageness that made her gasp.

"*Huh-UH!*" One of its talons had her around the heart; the pain was excruciating. That most essential of organs stopped...for several seconds. Then the thing let go. It was toying with her.

She called out, more a phlegm-choked rattle, really. "Bruce! J-Jack-ie! B-BRUCE!"

Oh dear Lord, her panic-stricken mind cried, *please HELP me!*

Bruce was there, on the pillow with her, watching her intently.

Save me, Lord. Forgive me,
(That we may be one, forever and beyond, we pledge to you)
Father, for I have sinned...
(Satan, our souls)

Bruce nuzzled her cheek, then began barking. And the barking—something he never did; he'd been taught not to—seemed both an irony and a mockery. It was Satan laughing at her. *(A dog, just a DOG; your soul for a dog...)*

But old habits and grand delusions both die hard, at least as hard as people. When the thing inside her chest, which in reality was nothing more animate or depraved than a great pooling of virus-laden mucus and phlegm, stopped her heart a second and final time by depriving it of oxygen, it was the dog, of course, that her startled yet knowing eyes turned toward. It was the dog, not God nor man, to whom she gasped out her final words. *"Bruce!* Don't let them... take *meee...*

Jack was up and most of the way dressed for work when Bruce started barking. He knew immediately that something was seriously wrong. Still, when he arrived downstairs, the closed door to her bedroom gave him pause, and he wasted precious seconds knocking before finally barging in. The scene he opened it up on was one that would add fuel to his nightmares in the weeks to come.

PADDYWHACK

His aunt was dead; he needed only to fix on her eyes—open, staring at nothing, *empty*—to accept that. But Bruce was trying to bring her back. Amid the same desperate groans and rumblings Jack had heard the day she fell, the dog was licking, nuzzling her face with an almost savage abandon while his fore paws scrabbled and clawed against her shoulder and neck in a steady tattoo.

Her head rocked on its lifeless neck from the onslaught. Gouge marks appeared on her throat, and her gown tore. The deepest marks colored in with a bare trickling of blood.

Something clicked inside Jack's subconscious, something not right. But by now he was transfixed by the desperate horror of what he saw, and it took a while for his conscious mind to make the connection. *Blood?* The marks were on parts of her anatomy that faced up; they shouldn't be bleeding at all, unless—

Unless there was a pulse, however weak, to make them bleed!

He whirled in the doorway to call for Judy, and was startled to find her standing behind him, eyes wide, just as mesmerized by the scene as he'd been. "Call somebody, quick!" he shouted, as if she were still upstairs. "Go on!"

The loudness was not for her—she had already turned to go—but for himself, to bolster his courage for what he was about to do. For what *had* to be done.

He moved to the side of the bed. Bruce paused in his frantic licking, bared his teeth and growled. It was the same as before—the skin around the animal's mouth and eyes seemed to melt and re-form into something demonic. It gave Jack pause, but only for a moment. Slowly, deliberately, as if it had all been planned out in advance and now he was simply following the step-by-step plan, he gathered up the bedspread, sheet, and blanket that covered the body.

Bruce slavered and growled. His eyes were mere slits now.

With the folds of cloth draped loosely between his hands and his face expressionless, Jack reached out cautiously toward his aunt. Close, closer... and finally Bruce would tolerate no more and sprang at him.

Jack caught him in the folds and, with lightninglike alacrity, wrapped the bedcovers around him till he was completely bundled.

Now his face became animate again, as if his real self had retreated to somewhere else during the unpleasantries and were only now returning. As he carried the heaving, struggling bundle from the room, he noted with a mixture of relief and concern—but with a predominance of the former—that Rachel was up and perched on one of the kitchen chairs, knees hugged against her chest, her face a frightened, confused mask. Good; it was necessary, for what he planned to do, that she be at this end of the house. "Honey," he panted as he walked past her, "shut the door between the dining room and kitchen, then get back on the chair. Shut it *tight*. Do it *now*."

He carried the bundle, from which an insane chorus of snarls and choking sounds now emanated, through the other door and into the living room. Judy was there, just hanging up the phone.

"Back in the kitchen. Quick."

He waited till she moved past him, waited a few seconds longer to make sure Rachel had had time to do her part, then flung the blankets and their snarling, raging contents to the far side of the room and stepped back into the kitchen. He slammed closed the door. Now the living room, the dining room, and the staircase leading to the second floor, which separated

PADDYWHACK

them, belonged to Bruce. The back half of the house was theirs.

Jack waited for the first familiar thud of dog flesh against hardwood. A total of perhaps ninety seconds had elapsed since it had first occurred to him that she might still be saved and he had come at Bruce with the blankets. Ninety seconds *plus* however long she'd lain there with no heartbeat before he'd arrived...

Not long! a voice inside his head railed. *The cuts still bled!*

KA-THUD! The door between the living room and kitchen shuddered but held, and he breathed a sigh of relief. He'd been most concerned about it; of the two, it was the one hung so that it opened inward, *into* the kitchen, and its effectiveness as a barrier was solely dependent upon the strength of its latch. There had been no sense to starting resuscitation efforts which, once begun, could not be interrupted until he was sure it was going to hold.

(Is that the real reason, Jackie? CPR, once begun, makes that life YOUR responsibility; you know that. And that's a dead body in there...)

KAT-THUD! He pushed away his fears with a giant, mental shudder just as Bruce hit the other door, the one between kitchen and dining room.

Smart little
(devil-fiend-goblin)
sonovabitch...

That, too, had to be pushed from his mind. Now came the hard part,

(your chance to be a hero, Jack)

the part that took real courage. Bringing the dead back to life.

The next ten minutes just happened. Jack didn't really experience them on an everyday, rational level of awareness; they were too supercharged with emotion

—horror, panic, and finally despair—for that. In a way it was like being in a really bad car accident (one which is prolonged, interminably) where you can only truly grasp what you've been through in retrospect. Too much, just too... *much.* He checked out, and for ten minutes, until some guy in white told him gently that *they* would take over now, the real Jack Lerille simply sat back and watched his physical self and the crisis interact.

He remembered lifting his aunt's rubbery-limp body from the bed (you can't administer CPR on a bed, he remembered; you lose compression) and onto the floor. He remembered how cold and, well... *dead* she felt. And then, for a long while, his mind went textbook:

Tilt head to clear the airway. Check for breathing; check for pulse.

No breathing. No pulse.

Pinch closed the nose, then four quick breaths.

The first real shock came when he tried to form a seal with his mouth over hers, and something moved and shifted inside the latter. A moment where panic and revulsion took over; then he realized what it was: simply her dentures, slipping.

(Nothing alive, Jack. Nothing that has crawled up her dead throat and wants out; deserting the sinking ship, you know...)

They had to come out, and he gagged just a little in the process. Afterward her lips sank in and it was like trying to mouth a doughnut made of raw liver. But at least he could form a proper seal.

Again he checked for breathing and a pulse. Neither.

Two quick breaths, then fifteen chest compressions...

"One-and, two-and—" Just before three there was a muffled, popping sound that he could actually feel beneath the heel of his hand. Had he remembered to measure two finger widths up from the xiphoid? He thought he had. He faltered but didn't stop. "Four-and, five-and..." The frail, bony latticework that was her chest continued to shift and emit an alarming series of crackles and pops. He prayed it was only cartilage being torn and that he wasn't actually forcing the jagged, broken end of a rib or two, separated from its anchor point on the sternum, into her heart. But there was no stopping now; the chest had to be compressed at least an inch and a half with each stroke, no matter what, or she was dead regardless

(alREADY, Jack; dead alREADY, al—).

KA-THUD! Bruce hit the kitchen/living room door again, harder than before. Jack shut it from his mind.

Then, for what seemed like hours, there were no other sounds but his measured breathing, the sound of old, brittle bones shifting beneath his pressure, and the spaced thuds of Bruce hitting the door.

Forming a proper seal around his aunt's sunken, cold-as-ice mouth became something he yearned, no, *lusted* for... as all-consuming in its own way as a kiss of passion between lovers.

He remembered agonizing over how little her chest rose and fell with each breath he puffed into her (hardly at all), how sure he was that he was merely finishing the job of killing her by impaling her on her own ribs...

And then the sound of heavy feet in the kitchen, a man's hand on his shoulder, a voice saying, "We'll take over now, buddy. You did good."

You did good! You did GOOD! Warm words, *wonderful* words. Words you could sink back against the wall with, sink *into* the wall... and ride to oblivion. For a while they were the only thing that got through to him, slumped there in his corner, though a part of him watched the proceedings, even marveled in a foggy sort of way at the machines they used—the terrible violence and power of the defibrilator, the way the breathing mask of the bag-valve resuscitator formed a perfect seal over her mouth and nose *every time* ...

Then one of them, the same one who'd told him he'd done good, said something that would save him much soul searching in the days to come: *"Damnit-all!"* he said. *"I can't get any air into her; her lungs are full of fluid! I can't ventilate lungs that're already full!"* The latter was said in a voice that begged both forgiveness and concurrence. Jack gave him both and amen. There was something else he said, something about suctioning them out with some kind of pump once they got her to the ambulance, but Jack didn't catch all of it.

There were three of them, three anonymous men in white whose names Jack never did learn, and at that point they began the complex, intricately choreographed process of transporting her to their vehicle without interrupting CPR.

Because they know she's dead, Jack thought. *Beyond reviving. They could stop now, but they've got to make it official, have a doctor say she's dead.*

He followed them into the kitchen, and as they paused momentarily, even with the living room door, Bruce smashed into it again from the other side. *KA-THUD!* Then silence for a moment, followed by a pain-wracked. *Ki-yi-yi-yi!* Then a bestial snarl.

"That dog is nuts!" one of the attendants said, and Jack realized he was one of those who'd been there last week when his aunt had fallen.

(Beyond nuts, WAY beyond!)

The finale, the finishing touch of horror to a morning filled with it, came a few minutes later and should have been anticlimactic, since Jack had been through so much by then. And it might have been, had it not been for the eyes, those staring, accusing, *condemning* eyes....

It, too, involved a death in the family.

It had been almost as if Bruce could see through the walls of his makeshift prison and measure their progress as they moved Blanche's body. He hit the living room/kitchen door one more time as they progressed beyond it; then, as they came parallel with the door off the dining room, he was there, too, slamming against it from the other side, his rage and frustration by this time having reduced his former snarls to a lunatic squealing resembling that of a slaughtered pig.

They carried her down the side steps and into the driveway, and as they loaded her into the back of the ambulance/van, there was a jarring crack against the dining room window facing that way. Only the fact that it was made up of very small panes and was reinforced to a degree by its heavy drapes, which were drawn shut, kept the demon that Bruce had become from breaking through. Still, two of the panes did shatter, and Jack told them they'd "better get going before he comes all the way through!" As if they needed the incentive with his aunt's body *(no breathing, no pulse)* in the back.

Thirty seconds later they were pulling out the end of the driveway and Bruce had redirected his attack so that it was now against the front dining room window—also small-paned and close-draped—with no better success, as Jack stood in the front yard, preparatory to loading Judy and Rachel in the car and following the departing vehicle. Something made him turn around at that point and look back at the house. Maybe it was the sudden and abrupt silencing of Bruce's squeals.

Maybe it was a premonition.

The first thing he noticed was the way the just-risen sun caught and glinted off the big, east-facing picture window in the living room, turning it a spectacular, lucent shade of gold.

The second—and this was as much a sudden recollection as it was an observation, having passed through the living room earlier that morning—was the fact that the drapes were not drawn on that particular window.

Even as his mind projected the probable consequences of that fact, they came to fruition: Bruce hit the window from the other side, and it shattered.

But the glass was thick, much thicker than in the smaller, paned windows, and Bruce weighed less than twenty pounds. It shattered, but it absorbed nearly all the animal's force of impact in the process. Rather than passing all the way through, he got hung up. His head on the outside, his body on the inside, a sickle-edged section of glass slicing halfway through his throat from underneath, he got... *hung up*.

He made no sound beyond a weak gurgle; that part of his anatomy wired for sound now had a serious flaw in it. No sound, but that is not to say he merely gave up and died either. He struggled valiantly to pull himself off the glass, all four paws flailing and scrabbling for a hold. But it was useless; the blood began to jet, and it was just too slippery.

Slippery with... blood; drenched with blood; *painted* with... blood. The two or three cupfuls that spilled down the window's outside surface (there was far more on the inside) were turned a red-copper shade by the rising sun. As Jack was drawn closer and closer to the window and the struggling animal, he was hardly able to tear his eyes away from all that blood.

But he finally did. Bruce's struggles gradually became less and less, and finally they stopped altogether. *Dead,* Jack thought. *He's dead.* And he raised his eyes to the animal's face.

At that moment the head swiveled, turned at an angle Jack would have thought impossible, considering the wedge of glass most of the way through the dog's neck. It swiveled, and their eyes met...and Bruce's hellbound ones, filled with a hatred so powerful it seemed as if it might transcend death, told him something.

Then and only then did the cold light behind those eyes switch off, and Bruce was truly dead.

What did they tell him? Jack wasn't sure; it was too terrible to put into words. A promise, he thought. Of bad dreams and sleepless nights. But whatever it was, it opened a gate, and all the horror and despair of the morning, which Jack had been struggling to keep at bay because he needed to be strong, flooded in on him. It hit him like a megadose of adrenaline in reverse, dropping him to his knees. He groaned. He groaned the way Bruce had groaned earlier—like an old man, tortured and near death, might groan.

It was the groan of a lost and frightened soul.

PART II

Such Are the Hounds of Hell...

"Who's *back? Not that dog—that dog is* dead! *Things don't come back from the dead!...They* don't!"
—Judy Lerille, to her husband

XIII

HENRY MALLORY DIDN'T REALLY KNOW THAT MUCH about his new neighbor, only that he liked him. Since the incident with the slaughtered kittens, there had only been two instances when their conversation had run much beyond "Morning" and "Cold enough for you?" called from across the yard. And on the second of those two occasions, when he'd said, "Tell me about yourself, Jack," almost casually but with a great deal of hidden curiosity, he'd been offered little more than a skeletal outline, and a modest one at that. Still, he could read the dreamer in Jack Lerille. Even if the man's wife and his Dolores hadn't hit it off so quick—since she hadn't opened up some, the way women friends most generally did around Dolores—he would have read it there. One recognizes one's own kind.

With Henry it had been football.

He'd been sixteen when Tommy Harmon won the 1940 Heisman playing for Michigan, which was just up the road a piece. Sixteen and highly impressionable. And already six-foot-two, two hundred pounds, and a hell of a football player himself. That year a vision began to form in his mind's eye, the kind of vision that shot little thrill-flutters up through his heart every time he thought of it and often made him stop whatever it was he was doing and just stand there with goose bumps on his arms...because maybe, just *maybe*, it was within his reach.

It involved glory, college football, and the pros.

By the time he'd graduated from high school in 'forty-two he was twenty additional pounds and two additional years of phenomenal football closer to that vision. College coaches were drooling over him, especially those out of Ann Arbor; some people from both the Lions and the Bears organizations had come to a few of his games—a 220-pound back with *moves* was unheard of in those days; and nothing could stand in his way. Nothing, that is, except a small matter of conscience.

The war was on; real patriots knew where their duty lay.

In September of 'forty-two he joined the Marines instead of Michigan's backfield, thinking with typical young-strong-and-got-the-world-by-the-balls optimism that America would put an end to the war quickly and that he could resume his football career as if he'd never been away.

On June 16, 1944, during the second day of fighting on Saipan, he got most of his left kneecap blown away. Surgery in 'forty-four wasn't quite what it is today; he was never able to bend the leg past thirty degrees again, which, eventually, was fine for walking but wholly inadequate for anything even vaguely resembling a run. His football days were a thing of the past.

Henry never talked much about his loss; only a few select people who were especially close to him, among them his high school sweetheart and future wife, Dolores, even came close to comprehending the enormity of his grief.

But inside he screamed; inside he cried for two years straight . . . though no one would have guessed it by his outward self.

And after those two years, he continued to grieve, only he forced it further and further back into the deepest, darkest parts of him so that he could make room in his heart for Dolores, who deserved as much of himself as he could give. But even so, it surfaced occasionally, kept surfacing right on through the years, right on up to the present. It would happen while he was watching a game on television... or when he saw someone run and run well... or sometimes when he was just plain sitting alone late at night with too much time to think. And each time it hit him the same: he'd lost his dream; his life would never, *could* never be fulfilled. And that was one tough revelation to live and grow old with.

He sensed some of that same hurting wistfulness in Jack, though neither one of them had ever talked about their respective problems to the other. There was no need; each had been filled in on the particular kind of cross the other bore by his wife, and the rest was pure... empathy. Maybe that was why he'd liked the younger man right off; they were kindred spirits. And the least you could do for a kindred spirit, whether you'd known him a lifetime or only a few weeks, a few brief conversations, was to offer help in those ways that you might be able to help. That was why, on Saturday morning, exactly one day after Blanche's death, Henry Mallory found himself walking the few blocks up Romeo Road toward Main Street and the library.

It was quiet when he entered. There was no one there except Jack, seated off to one side at a small children's table. The whole of the table's round surface was cluttered with old, ragtag looking books, most barely held together by their bindings. Jack was hunched over one of these trying to apply glue to where the cloth of its backing bulged away from the cardboard beneath.

Henry walked over to him, and in this place his footsteps sounded loud and ponderous, the way they used to when he was still farming and would forget to change from his heavy, high-top work shoes before coming into town to the bank or drugstore. Libraries, even small ones, had that effect on him—a feeling of overwhelming cloddishness, a shameful awareness of all that knowledge, all that culture, housed around him, and his being too stupid and/or lazy to grasp even a thousandth of it.

Jack looked up from the book he was working on. "Henry," he said. "My first customer."

It threw the older man. He felt more than ever out of his element, and he glanced down at his hands, dangling at the end of their big-boned wrists, as if they might deliver him an appropriate answer. "Yeah," he said finally, aware he was only encouraging a direction of conversation at odds with his purpose. "I s'pose I *should* do more reading..."

Jack looked down at the book he was holding, then back up at him with the flicker of an idea in his eye. "Have you ever read Burroughs, Henry? You know, Tarzan, Pellucidar, that kind of stuff?"

"Can't say as I have."

He nodded in the direction of the cluttered tabletop. "That's what these are. A Mrs. Delaney brought them in a few days ago. Said they'd belonged to her husband. He died. He was in his eighties, I guess, and—"

"I knew Jake. He was a tough old bird." Henry frowned. "'Bout as much imagination as a stone, though. You mean he actually read all these?"

Jack nodded. "A lot of them over and over again, according to his wife."

Henry chewed this bit of revelation over before he answered. "They sound my speed, then. Jake and I thought a lot alike."

"I'll *bet* you did."

Henry's eyes widened a little in surprise. He'd just

claimed the man had no imagination. But then he saw something in the way Jack met his stare, straight on, that told him the basis for the remark might be something good, even admirable. Never one to angle for compliments, he reached for the book nearest him and said, "Is this one okay, or do you have to assign it a code number or something first?"

For answer Jack reached over, took the book from him, and handed him another in its stead. It was titled *Tarzan of the Apes*. "This one's the first in the series. Try it. By the time you get to where he meets D'Arnot and learns he's human instead of an ape, it's my guess you'll be hooked." He shrugged. "If not, don't be too polite to say so; we'll try something else."

Henry looked down at the book, turned it over several times in his hands, as if by weight and texture he could best judge its worth, then glanced back up. "All right. That takes care of me. Now... what about you?"

It was Jack's turn to frown. "What do you mean?"

"I'm kind of surprised you came in today. Knocked at your door first, and your Judy told me. Are you sure you're up to it?"

Jack looked away and reached for another of the books in obvious need of repair. He was quiet a moment. Then: "It's one of those things. You keep replaying it in your mind every time you're not busy, keep going over every detail, wondering..." His voice trailed off for five, maybe ten seconds. Henry waited patiently. "Wondering if you did everything right."

He gave the younger man's shoulder a pat. "You did. More'n most anybody else around here could have done, I'll guarantee that."

Jack was gazing off into space now, and Henry figured that was not good, so he kept talking. "I seen what that asshole dog of hers did. Even taking into account how much you admired the beast, I know it must have bothered you some."

The dry sarcasm, used intentionally to cut through the other's unhappy reverie, accomplished its purpose. Jack smiled ruefully. "Jesus, what a mess! You're right, I could've done without it."

"He was crazy, Jack. And real craziness is a helluva thing. I remember seein' a dog once that was so far gone with rabies it was after its own tail. Sounds kinda funny, I know, but believe me, it wasn't a'tall. Wasn't anything but sad." He paused. "I shot it. Put it out of its misery. Bruce is out of his."

Jack thought about it, then nodded. "As is Aunt Blanche."

Then they were both silent for a while, and Henry wondered if Jack was thinking the same thing he was, that it seemed perfectly natural to lump both deaths together as one inseparable demise.

Henry was the first to break the silence. "Any problems with the funeral arrangements? Anything I could help you with?"

Jack shook his head. "I guess not. Not now, anyway. Yesterday afternoon was rough, though." He looked up, and there was a puzzled-hurt look in his eyes. "It seems that none of the good ministers in this town wanted the job of burying her."

Henry blinked. So, it had come to that. Well, he wasn't really surprised.

"I went to the Granger Presbyterian, the Congregational Something-or-other on Main, and the First Methodist," Jack continued, numbering them on his fingers. "And each steered me right on out the door to the next. Said they thought it would be more 'appropriate' if so-and-so did the service. Finally, at the last one, the Methodist, I got mad. He told me I should go over to Manchester to the *Catholic* church. I told him that, to the best of my knowledge, Aunt Blanche was about as Catholic as Billy Graham."

Henry snorted. "Glossman, the old hypocrite! Old Powderpuff. I bet *he* turned red!"

"He did when I told him that in my opinion if you're not specifically Catholic or Jewish or partial to the hubba-bubba sun god, you must be Protestant... and Methodist was close enough. I even lied a little and said that Aunt Blanche had spoken of him before, and so I thought it would be most 'appropriate' for him to bury her. That seemed to upset him more, but when he saw I wasn't going to leave, he finally agreed."

Henry chuckled. He'd played ball with Coleman Glossman in high school, and even as an eighteen-year-old the "reverend" had managed to be pompous. He'd been a candyass, too, hence the nickname Powderpuff. But then he stopped laughing, because by the expression on Jack's face, he could tell what was coming next, and nobody likes to be the one to tell their buddy his sister is banging for the troops.

There was a momentary lull, then he was hit with it:

"What's the deal here, Henry? Why do they get so ...*uncomfortable* when I ask them to do the service?" He tried for a just-kidding kind of grin, but it was weak. "What, is there a family curse or something?"

Bingo, Henry thought. He made a show of taking a deep breath. "This is hard, Jack," he said finally. "Especially since I don't know how close you and your aunt was. If you was real close, the way I was to one of mine, almost like a second mother, I'd just as soon—"

"We weren't. I saw her once in five years."

Henry nodded; he could no longer put off the inevitable. "All right. Okay." He took another breath. "Put bluntly—and I guess there *is* no other way to put it—

most folks in this town believe your Aunt Blanche was a Devil worshiper. A satanist."

Other than a minute bunching of the muscles around his jaw, there was no way of reading in Jack's face how the statement was affecting him. He blinked several times, but that didn't tell Henry anything. Then he spoke, and his voice was tight, cautious. "What makes them think that?"

"It's a long story, all of it. The bones are this: about four years ago there was two couples that moved into town. Outside of town, really; they rented out what used to be a little Friends of Christ church about half a mile east of here on Plank Road. You may have seen it."

Jack shook his head.

"Kind of different-acting, they were... in a strange sort of way. I couldn't quite put my finger on it back then. You know, put it into words. But since then I've settled on 'serene.' They were serene. That pins it about as close as it can be pinned. They were well-mannered and all—but you got the impression when you saw them that they was seein' things you weren't seein', hearin' things you weren't hearin'." He paused. "Good things, *pleasurable* things..."

"Could've just been drugs," Jack offered.

"No. No, this was different. Don't ask me how, 'cause I don't know how. It just was. You'd know what I meant if you seen them."

Jack didn't comment, but he looked skeptical.

"Even a deputy sheriff who used to work narcotics with the Detroit police said he didn't think it was drugs. Your good buddy Michaels asked him to stop by, by the way, and to kind of 'discreetly' check them out. They were the same 'serene' way all the time he was here, too, and he didn't know quite what to make of it. Said it wasn't drugs, though. Said they were just peculiar and would bear watching."

"How did you know all this?"

"Bob Michaels likes to brag about how hard he works as city manager. How he looks out for the interests of the town. He likes to brag to me in particular cause every Fourth of July I beat him at arm wrestling. There's an open contest right after the chicken barbecue, and it bugs the shit out of him that he places second each year to a man who's old enough to be his father." Henry could feel his ears redden as, halfway through, he realized that what he was saying could be judged as a bit of brag in its own right. He went on with his story, looking away for a minute because he didn't want to see whether Jack thought so too.

"Anyway, after a while we all just kind of got used to 'em, these new people. Then they started approaching different ones of us, mostly some of the older folks, telling them how they followed a religion where you could 'come to terms with yourself.' They talked about things to do with 'life beyond death' too." He looked back now and shook his head. There was a half-sad, half-bemused set to his eyes. "You better know those are the right kind of words to strike up interest in an old person's heart. Some of 'em went out to the converted church when they were invited, your aunt included."

He just plain stopped then, in the middle of his story, aware by Jack's expression, all tense and anxious-expectant, that waiting was a strain on him. But he had to get it right, say it in a way that was not overly condemning of Blanche Lerille, and he needed the right words. To the younger man's credit, he tried his best to be patient, simply sat back and waited. Yes, he did like this Jack Lerille.

Finally he thought he had it right.

"It didn't take most of them long to figure out what they were all about, once they'd gone out there. The whole interior was painted black, and right away the two couples would start talking about man's 'true nature' and how the 'deity' they served wasn't at cross-angles to that nature. They talked about 'giving in' and 'pledging your soul.' It was the same with each person that went out—they only invited one at a time, you understand—and what they were getting at, pure and simple, was worshiping the Devil."

He was tempted to look back away for the next part, but he didn't; he met Jack's stare straight on.

"Only your Aunt Blanche kept going. Everybody else—and there were eight or nine of 'em—quit after one visit, but your aunt kept going back. Even after they moved someplace else—I don't know where—their car, a big, black, mid-sixties Chrysler that was unmistakable, would stop by her house once a week and drive off with her for the evening."

He paused and let Jack work that much over in his mind. If it had been his relative, regardless of their closeness, what he'd just said would have been a tough pill to swallow.

"How long ago'd they stop coming? She's hardly gone... she hardly *went* out of the house since I've been there." Jack's voice was flat, void of emotion, as if he were very, very tired.

"About a year. Right before Dolores and I moved next door. Nobody knows why."

"Anybody ever ask her?"

"Nope. Nobody even talked to her anymore except Dolores and me."

"A social pariah, huh?" Now his voice held just a bit of something, anger maybe. Or reproach.

"I don't know the word."

"An outcast. Like she had leprosy of the mind."

"Oh. Yeah, I guess with a lot of folks it was that way."

A sudden thought occurred to Jack. "And not with

Michaels? I'm surprised he hired me, being I'm her nephew."

"He knows your dad pretty good. I guess—"

"Never mind; I don't want to know."

Henry looked at him oddly, then he understood. "Let's just say that, from a personal standpoint, it wouldn't matter *whose* nephew *or* son you were to Michaels. He goes with efficiency and whether or not the person needs the job bad enough to follow orders, *always*."

Jack grinned sourly. "Thanks."

"Hell, I'm not telling you anything you don't already know."

"Yeah, but it sounds so sweet to hear another man's rendition."

It took Henry a few moments to catch the real tone, it was said so seriously. Then he grinned back. "The way I figure it, both Michaels and your dad have a few surprises coming some day."

"Thanks...again."

They were both quiet for a while then, but it was a satisfied, comfortable silence. The kind that can only occur when you suddenly realize the person you're with expects nothing from you, absolutely nothing, other than that you be yourself; because he likes that self just fine. Henry believed it was a mutual realization. "Well," he said at length, "I just stopped over to tell you how sorry I am about Blanche and to offer to help in any way I can with the arrangements. You need some help?"

"I guess not, but thanks."

"What about the *Reverend* Glossman? Old Powderpuff. I played football with him, you know. If he gives you any more trouble, tell him the 'Dozer' might just want to stop over and relive old times. He'll know what you mean."

Jack grinned. "I'll tell him... if he gives me any more trouble."

He turned to go then, before he turned this into a full-fledged brag session. When he was halfway to the door, Jack asked him, "What made them leave Granger? The 'Devil worshipers.'"

Without turning, he said, "The building's owner only gave them a six-month lease. He wasn't that much interested in renting it in the first place; he only had it 'cause it came with a twenty-acre parcel of farmland he'd bought six years earlier. By the time the lease was up, he knew what they were doin' and started raising the rent by about a third each month." He chuckled. "By the time they finally realized how much they were appreciated around here, he was gettin' eight fifty a month for the place."

There was a pause, before Jack said, only a little conspiratorially, "May as well turn a profit when you're cleanin' your backyard of vermin. Smart."

Henry continued on toward the door. "That's the way I saw it too. Thanks."

XIV

ON A HOT AUGUST AFTERNOON TWO YEARS BEFORE her death, Blanche Lerille paid an in-office visit to a man named Walter Stone. Walter was the owner of a John Deere sales and service center just outside of town, and a fair and reasonable man (although he was suspected by some of secretly being an MSU fan, what with all that John Deere green around—a proclivity which, had it been proved, would have been about as bad for business in this pro-Michigan, go-blue-and-gold town as if it had been revealed he was gay). Walter was also the owner and manager of Pine Grove, Granger's only unfilled cemetery.

Blanche did not bring Bruce along on this particular outing, because she was convinced the matters she had come to discuss would only upset him. She was equally sure that if she approached these rather unpleasant matters in an honest, straightforward, businesslike manner, they would be settled once and for all and in a matter of minutes. She was wrong. Very shortly after she entered Walter Stone's office and closed the door, an argument ensued. No one but Mr. Stone himself ever knew exactly what the argument was about, but Jim Fresner, who manned the front sales counter, told everyone *he* knew that, after about ten minutes, Old Witch Lerille came buzzing out of his boss's office as brisk and rammy as someone her age could afford to be. Ol' Walt followed her, all tight-lipped and flustered. Before she slammed the outer door, practically in his face, she had turned back to him and said, "What's 'human'? *You're* certainly not, you—you stuffed shirt! You can't keep us apart!" Walter never said a word.

From there Blanche proceeded directly to the home of Frank Russell, a dairy farmer whose 220 acres included the field directly adjacent to Pine Grove's northern boundary. It is to be assumed that here she fared better, because when she left the Russell's place she appeared positively relieved, as if a giant weight had been lifted from her shoulders.

The funeral went about as well as a funeral can go on a cold, sunless early-December morning. Without a hitch, really. Well, almost without a hitch. There had been a moment when Jack had glanced up at the minister, Old Powderpuff, a pug-faced man whose head grew directly from his shoulders without benefit of any visible neck, and had discovered he looked alarmingly like Bruce, dressed in a black suit. Alarmingly? *Exactly.* But only for a moment. And that had been after thinking about the dog, staring across the fence from *her* grave, which was as close as cemetery restrictions allowed to the north boundary of Pine Grove, to *his*, right up against the fence but still legally on Frank Russell's property.

But all that was behind him now, Jack thought as they filed somberly back to their cars—all seven of them who had attended the graveside ceremony. Besides, what was a little hallucinating compared to being stuck in the same house with his father, Jack Lerille Sr., for the next twenty-four hours? One thing; his father wouldn't stay for too long past the reading of the will, which was tomorrow at ten A.M.; Jack could count on that. But in Jack's present frame of mind, he didn't know whether that was a drawback or a blessing.

XV

IF HIS FATHER GOT THE HOUSE, JACK WOULD PAY HIM rent, whether asked to or not.

The decision was made as he sat across from the senior Lerille on one of several folding chairs arranged in a semicircle in front of lawyer Exman's desk, awaiting the reading of the will. They both wore similar expressions, Exman and his father: down-turned mouths, lips pursed but pressed tightly together, the kind of expression one wears while cleaning up after someone else's mess. It made them appear as if they might be related, although they weren't and in most other aspects of their appearance they were completely different.

His father was a meaty man, slightly shorter than average, with nothing whatsoever to suggest delicacy or frailness about him. From his high, extra-broad forehead, which, even when Jack was little, had reminded him of a buffalo (no malice intended...then), to his ham-shoulders and his forty-four-inch waist, he was sturdy, solid. Physically capable. And he would never *ask* for any kind of rent from his son...just let him know how much the house *could* bring in if it were anybody else.

Exman, on the other hand, was frail indeed. On the phone he'd sounded old. And *dusty*, somehow. Like maybe he lived and worked in a place that had dried-up flies on the windowsill. In reality his office was clean and relatively modern...which did little to alter Jack's original impression of a man who seemed as if he'd be most at home in someone's attic. He was tall, gaunt, and if Jack Sr. brought buffaloes to mind, Exman was a vastly down-sized version of Lurch on the old *Addams Family* television show *(You RANG?)*. He moved with the same dead-from-the-neck-down stiffness, too, as if his body were an empty suit still hung on its hanger. Or perhaps, considering his almost *painfully* serious manner and his dour expression, the method of suspension might more appropriately be a pole run up through the center of his body through his rectum.

Besides the lawyer, his father, and himself, there was only Judy. She had a hand on Jack's shoulder even though she was sitting down next to him. The hand, the expression she wore as they sat there under patriarchal scrutiny, said clearly, *He's mine, I'm with him, and* I *think he's great,* and Jack loved her for that.

The lawyer Exman cleared his throat. "I, uh—" When that much swung all heads in his direction, he stopped abruptly, mouth partway open, as if it were almost too much that they should look at him as well as listen. "This will was originally filed eight years ago. Since then it has been revised. Twice. Once three years ago and, uh, once very recently." He cleared his throat again. His Adam's apple moved remarkably. "In point of fact, three weeks ago. The revisions, uh, may prove upsetting... to some."

Then he was quiet for such an extended period of time—a full minute at least—that Jack wondered at first if he might need prompting. Upsetting? What was there that could be upsetting? Blanche, *Aunt* Blanche, had next to nothing beyond the house itself. The money she had inherited from Grandpa Lerille, back in 'forty-three, had run out just about the time she'd started receiving her SSI checks. She'd simply lived on it till it was gone, as his father—who had used his half to start a hardware store, which was now *five* hardware stores—had always pointed out with the same kind of loathing in his voice as when he spoke of women's libbers, welfare recipients, and black athletes with million-dollar contracts. Jack glanced over at him now, the man who had always (forever and amen!) made it clear that he ranked Jack's own dream of an acting career as only slightly less frivolous, and therefore deplorable. He was leaning forward on the edge of his seat.

"... being of sound mind, do leave all my worldly goods..."

PADDYWHACK

Jack's mind snapped back from its bitter and fruitless musings. Exman had finally begun.

"... sole ownership and title to all properties and structures located at the legal address designated as 115 Romeo Road, Plot forty-seven in the Township of Granger, County of Lenawee, State of Michigan, to my nephew, Jack Joseph Lerille Junior, with the single yet binding condition that he should feed, house, and care for my loving companion Bruce, existent in this world as a male Boston bullterrier, marked black and white, should Bruce survive me; and that he should deliver said terrier's remains, upon death, to Mr. Frank Russell, residing at 100 Chelsea Road in this same township for burial.

"To my only other living relative, my brother, Jack Joseph Lerille Senior, who has forever judged people solely by their earnings and their industry and has therefore damned me in his mind all these years, I leave nothing but the following piece of advice: There are many roads to hell, not the least of which are pride, greed, and lovelessness."

The room was silent. Judy, who was hanging onto Jack's hand now, rather than his shoulder, was unconsciously gripping him so hard that at any other time he would have complained aloud. And he understood why. It had little to do with the fact that they had the house, that they needn't worry anymore about such things as rent or finding another place to stay. Or that, with the reading of a single sentence, their net worth had more than doubled... It had to do with a sudden and powerful sense of malignancy in the room, with an abrupt change of climate with the reading of the will and its talk of Bruce being "existent in this world" *(only?)* as a dog, its use of words like "damned" and "roads to hell," from an atmosphere that was frosty and unpleasant to one that fairly reeked with madness and Cimmerian premonition. It was as if his dead aunt had laid a cold hand on each of their shoulders and whispered, *Along with my property... insanity. Or worse.* And he didn't understand why. Any more than he understood how he should *know* that Judy was feeling it too.

Words, just words, he reassured himself. *And we knew all along that she wasn't all there when it came to—*

Exman cleared his throat. Loudly. "I, uh... that's it."

Jack Sr. came to his feet with a single, quick, almost explosive motion that belied his considerable bulk. His expression was brisk. *"Well,"* he said in a mildly surprised tone. He took a step in Exman's direction, his hand partway extended, as if unsure whether he was supposed to shake hands with the man, the way you would at the conclusion of a business deal. Then he stopped, apparently deciding against it, and turned toward Jack. For a fraction of a second his face registered hurt and confusion, and for just about that same length of time Jack felt sorry for him. But the moment of vulnerability passed, and the old Jack Lerille Sr. was back: arrogant, judgmental. "Well..." he said again. "Congratulations. Lord knows you need something like this—even from a crazy—after the mess-up in New York and the job you've got now."

Jack didn't answer. A still, small voice was speaking to him inside his head. (His own? Blanche's?) It said: *See? See? It all fits. Good is good, damned is damned, and everything bad you're feeling is true.*

XVI

HIS FATHER WAS GONE. LEFT DIRECTLY FROM Exman's office within sixty seconds after they had stepped outside. He'd mumbled some awkward thing about not being able to be away from the business for too long, and hopped in his car and driven away. Jack had stood there watching him go, feeling helpless and resigned. It wasn't until they were most of the short walk home themselves that he had turned to Judy with mild surprise and said, "He must have had his suitcase packed and with him before he even left the house."

She nodded, avoiding his eyes, as if the uncrossable gulf between Jack and his father were somehow her fault and she was ashamed of it. "I thought you knew."

No, he hadn't known. In fact he'd had it in his mind since yesterday, before the funeral, that once the matters at hand were taken care of—the service itself, the reading of the will—they would talk. That he would say something like, *Look, Dad, I know we're two entirely different people, but that doesn't mean we're enemies...does it?* and that somehow that would open things up in a way they'd never been open before. Well, it wasn't going to be. Fine. He could live with that too.

But the ache in his heart, as palpable as the premonition of doom he'd felt earlier, said it wasn't fine.

It told him what he already knew but, till now, had refused to admit on a conscious level: every man needs a father. Or a least a father *figure*. Someone, who may or may not be older than himself, whom he perceives as being exemplary of what a man should be and with whom he can communicate his hopes... his fears... and seek affirmation that these are normal, acceptable parts of the male condition.

Judy, with all her love and that special psychic bond some, but not all, married couples share if they remain together long enough, couldn't fill that particular need. Maybe that was why, when he split off from her and went to the Mallory's front door to collect Rachel from Henry and Dolores—who had kindly volunteered to babysit for them while they were at the lawyer's—and Henry said, "Whyn't you stop back over later this evening. We could play some cards, talk... whatever..." he'd answered immediately, "I just might do that." And he knew, once the small talk, the preliminaries were out of the way, just what his opener for the evening's "whatever" would be. It would start out with something like, *Did you ever get a feeling of dread, a premonition so strong...*

He tucked Rachel in her bed around eight. It had been a long day for a six-year-old. So had yesterday, with the funeral and Jack's father being there...

She stared up at him with round, solemn eyes, as if she were waiting for something. He leaned in closer for his kiss, and her little arms practically flew around his neck, squeezing him with a desperate strength. She clung to him for maybe thirty seconds that way, while he stroked her hair, then she let go. And watched him again with those solemn, expectant eyes.

He knew what she was waiting for: someone to make sense of all this.

"So..." he ventured. "What does a junior-sized pumpkin make of all this?"

She'd been right there, hovering in the kitchen, through it all: his working on Blanche's body, administering CPR; Bruce's throwing himself at the door; the arrival of the paramedics; the wheeling of the body out... The only thing she'd been spared was the gruesome detail of just how Bruce had looked, hung up there halfway through the window like sliced meat. And he'd never even talked to her. He'd held her, comforted her; but he'd never talked things out. Nor had Judy.

"I think..." She paused, frowned. "I think I don't know what to wish. About Bruce."

Jack felt himself tighten at mention of the dog. It wasn't at all the point of departure he'd hoped for. "What do you mean?"

"I don't know if to wish Bruce is alive or dead."

His own uneasy frown had little to do with her first-grade syntax.

"I think dead, 'cuz they were in love, and he committed sewer-side, but—"

Ka-THUD. Jack's heart did a double flip. Out of the mouths of babes...

"—but maybe not, 'cuz he's sooo mad."

"Mad?" It came out sounding too much like a croak. "How can he be mad? He's dead."

"Yeah, but—"

"But what?" He didn't like the way this conversation was going. The first trickle of cold sweat let go beneath his right arm; he could feel its icy progress down his side. No, he didn't like the way it was going at all.

"But he still talks to me. All the time. He says he hates you 'cuz you kept him from Aunt Blanche when she got her heart attacked. He'll *always* hate you, and—"

"Rachel, that's not true! Dead animals, dead *people*, don't talk! You're imagining things—and I can understand why. This has been hard on you..." He tried to say it calmly, rationally, but inside he was about as calm as a man facing a firing squad. The same sense of malignancy, of rushing—or being drawn—toward some grim-visaged destiny he'd felt during the reading of the will, was on him again, drowning out all sense, all purpose, so that he was barely aware of Rachel's argumentative, "Noooo. He *talks* to me!"

"Now I want you to put all this out of your mind," he went on, saying the words but not really feeling them. "Your aunt had a heart attack; Bruce had an accident. That's all there is to it. You don't need to worry. And if you *still* can't keep your mind off it, think about the fact that both of them were hurting—a lot—and now they're not hurting anymore. And about the fact that your mother and I both have very strong, very healthy hearts."

Except for the last, it was a chant, a kind of parental incantation patched together from the distilled *non*wisdom about death recited for his own benefit when he was a child; and as such, it was next to worthless. But it would have to do, because it was better than nothing, and far better than if he were to stay there and keep talking. And allow her to see how gut-watering spooked he was.

As it turned out, Jack didn't have to do much steering of the conversation in the direction of premonitions or otherwise. Henry Mallory was remarkably in tune with what Jack was going through, what he was feeling that evening. In fact, when Jack thought about it much later, there was never a time when he and Henry *weren't* of at least similar minds.

He stopped over around eighty-thirty. Alone. Judy

had claimed she was exhausted and was going to bed, but what was much more likely was that she had intuited his need for some more "fatherly" companionship right now and had stayed behind for that reason. He hadn't put up much of an argument.

Henry answered the door—not at all surprised, it seemed, to see him—and ushered him into a house which, structurally, was almost identical to their own. *It's like ours*, Jack thought, and wondered at how easily his mind slid over the "ours" without a hitch. Structurally. They were both Cape Cods, very obviously built at the same time by the same builder. Even their interior layout was the same. But the house had a different flavor, a different feel to it. Standing there in the middle of what, in the other house, was the formal living room but in this one was more of a cozy blend between well-used den and family room, Jack was reminded of the night he had been drawn downstairs by the sound of his aunt's voice doing her insane monologue with Bruce as sole audience... and how everything in the living room had appeared alien, out of dimension, and, yes, *conspiring* in the leeching moonlight. This room would never look that way; it was a solid, *friendly* room. The kind of room where you could imagine you heard the crackle of a log burning in a nearby fireplace even if there wasn't one... which there wasn't, he noticed.

Henry motioned for him to sit down on a low-slung, deeply padded sofa, which was covered in some kind of chamois. He himself chose a straight-backed cane, which he swung up close to Jack and straddled backward, forearms resting on the top of its back. A young man's posture, which for most sixty-year-olds would have seemed both uncomfortable and affected. With Henry it seemed neither.

"Well," he said, "do you stay or is she turnin' it into a home for wayward pooches?"

Jack smiled. "Only on weekends. We stay."

Henry clenched a blocky right hand into a fist and raised it a little ways off the back of his chair in a mini victory salute. And somehow that hand looked more powerful, more impressive... more when-the-chips-are-down dependable than all the Rocky/Rambo pumped-up pectorals and deltoids in the world. "Good," he said. "Good." Then he just sat there for a moment, smiling through his eyes in a genuinely pleased way. Meanwhile the pastoral home fire crackled and popped companionably in Jack's mind, putting him at ease. "Was it rough?"

"Which part?" But Jack knew which part. Like minds.

"All of it. The reading of the will."

"It was... worse than I thought."

"Who was the lawyer?"

"A man named Exman."

Henry snorted, caught himself, then laughed outright. "First *Gloss*man, then *Ex*man... and neither one of 'em much like a *man* a'tall! Both of 'em farts of a different color, actually... if you know what I mean."

Jack nodded and grinned a little himself. He knew exactly what Henry meant.

Then Henry's face went serious. "They ain't typical, Jack. Neither is your so-called boss, Bob Michaels. Most folks in this town are good, ordinary people you'd be at home with." He tilted forward on the chair. "But Exman's not all of it—the 'worse than I thought'—is it?"

Jack opened his mouth to answer, frowned, then closed it again. Here was the opportunity he'd been waiting for, so tailor-made, in fact, that he could almost have used verbatim the opening line he'd carried, half formed, in the back of his head since earlier that day, when he'd picked up Rachel—the one that began, *Did you ever get a feeling of dread*... And yet he hesitated. And during the hesitating Dolores came in from the kitchen and the moment was lost.

She didn't stay long. In fact, Jack thought it possible that Henry signaled her *not* to with some subtle movement of his head or his eyes, though he couldn't be sure. He thought he caught that in *her* eyes. The train of thought was effectively shifted, though, and before she went back in the other room to "tend to some sweet rolls for you boys," it had settled on how "little Rachel" had been affected by both Blanche's and Bruce's deaths.

He didn't bring up his most recent conversation with her, though, until *after* Dolores had left the room. Then he told Henry everything Rachel had said just a half hour ago, as he was tucking her in: the part about her aunt Blanche and the dog being "in love"; her insistence that Bruce still "talked" to her; and her belief that the animal hated him for keeping it and Blanche apart.

About halfway through, Henry stood up and moved to the window. He remained there, looking out in such a way that he was in profile to Jack, and it was impossible for the latter to see his eyes. "Well...?" Jack asked when he was done. "What do you think?"

Henry was quiet a moment, still gazing out the window into the darkness. Then he said, "I think she's a smart little girl. Not afraid to talk neither—and that part's good." Now he moved back to his chair, resumed his backward perch on it...and that's when Jack knew that the topics of premonitions and feelings of nervous dread would be entirely appropriate with this man, this night. Because there was deep concern —and maybe something else—in Henry's eyes.

"And I wouldn't set much store in the 'in love' part," he went on, " 'cause that's natural. A six-year-old is *gonna* lump animals and people in the same

boat with regards to feelings. But the suicide part...
and the piece about Bruce *tellin'* her how much he
hates you..." His voice drifted off. "I think you better set her straight on those things." Then he finished
with, "What do *you* make of it?"

What do I make of it? Jack thought to himself with
surprising bitterness. *I'll tell you what I make of it.
But you won't get it; you won't feel the same sick,
SURE dread I felt this morning. Or felt again a half
hour ago. The kind you might have last felt as a child,
waking up in the middle of the night, listening... and
knowing,* knowing, *that you hear someone breathing
in the room besides yourself... Because to feel that
way, you would have had to be there, late at night,
when Blanche and Bruce "talked". Or have seen the
way the dog looked at me. Or dreamed my dreams.
Or have been there when he died...*

But aloud he said, "I... I don't know what to make
of it. All I know is I need to talk. Not just about what
Rachel said but... other stuff."

He stopped then, still unsure of himself, waiting for
some sign from the older man. Henry didn't say a
word. But he did stand up again, turn the old straight-
back around the right way and settle on it as if he
meant to stay there awhile and do some serious listening.

Jack took a deep breath and began: "Did you ever
get a feeling of dread, a premonition so strong..."

Henry listened just right. He didn't interrupt, except
to ask a few questions that really did help clarify
things; he wore the look of someone who is genuinely
listening, rather than the preoccupied, somewhat impatient expression of someone most concerned with
what *they* will say in reply; and, a minor thing, he
didn't laugh in Jack's face or suggest he was crazy
when Jack was done. As well he might have. Because

Jack told him everything. Not just the factual stuff, like the way Blanche had talked to Bruce late at night, or the way things had gone with the dog when she'd taken her fall (he could still vividly see Bruce licking the protruding bone end), or the way both of them had died... but the things that were more a matter of interpretation. Like the way Bruce had always looked at him, so measuring, so knowing, and, at the end, so full of hate. And the dreams. And the sense all along, from the day they'd moved in, that there was something spiritually wrong in the house, something that had as its source the unnatural bond between an old woman and her dog.

He began and ended with the almost incapacitating sense of dread, the feeling that something right out of his worst nightmares was about to happen, which had gripped him like a cold, dead hand immediately following the reading of the will.

When he was finished there was a drawn-out silence. Even Dolores, out in the kitchen, seemed to have ceased moving about. The only sound at all was the steady *whisk-whisk* of Henry's callused hand rubbing back and forth, back and forth, across the day-old stubble on his chin. It was an unconscious thing, and Jack had one of those flash moments of total recall during which he could see the older man doing the same thing on that day, which seemed so long ago, when they had entered the Mallory garage and found the kittens... or what was left of them.

Then Henry spoke.

"A man my age'd be a fool not to put some credence to... 'feelings,' Jack. What you call premonitions and what we 'farm boys' used to call 'skunk hunches'—but only when we was young and would've made light of the Devil himself. I've had 'em. So's the Missus. And sometimes they're nothin' more than a sour stomach or the first scratchin' of the flu." He cocked an eyebrow at Jack. "And sometimes they're more.

"When I was a boy—ten years old, I think—I had one, a skunk hunch, that was bad. Me and the neighbor girl, Maggie Fisher, used to walk to and from school every day. It was a little more than a mile each way on a dirt road that saw more tractors and horse manure in those days than it ever did cars, and there was an old, deserted gravel pit along the way. It dropped right off from the road on the one side, though you couldn't see into it except in the winter, 'cause of all the sumac and weeds. Anyway... one day, just before school was out for the summer, Maggie and me was walkin' just about there on our way home when we heard some digging sounds..."

He paused with his lips parted as Dolores called in from the kitchen, "Jack, you want apples or raisins in those rolls?" For just a moment, the grave, serious look on his face disappeared, and he winked at Jack. "He wants both!" Then it was back.

"It was *somethin'*, Jack. It was just diggin' sounds ... and yet Maggie looks at me and I looks at her, and our eyes was both big as saucers. And talk about *scared*... It was like we'd both just looked over our shoulder and seen the headless horseman comin' for us."

His gaze took on an unfocused look, the look of a person viewing their own private movie, on the *back* side of their eyes. Jack decided, after a while, that he needed prompting. "What'd you do?" he asked.

"Why... we ran. We ran to beat hell. All the rest of the way home to my house, which was still a good half mile. And, Jack, it was just *diggin'* sounds. From a *gravel* pit."

Again he paused, as if seeing things that weren't there, then pulled himself back, with an effort. "But I'll never forget the feelin' that come over me—Maggie, too, I'm sure, though we never talked about it, not even after we found out. It was like... like somethin' dead had just whispered in my ear, invited me to do somethin' or go someplace... someplace *evil*. And while it was whisperin', it was slidin' a dead hand right up inside you, through your bowels, through your stomach, gropin' for your heart. And it all had to do with that diggin' sound. Somehow we knew, we *knew* that it meant somethin' read bad. *Real* bad."

Now there was not even the sound of a hand rasping on whiskers. Nothing. Jack cut into that silence, feeling almost irreverent in so doing. "What was it? You said 'after we found out,' so you must know. Or don't you want to say?"

Henry regarded him peculiarly again. "No. No, I want to tell you. It'd defeat the whole purpose if I didn't tell the end."

Jack waited. Henry took his time; mapping it all out in his head first, Jack supposed.

"It was the sound of a murderer," he said finally. "Not *just* a murderer, but a real sick-un. What you might call a 'psychotic killer' nowadays."

He paused, possibly for no other reason than effect, but it seemed to Jack as if he expected some kind of challenge from him. When he got none, he went on.

"Now, you may not think we had such a rare animal back then, but we did. This one started out by murderin' his wife and seventeen-year-old daughter over by Monroe. He beheaded them in their sleep, with some kind of machete knife.

"The one he was buryin' here, though, was number five on the hit parade—two more in Ohio, a mother and daughter again, and then this poor girl. They finally caught him after number six, but that wasn't until the end of that same summer. He owned up to everything then, even showed them where the bodies was buried and told them *when* he buried 'em...."

Henry let the last words simply hang there, and Jack tried to imagine how it must have been, reading that in the newspaper or having your friend stop over on his bike. *Hey, Henry, didja hear what they found over in the pit? Didja...?*

Finally, Jack said, "And you never talked about it ...with this Maggie?"

"Nope."

"Why not?"

He leaned forward, deliberately. " 'Cause we was scared. Or at least I was. And I was too busy denyin' it, denyin' it happened that way at all! 'Cause... 'cause if it did..." He sat back again, just as deliberately, and there was old hurt in his eyes. "If it did, it seemed like that opened up a whole lot of other possibilities and made the world a whole lot less cut-and-dried than I wanted it to be."

Jack thought about it, thought about a ten-year-old and how nobody sees things more black-and-white, more in clear-cut terms of what *can* and *can't* be, than someone who is ten and who has finally mastered Santa Claus, where babies come from, and the reality of the diplomatic lie. "Oh," he said. "Yeah, I guess that—"

"But I *should* have. I should have talked to Maggie. She was older—country school went up to eighth grade back then, and Maggie was seventh at the time —and it definitely would have helped to talk things out. 'Specially with someone older..."

Jack nodded, even though Henry didn't see him do it because the older man was studiously avoiding his face at the moment and seemed just a little embarrassed. *(It's good that you came to me, Jack...)* Only he wasn't so sure how good it was. In the story, Henry's premonition had become reality in the worst possible way.

"And... what would this *older* person have told you... that would have helped?"

Henry chuckled. "That sometimes a skunk hunch is on and sometimes it's not. That they're not to be ignored, but that at the same time you can't overreact to one neither. Or let it turn you chickenshit for a season, the way it did me. Because they seldom tell you just *what* to be wary of anyway."

He chuckled again, but this time it ended in a self-derisive snort.

"Hell, I'm one to talk. I did it again a few years later, when I was thirteen. This time one grabbed me just about as hard, only in a different way. A lot more long-lastin' too. For all of one night and most of the next day I was *sure* my mother was gonna die. Just as sure as I was three years earlier that there was somethin' terrible in the gravel pit. The knowledge just come over me, and it was so much like real fact that I cried, told her stuff a thirteen-year-old boy *never* tells his mom, like 'I love you' and 'I been selfish and mean to you,' and generally behaved in a manner unbecoming any self-respectin' hell raiser."

He paused for a moment, long enough to break into a half smile, then looked serious again. " 'Course she'd been sick to bed for two days with what musta been pneumonia and was weak as a kitten, and none of us kids had ever known Momma to be weak *or* in bed past six A.M. our entire lives..."

He flashed the half grin again.

"What happened? I take it from the grin she didn't die."

"No. No, she didn't die. I don't rightly remember what happened next, or how I saved face on the whole thing—what the *Reader's Digest* calls 'selective memory,' you know—but I'm sure Mom would remember. We could call her'n find out; it's not that far. She lives over by Onsted now. She's eighty-eight and sees, hears, and thinks as good as I do, though I do believe I could edge her out in a foot race these days."

Jack joined him in his grinning, and the thought of that old woman still carrying around in her heart what a thirteen-year-old boy had told her when he thought he was going to lose her warmed him in a way he knew he would be able to draw on in the future.

"The thing is, Jack, it was the *circumstances* that second time. I was worried. Our house was off its routine... I think my subconscious added it all up and drew its own conclusion: She's gonna die. And from what I've read, the subconscious doesn't deal in *mights* and *maybes*..."

He paused to let that much sink in, and then, perhaps because he saw the doubt in Jack's eyes, he went on.

"Now the first time, that was different. That was like a bolt from the blue. We wasn't worried or scared ahead of time. No ominous doings... Just walkin' along feelin' pretty good about the day and school bein' almost over for the summer and... *wham!* If I got one like that today, I'd still be scared as hell." He paused again and eyed Jack shrewdly, one eyebrow slightly cocked. "But that's not you, is it, Jack? I mean, look what you'd just gone through. Where you were at. What you were *there* for..."

Jack thought about it... and he could almost allow himself to feel better. Almost. Logically it made sense; it would have been unnatural for him *not* to have suffered some kind of reaction, some kind of emotional shake-up or letdown as a consequence of the horror and stress he'd been through this past week. And he knew that, often as not, those kinds of reactions came after the pressure was *off*—people held themselves together while they got done what had to be done, and *then* they collapsed. The reading of the will had more or less capped things, put it all officially behind them.

"... worth keepin' in mind. Anyway, I'm glad she didn't give the house away from under you."

What? Jack gave a mental start. At some point during his musings Henry had begun talking again, and now Jack tried frantically to recall just what had been said prior to his tuning back in. It was very important to him, he realized, that he impress the older man as being good company.

It must have shown, the lapse in attention; he hoped not the eager need to please as well. "Sorry," Henry said easily. "I seen you were doin' some heavy thinking, and I started up anyway. Go ahead, finish your thoughts. I can wait." And his eyes said to Jack that it was the truth, that he wasn't the least bit offended.

"They're finished. I was just thinking about what you said, how your 'skunk hunches' can be different."

Henry nodded, but remained quiet anyway. It wasn't an altogether uncomfortable silence, but still, Jack felt the wheels should be turning, and they weren't. Instead, he felt strangely content and determined *not* to be content at the same time.

"I see your dad didn't come back with you after the funeral," Henry said at length. "Was he peeved at the way the will went?"

Jack shrugged. "I don't know. Probably. He probably wouldn't have stopped back anyway. We don't have that much to talk about."

Henry nodded once more, as if he understood completely, and the corners of his mouth turned down momentarily like he'd tasted something sour. "Life's a bitch," he said. "Man and woman, man*kind* and the Almighty... a father and his son... It seems like all the pairings that should be in harmony, that should be of like minds and able to communicate just fine, actually understand each other about the way I understand Chinese." He reached across and slapped a big hand on Jack's knee, giving it a squeeze like you might squeeze a little boy's knee. Then he let go. He did it almost absently, and it seemed the most natural thing in the world. Jack found himself thinking that it probably was.

"I'm sorry for you," Henry went on. "But don't let yourself think you're the Lone Ranger. I never saw eye to eye with my dad either. And my own boy—though we get along when we see each other, which ain't often—it's pretty much surface stuff we talk about. It's almost as if parents're forever just a little bit pissed at their kids for growin' up and not at least havin' the decency to turn out like carbon copies of themselves. And kids... kids I think know that, deep down inside, so when they're around their folks, they never feel all the way good about themselves. And they resent it. Deep down inside..."

Something inside Jack let go then, and he didn't simply want to talk, he wanted to confide in the older man, to unburden himself in a way that till now he'd only been able to do with Judy. And how the hell did Henry sense that? How did he know just where to begin? Was he, Jack, that transparent?

But Henry did know, because he said, "With me it was football, always football. The 'seed of my discontent,' you might say. Also the thing that most kept my dad and I at odds... or at least the most convenient excuse for us bein' that way. It was my dream, and as such, much of times made my life hell." He paused. "Just the way *your* dream, that of bein' an actor, does for you. Am I wrong?"

Jack blinked, but somehow he didn't feel all that surprised by the other's insight. "You're not wrong," he said.

PADDYWHACK

"I thought not." Then, over his shoulder, in a louder voice: "Dolores, how long before those rolls are done?"

"Oh...twenty, twenty-five minutes," came the reply from the kitchen, and in glancing in that direction, Jack noticed, above the door, a framed photograph of Eisenhower and Harry S shaking hands, presumably on inauguration day—a moment in history that had occurred before he was born but would have found his hosts of an age close to what he was right now. It gave him an odd kind of start.

Henry turned back. "We got time," he said. "Tell you what. You tell me about acting—not just *about* it, but what it means to you—and I'll tell you about football."

And that is how it got started. That is the point at which Henry Mallory began the rather rapid transformation from neighbor and acquaintance to friend. Then to friend/surrogate father.

Jack told him everything. All the things that counted for much, anyway. Among them the fact that when the off-Broadway play had flopped and he'd made the mistake of telling his parents, the first and only words of consolation he'd heard from his father were, "Now maybe you'll grow up and take a real job."

And the way he felt about his job here at Granger: almost as if he were caught in some kind of time warp from which there was no escape and where the only possible emotion was a kind of empty despair (it turned out that Henry was something of a *Star Trek* fan, so the warp analogy was a good one).

And, painfully, awkwardly, his need, the *ache* inside him to be some kind of hero—and how making it as an actor would have fulfilled that need, at least in the "larger than life" sense of the word.

Henry never once laughed. In fact he went one better, he understood. It was partway evident by his expression, by the way he nodded, but it went beyond that too. It was a feeling Jack got as he spoke that still would have been there had he spent the entire time with his eyes closed.

Then it was Henry's turn, and he could have done it easier, if less honest, but fair is fair. The part about him crying on the inside, for example, *needing* to cry on the outside, too, for the first two whole years after he came back from service with a leg made useless for football, must have been at least as tough as the hero bit was for Jack.

Then Dolores was there with the rolls, just as Henry finished, and what could have been one of those awkward moments that occur even among friends when they've each said as much as can be said on a subject but aren't sure how to move on, was saved by her cheery effusiveness.

The rolls were warm and delicious. The atmosphere was the same. So much so that by the time Jack bid the two of them good night, a kind of happy-sad nostalgia had supplanted the ominous forebodings he'd carried with him into the house. He would draw upon those good feelings, much the same as he would draw upon the image of Henry's octogenarian mother, still carrying in her heart a distraught little boy's words of love... in the bad times that followed.

XVII

WHEN JACK GOT BACK HOME, JUDY WAS ALREADY IN bed, despite the fact that it was barely past ten, and the empty solitude of the downstairs robbed him of the good feelings he'd brought with him from the Mallorys in much the same way that sub-zero cold steals the heat from unprotected flesh. This house, *his* house now, wasn't the same as the house he'd just left, Jack decided. It was not a loving house, a wood-and-brick giant that held its occupants willingly, gladly, in the cupped palms of its sheltering hands; it was at best a neutral structure, incapable on its own of fostering good *or* bad. And at worst...

But the house wasn't the problem, really; it was the attitudes he came and went with *in* the house—the depression, the anxiety, the self-doubt and guilt—*they* were the problem. Jack knew that. It was those things... and the ghosts.

Ghosts?

Ghost. Maybe the singular was more proper. He'd visited his aunt Blanche only infrequently as a child, had not taken the time to know her as an adult, even during this recent, more prolonged stay... and yet her ghost was everywhere.

It was standing at one end of the living room, where she had stood the day she'd 'caught' him playing his little game with Bruce and the toy rat.

It was with him as he strode into the kitchen and

snapped on the light, trying not to move, as if he were *(damnit, STOP it)* in a mausoleum.

It was there, in the cupboards, among her cups and saucers, as he reached for one of the former to hold the milk he'd decided to pour for himself. *(Skim milk, Jack—it's still there, on the refrigerator door—or regular? And, by the way, it's not really* her *ghost you're uneasy about anyway, is it, Jackie-boy?)*

Just like it wasn't really the house. Which ticked and made other settling sounds on this, the first really cold, single-digit temperature evening of what wouldn't "officially" be winter for another ten days. And if, as he poured his milk then sat down with it at the kitchen table, it seemed as if most of those noises —no, *all* of them—were coming from behind the closed door at the opposite end of the room, the door which led to

(their)

her room, so what? Why should he feel compelled to scramble to his feet, rush over to it and fling it open with the same falsely brave, genuinely stupid battle cry as witnessed in a thousand horror movies: *Who's there?*

He fought the impulse and remained where he was. But even in this act of rationality there was no comfort, no relief from the terrible sense of unease that had reclaimed him almost the moment he'd entered the front door... because he suspected that what kept him glued to his end of the kitchen while he finished his milk, what *really* kept him there, was something far less rational than the mere desire to avoid looking stupid.

He finished his milk, deliberately forced himself to rinse the glass at the sink, then headed upstairs. The sounds did not follow him. (Did he think they would?)

At the top of the steps, on impulse, he turned right

PADDYWHACK

instead of left and looked in on Rachel. And smiled. Here, at least, the good feelings still abided.

She lay high on her pillow, the world's most perfect six-year-old, with her dark hair fanned out around her like a still from a shampoo commercial, and something stirred deep inside Jack. The innocence, the angelic beauty and grace etched on her sleeping countenance, made the back of his eyes burn with unformed tears, and he was sure that if the rest of the world could see her as he did at that moment, whole nations would throw down their armaments and dictators preach the brotherhood of man.

He stepped forward into the moonlit room, meaning to kiss her softly on the forehead, fix her covers, because—

The smile froze on his face.

Because there was something *on* those covers, crouched at the foot of her bed! Something small, but not too small... Something with animal lines, animal curves and angles.

(Ghost! If Bruce had been human he would have died cursing my—)

Ka-thud. His heart reached out and punched at him, connecting solidly with the low end of his sternum from the inside.

(No, it can't be! It—)

Ka-thud, ka-THUD!

Then he saw it for what it was: his daughter's oldest and dearest friend, a black and white teddy bear named Grumpkins, with a mashed-in, melancholy face, and his limbs went leaden with relief. He stood there uncertainly, a shadowy silhouette for anyone glancing up through the room's dormer-style window to see.

Then would have been the time to lay certain thoughts, certain fears to rest. For good. Maybe even laugh at himself a little, at the *idea*. He could do neither. Instead he checked all the corners of the room, all the little hidey-holes...and then crossed the hall to his own bedroom.

The sound of Judy's breathing, deep and regular, brought him a little closer to rational thinking, and he undressed with exaggerated care, so that not even the rustle of his clothes would cut him off from it. Good sound, comforting sound. Then he climbed into bed and immediately slid over against the curve of her hip where she lay on her side, facing away from him; and for the first time since entering the house that night, he felt complete.

There was something magic in those hips, mystical power in her loins. Whenever he touched her there, whether it was the sensual, intimate, inside-outside touch of their lovemaking or simply a hand placed casually, appreciatively over the curve of one buttock, he felt more solid, more right with the world than at other times.... And in the last four days, since his aunt's (and, let's face it, Bruce's) death, he'd awakened early each morning to find his hand resting, comfortable and secure, on her pubis, in much the same way, he supposed, as a one-year-old Rachel had finally slept through some of her rougher nights with one hand resting firmly on her bottle. It had made for some interesting mornings, and he smiled now at how Judy had asked teasingly if he were worried that that particular part of her was going to run away.

He was still smiling when he drifted off to sleep. Except for a brief moment when it occurred to him that he'd forgotten to brush his teeth. But the bathroom was downstairs, next to Blanche's room, and he dismissed the thought of getting up and going all the way down there again almost immediately. Put it right out of his mind.

* * *

PADDYWHACK

While Jack lay sleeping in his bed, Henry was wide awake in his, struggling with his conscience. He hadn't really lied, he told himself. Just smoothed things over a little when maybe they shouldn't have been smoothed over. It had seemed like a good idea at the time, because Jack had looked like he had about all the worries he could handle for one night. But now he wasn't so sure he'd made the right decision.

Then again, what good would it have done to tell him? It wasn't as if he had something concrete that he could warn Jack against. And, feeling the way he did, Jack would no doubt be as careful as a man could be... as if carefulness had anything to do with it. In these things, whatever would happen would happen if the feeling played true; inevitability was at the very heart of it. When it came right down to brass tacks, he finally decided, it didn't make a damn bit of difference, in any preventive kind of way, that he'd been having the premonitions too. Or that, last night, he'd dreamed that Blanche and Bruce had come back.

Six-year-old Rachel had had no trouble falling asleep that night. As with adults, some small children are worriers and some are not. Rachel wasn't. The transition from wide awake to drowsy-eyed somnolence to full-fledged slumber was but a three-minute journey with no stops or layovers along the way to allow for the boarding of hijackers, particularly those repeat offenders, Unvoiced Fears and Troubled Conscience. In this she was more fortunate than her father or Henry Mallory. But if getting there is oftentimes an easier task for the young, that is not to say that, once arrived, the stay will be any more pleasant. It was well for Rachel, in the days that followed, that she was not a worrier. Because she dreamed. She dreamed often and badly.

This first night the dream was not personally threatening; at least she felt no personal sense of danger. But it was disturbing in its ghastly import, even for a six-year-old.

It was summertime. She had never been at Daddy's aunt's in the summer before, and she felt good about how nice things were. It was an excited, can't-wait-for-the-real-thing kind of feeling, because now the part of her that *knew* she was dreaming also knew how pretty things would be once warm weather really came, and that double awareness spilled over into the dream.

She was playing with Bruce, who hadn't died after all (but of course she knew that), out in front of the house, and everything was flowers, green grass, and sunshine. It bothered her not at all that some of the flowers were animator's flowers, cartoon flowers, something right out of Snow White's garden. Or that the oversize butterfly on one of them was actually smiling at her. Bruce was real, very real. And she was real. And the thing she held in her hand, ready to throw yet another time for Bruce to chase and fetch back to her, was—

But wait. That *did* bother her. And for the first time she looked at it closely. It was a doll, a "Daddy-doll". Not *just* a daddy-doll, a *her* Daddy-doll, and, oh, it was real and lifelike indeed! Her father's features, in miniature, stared up at her from a face no larger than the end of her thumb; and hadn't he screamed a tiny, tinny scream the last time she'd thrown him out for Bruce?

No. He was just a doll. Plastic and paint and—

And she threw him again because Bruce was dancing a moony-eyed, front-feet-only jig and groaning, *groaning* for her to do it, and she had to because this was a dream, Bruce's dream too. He was in control as much as she was. An amazing thing happened. The Daddy-doll's body, which had been as stiff and hard-plastic in her hand as her Barbie doll, now pinwheeled through the air as a living person might, arms flailing, its back arching then bending just like the woman in the scary movie when King Kong had picked her up, discovered she wasn't the lady he was looking for, and flung her away.

The tiny scream again.

(Pain in the neck. No! Break his neck, you'll—)

Bruce leaped for him and caught him daintily between his teeth before Daddy-doll could hit the ground. He trotted back to her with his prize, eyes rolling the way they did when he was wiggly-happy. His tail was wagging too.

But when she went to take Daddy-doll from him, he clamped down momentarily with his teeth before letting go. There was a wet crunch that didn't sound anything at all like plastic. And in that moment his eyes didn't look happy at all; they looked scary.

But Daddy-doll's eyes, *his* face scared her more. Because now the plastic and paint had shaped themselves differently; his mouth was drawn down and open in a frozen rictus of pain. Frightened yet concerned, she tapped a fingernail against the side of his face experimentally. Still hard plastic.

It didn't matter; she decided then and there that she wanted out of the dream.

And Bruce wouldn't let her go.

Finish it, he said, yet his mouth didn't move at all. He simply stood there, tongue hanging out, laugh-panting, pant-laughing. *One-more-time-he's-mine-he's-mine!*

"No!"

It's either him or the kitten.

"No!" She didn't know what he meant... and yet she did.

He's only a doll, he's not YOU.

And then the thing in her hand came to life, twisting and squirming, and her hand, her arm, betrayed her. She threw it as far away from her as her strength would allow.

From that point on, things slowed down. When Bruce left the ground to soar through the air on a trajectory that would intersect with the doll at its high point, he did it in slow motion.

When his mouth finally closed around the screaming, flailing Daddy-doll in midair, that was in slow motion too.

As was the remainder of their flight time.

And her own hands slowly rising to her cheeks in the age-old posture of horror as she saw where their inevitable plunge was taking them...

The wall with the window hadn't been there before. *It hadn't been there before!* Only green grass. Green grass, cartoon flowers, and sunshine. And they hit it, the window part, with all the force of an airborne bowling ball.

The glass shattered, they passed through!

But not all the way through.

They got hung up, or rather, Bruce got hung up, on the jagged remnants. A piece the length of a butcher's knife and twice as wide sliced through his throat so deeply that it was amazing there was enough connective tissue left to keep him suspended there, to keep his almost decapitated body from tumbling off the glass on one side and his severed head on the other.

As for Daddy-doll, the impact must have forced Bruce's jaws shut. All the *way* shut. Daddy's legs still hung limply from one side of Bruce's mouth, most of his upper body from the other in a grotesquely limber backbend; but it was obvious there couldn't be much left between.

PADDYWHACK

Time passed, or rather, it *refused* to pass; the moment seemed frozen forever.

Blood dripped and ran down the jagged shard. It dripped also from the sides of Bruce's mouth.

Then, with the disjointed continuity of a dream, which of course it was, Bruce had somehow pulled himself off the glass and was running toward her. His nearly severed head flopped erratically, like a ball on a short string, as he ran.

No, that wasn't entirely true, because now she could see there was a pattern to it. He was bounding now, more than running, and with each forward lunge, each powerful thrust of his hind legs, the head, the moony-eyed, grinny-faced head, flopped up and backward like some macabre, living flip-top box, so that it lay momentarily atop his upper back and shoulders, staring skyward. And in those moments, Rachel noticed with a raw, sickening horror even a six-year-old could appreciate, it appeared as if Bruce had two mouths: one that still held what was left of Daddy... and another, larger, more gore-filled maw, which was, of course, the gigantic "smile" slashed across the animal's throat, stretched to its widest, most "accommodating" grin.

With a great and concerted effort she pulled away from the dream then, coming very nearly awake before drifting back to a less troubled sleep. She had to. Not because she felt, even at that point, that she was in any physical danger, but because she knew what would happen next:

She would feel compelled to reach down and take the "prize" Bruce had fetched for her, and one of two things would happen. Either she would find herself holding a torn and bloody *half* of her bitten-in-two daddy *(doll?)*... or, if Bruce could not or would not let go, the remaining flesh holding his head in place would give way at that moment so that both the severed doll body *and* the severed head would be her prize....

And if either of those two things happened, she felt quite sure, in her dream, that she would still be holding them when she woke up.

XVIII

THE NEXT DAY WAS WEDNESDAY, DECEMBER twelfth. Blanche had died on Friday the seventh, been buried on Monday the tenth, had her will read yesterday ... and now it was Wednesday, the twelfth: Everything Back to Normal Day.

Except that it wasn't very normal to Jack. The term "normal" implies something one is used to, procedures, actions one has done before and will, in the regular course of things, do again. And standing stooped over in the city's makeshift bookmobile for two hours (which seemed more like eight) while an endless succession of rude, impossible-to-please middle-school English students ("We have better stuff than this in the *school* library") and their condescending teachers filed through, was something he was neither used to nor wanted to do again. And he would have to. Every Wednesday. Which made it all much more depressing than any "normal" day should ever be.

He should have begun on Monday with the elementary school, where he might have been broken in more gently simply because kids are more impressionable, less "sophisticated," and easier to please at that age. Thirteen-year-olds are as tough an audience to open to as there is, he tried to tell himself. But on Monday he'd been at the funeral, and so he'd hit the middle schoolers first. And the high schoolers were next, on Friday, where he and his tiny bookmobile would be regarded as some kind of pathetic joke.

Damn Bob Michaels...

He'd called, of course, shortly before Jack had closed things down at Granger Public (10-6 Mon. thru Thurs., 10-5 Fri. and Sat.) for the evening, and that had been the kicker. *"Jack,"* he'd boomed into his end of the phone, and Jack had had to move the receiver a safe distance from his ear. "Michaels here, your ever-on-the-job boss." Hardly a missed beat, then, "Say, I happened to run into Dick Pauley at the bank this afternoon. Dick's an English teacher up at the middle school..."

A genuine pause then, and Jack was compelled to fill it with a guarded, "Yeah?"

"Yeah. So I asked him how he thought you did. Just so we could get some feedback."

Jack's hand tightened on the receiver and he had to wait while the instant white-hot resentment he felt ebbed some from where it had lodged in his throat. "So..." he finally managed to croak. "What'd he say?"

"Well, to be honest, he didn't think it went all that good. He thought the whole act needed a little snazzin' up. You know...to catch the kids' interest?"

Jack clenched his teeth then unclenched them. "It wasn't an act."

A pause, then, "Oh? Well, maybe it should be. You're an actor, Jack; that shouldn't be too hard."

"But that's not the purpose—"

"The purpose, Jack, is to turn them on to books and reading 'stead of TV all the time."

Jack winced. He hated the Gomer Pyleish way

everyone in the Granger area said that one word. *TEE-vee.* It worked like an electric prod to keep him reminded of where he was and where he'd like to be instead.

"...used to TEE-vee; that's what gets their attention. And why...? Because TEE-vee entertains. It's snazz'n pizzazz all the time! That's what you gotta do, Jack—be a little bit snazzy! You know... 'gimmicky.' Like *you* was on TEE-vee."

There was a lengthier silence then. Jack was vaguely aware that some kind of reply was expected, that it was rebuttal time, but some kind of circuit breaker had switched to INOPERATIVE in his brain after he'd heard the word TEE-vee for the third time. He felt removed, a third party, laid back and observing how pissed off and frustrated this guy made him feel.

"...you think? I'd like some feedback on that."

Michaels was talking again. God, the guy talked a lot! All Jack could muster from his closed-down brain was, "Huh? Oh...yeah."

Then somebody fixed his circuits. All of them. All at once.

"Ideas? Yeah...I got one." *Oh, shit.* "How 'bout if I have a friend of mine from Detroit stop over? She works for one of those strip-o-gram places, but she's real tasteful, Bob. Only goes down to tassels and a G-string. Her specialty's a 'cheerleader' act where she bumps and grinds to rap music. You know: 'You gotta *read* every *day* to suc*ceed* all the *way*!' She could even wear a Granger uniform! How's *that* for a gimmick? It'd be *great*!"

Another lengthy silence, and, *damnit*, had he really said that? His only hope was—

"You're...kidding...aren't you?"

Think-fast-think-fast-fast-THINK-think—"Jeez, uh ...Bob, what do *you* think?"

"I mean, I know you were kidding, but... were you... *kidding*?"

"I don't follow," he said in a voice as innocent and mystified as that of the man who says to his wife, *What blonde? I didn't even notice any blonde.*

"Never mind. Skip it... I guess." He laughed, a little nervously. "You New Yorkers are on a different wavelength, I guess. But a word of warning: I'd take the cutting edge off that sense of humor. Your just-plain-folks around here aren't gonna be sophisticated enough to not take it the wrong way."

A vast sense of relief swept over Jack. It was like being wrapped in a heated blanket after having just swum in ice water. *He'd bought it!* It was too powerful an emotion for him to appreciate the comedic irony in what Michaels had just said. He filed it away for future enjoyment. "Really?" he said. "Jeez, I never thought of that. Okay, I'll be careful."

"Good. Good. Well, give some thought to Friday. See if you can come up with somethin'. I gotta go now; the wife's got supper on hold."

They had said good-bye, Jack had hung up and closed the library shortly after. Then he'd walked home, bemused. The fact that he would never allow Michaels to get to him again in quite the same, ego-threatening way, now that he knew he could keep him off balance, wasn't quite enough to override the fact that he did indeed have to come up with something for Friday—and for the other days too—or this job, this simple, picayune job of his, could walk all over him.

And then there had been the incident at supper. Supper at the Lerille residence on Everything Back to Normal Day. Again, the mix was between the laughable and the deeply disturbing:

Judy had been teaching Rachel to say her prayers. Both the grace-before-meals and the bedtime varieties. They had sat down to one of Judy's specialties, a kind of taco salad/casserole, and she had given Rachel the nod.

"God is great, God is good..." Rachel began.

"And we thank Him for our food..."

She hesitated, frowned a little, then brightened.

"If I should die before I wake...

"I pray the Lord my soul to take."

There, if she could have just stopped there; Judy and he could have glanced at each other surreptitiously, smiled, and felt good about the day because they had each other and they still had Rachel, who gave them moments like this from time to time to remember and cherish and maybe even laugh about in the warm afterglow of their lovemaking. But she didn't stop. She was on a roll, and she went on:

"And Godbless Mom and Dad, and both grandpas and grandmas, and... and Bruce. And... and if he *has* to come back, make him not so mad at Daddy."

XIX

THERE WAS NO REASON FOR HIM TO ENTER THE ROOM. Absolutely none. He'd gotten up early, he'd told himself, because he wanted to put in some hours at the library before it opened, mapping out some kind of long-range plans and goals that might still turn the bookmobile idea into something positive... and *not*, he'd also told himself, because of what Rachel had said last night at the supper table, which had allowed him to sleep only fitfully. But all through his solitary breakfast (it was amazing and a little disconcerting how much noise the rustle of forty-percent bran flakes and the clink of spoon against bowl could make at six-thirty in the morning) he'd sat facing her door.

It wasn't his usual spot. His usual spot was on the opposite side of the table with his back to that door. The door that led to her room. Her bedroom. The room in which she had died and she and Bruce had...

(Had what?)

But alone now, in the small hours of the morning, he had no desire to sit in his usual spot; and although he *could* have, in much the same way as a person *can* make themselves walk a steel girder forty stories up, he was sure the experience would have made the skin crawl beween his shoulder blades and the small hairs at the back of his neck move as if they were being breathed upon. Hell, even sitting where he was, facing the door, gave him an uneasy feeling.

He got up and, with footsteps that were deliberately heavy and loud *(to give warning?)* crossed the kitchen. But as his hand actually gripped the door handle, he hesitated.

(Ready or not, here I come.)
(S'all right?
  S'all right!)

He opened the door and took a step inside.

The *slide-tap, slide-tap* of doggy claws scrabbling over hard floor became the sound of old linoleum, which was working loose in places, shifting and crackling underfoot. Or was it vice versa? He didn't know yet, and in their panic his heart and stomach collided with each other with a queasy kind of impact that spun him in a frenetic half circle.

But there was nothing. Nothing on all sides. Just the room. And the room simply watched him, amused.

He stood there, waiting for all systems to return to

normal, waiting for some semblance of logic to seep back into his brain, and after a minute or so he was reasonably calm. But the impulses he felt—to look under the bed, to fling open the closet door to see if there was anything there—were as illogical as before. He decided to humor himself the rest of the way and give in to them.

First he searched the closet, and there was nothing there, of course, except that sad, oppressive air of abandonment and futile irony that must always emanate, like an invisible vapor, from a recently deceased person's belongings, especially their clothes. The whole room, in fact, had that same feeling to it: detached, out of the mainstream, decades abandoned and forgotten, and yet vitally sentient in the way it mocked you and your pitiful treasure called life.

By the time he had progressed from the closet to beneath the bed, he was completely caught up with the feeling, and his mood was as much melancholy as it was wary or fearful. Which, he decided later when he had recovered enough presence of mind to evaluate what happened next, was an argument for its having been completely real and not imagined.

Because he saw Bruce. Saw him and then didn't see him. Not under the bed but *on* it, on the pillow that had belonged to the dog and where he'd spent a great deal of time while Blanche either rested or slept.

It was a split-second thing, far more rapid in terms of elapsed time—and yet similar in other ways—to the experience of catching a glimpse of one's own face in a mirror in an otherwise pitch-dark room as lightning flashes. Only this wasn't a darkened room with sudden and blinding light to play tricks on one's optics. And the face wasn't his own face or anyone else's face; not even his aunt's face. It was a face straight from hell, *Bruce's* face, and it was straining, his whole animal body straining to come at Jack. To break... *through.*

Break through. Jack thought about that later too. Because, in that split-second, that *milli*second, it seemed there was something between himself and the beast, something that prevented it from reaching him. A barrier of sorts, something like stretchy, clouded-over saran wrap; and yet nothing so mundane, so... corporeal as that. Even in that moment of absolute terror, the word—or at least the concept—"placenta-like" came to mind.

Bruce strained for him, stretching but not breaking the barrier. And—amazing that he was able to catch it all in its shutter-speed brevity—the more progress he made, the farther Bruce stretched the barrier, the *less* visible he became.

That would bother him too. Later. In the incident's aftermath, that fine point of perception would bother him almost as much as the feeling, no, the *conviction* that the barrier would not hold for much longer.

But right now his reaction was more visceral, and the absolute quiet (there was no noise; Bruce's lips were pulled back, his teeth bared in a snarl of utter silence) was torn by a single, gutturally-explosive *Ungh!* before the vision disappeared.

That evening it was the rat toy he'd bought for Bruce to play with just a little over a month ago.... He found it, thoroughly chewed, in the bathroom, which was next to his aunt's bedroom and also opened onto the kitchen. When he'd thrown it away, that same day he'd purchased it and immediately after Blanche had made it clear she loathed such toys, it had been almost like new.

Until now he'd spent the whole of the day in a kind of a daze, no more than going through the motions of his job at the library. His mind had been completely and totally absorbed with the nightmare vision he'd experienced that morning, striving with an almost frantic diligence and more than a little imagination to rationalize it away. To deny its reality. And he'd almost succeeded. Except for that deepest part of himself which could not be tricked. That part knew the difference between real and imagined, and no amount of fancy footwork or mental sleight of hand would completely put it to rest.

Which in some ways made finding the toy less of a shock than it might have been otherwise.

Still it was the same kind of feeling, the same kind of ice-water-down-your-ribs feeling, as coming awake from what you thought was only a convincing nightmare about axe murdering your neighbors... and finding blood on your hands. And the axe lying next to you.

He was still standing there, staring at the chewed-up toy, which peeked up at him from behind the toilet, that invisible, liquefied cold trickling down and pooling in his belly now, when Judy called in to him, "You 'bout through in there? I'd like to get Rachel her bath *before* supper for once."

He hadn't said anything to Judy about this morning. And he didn't say anything now. She'd subbed at the elementary today, then picked up Rachel and gone shopping, so she'd only been home a few minutes longer than he had. She wouldn't have been in there yet, she wouldn't have seen it. He did what had to be done. What any self-respecting adult, desperately clinging to their "safe," compartmentalized canons of reality would do. He hid the rat toy. He picked it up as if it were a seven-inch slug covered with slime and shoved it deep in the wastebasket, covering it over with Kleenex, an empty tampon box, then more Kleenex.

Then he began the process of rationalizing all over

again. Not the rat's being there, but the circumstances by which it had arrived. But it was a little like a distance runner knocked flat onto the track, who has to get up again and try to catch up: there was a bit of a slump to his shoulders. And not much of anything resembling "pluck" in his heart.

XX

JACK ALMOST MADE IT. IF THE MONUMENTAL STRUGgle he was going through to make sense out of everything, to avoid panic, could in any way be likened to a distance runner's against-all-odds efforts to come back from a fall and still win, then what happened the following evening was the point at which the runner finally pulls even with the front man, a scant ten yards from the tape . . . only to go down again, this time with a blown hamstring.

But he almost made it.

A man fights hard to keep intact his most basic tenets of reality. Of what can and cannot be. Jack fought hard. There were a million and one possible explanations for what had occurred since that first especially dark premonition in Exman's office, and he played through them all. Plus which, there was still—there was always—the option of just plain ignoring it, walling it off, blanking out that part of his mind that insisted upon remembering. He was prepared to do that as well. After all, he was pretty good at it; growing up with Jack Joseph Lerille Sr. had assured that fact.

And he had *seemed* to be winning.

Oddly enough, his Friday Is Bookmobile Day visit to Granger High School appeared as if it might be the turning point.

He was, of course, woefully unprepared for that visit, having been unable to concentrate even for a minute on anything beyond what he was going through at home. He'd been left with no other choice but to stand and wing it. All the bookmobile's potential patrons, which included every student in an English, literature, or expository writing course, had been gathered in a large, double-sized classroom to hear what the vice-principal introduced as some "introductory remarks" from Jack. What had come out was one of those straight-off-the-cuff, sometimes corny, sometimes not, "Look I'm new here here's who I am and this is what I can do for you" speeches. And they had bought it! No gimmicks, no "snazz and pizzazz," as Michaels would have said. Just Jack Lerille, telling it like it was about his experiences in New York and how he'd been very good at his job with Acquisitions and how maybe he could help them find what they were looking for too. And they'd bought it!

Somehow that one small success had, more than anything else, reestablished his faith in the real world —a solid, well-ordered world with no room in it for the kinds and degree of anarchy he'd come most of the way toward believing in the last few days. He'd left the high school fortified by that thought, and by the time he'd closed and locked the library at six, he'd had it all worked out, an explanation that was plausible, that had no holes, for each of the events.

By later that evening, when he'd gone up to tuck Rachel in for the night, he had accepted those explanations and closed the door on that noisome, persistent *Yeah, sure* voice in the back of his head, muffling it to the point where, if he concentrated hard on other things, it was unintelligible, if not totally absent.

A scant ten yards from the tape.

And then...

TWANG! The runner goes down, and this time there is no way he is going to get back up again. God or the Devil has just strummed his hamstring like an overtuned guitar, and the sound He has produced is a two-note chord: First, the God-awful *twang*, as much felt as heard, as the muscles and tendons tear; and then, along with it, a scream of agony and, worse, despair. He goes down as if someone has just put a bullet in his head, and he lies there, writhing, beating his fists. And nobody in the bleachers understands, nobody knows how bad it can be. Because they've never been there...

Or, in Jack's case, five words, five simple words, said sweetly, singsong fashion, in a little girl's voice. Five words that made his blood run cold and brought to mind images that belong in a Spielberg movie but, please God, not in the real world.

"He's still *maaaaaad* at youuuu."

And the touch of something cold and invisible against his throat.

She hadn't been in her bed when he'd gone in to tuck her in. At first he thought maybe she'd gone across the hall and climbed into their bed instead— she did that sometimes, on nights when she couldn't get to sleep. But then he saw her. She was standing in the dormer, a still, calm silhouette against the moonlight, staring out the window. And just as he saw her, she turned around to face him, turned with the slow, moveless grace of a sleepwalker, as if the floor beneath her were a revolving pedestal. Ghostlike. In that half instant Jack imagined that she had died somehow and that this was her ghost. But even before the full import of that awful thought could color his thinking, and thus be clutched at later as some sort of lame rationale for once again denying the proof of his own senses, she spoke.

"He's still *maa^aaad at youuuu*."

Sweetly. Singsong fashion.

And in the same instant she finished, Bruce tore through the barrier between life and death and came for him.

It was as if all of life, *his* life, was nothing more than a single channel on some sort of cosmic television set. And somebody, for no more than half a second, had flipped channels on him, then flipped back again. With the sound off. Out of the fabric of the air itself Bruce lunged at him, a soundlessly snarling demonhead. And like before, that air took on substance, became a membranous barrier, stretching against, distorting his devil-dog features into something even more hideous, more grotesque. Only this time, though he was there for only a fraction of a second, if that, three things occurred that made all the difference, all the difference in the world:

One was that the barrier tore. It tore not the way paper, or even cellophane (which was the inanimate material it most closely resembled: clouded cellophane) tears, but with the wet, fibrous, yet nonetheless soundless parting of living tissue.

The next was that Bruce came through that opening. And as he came through he dissolved... into *nothingness*. It was as if the air on this side of the barrier was, for him, for one of *his* kind, not a clear and guileless thing but an opacity that swallowed him whole.

The third event, or occurrence, was that something, some force or some*one*, literally yanked Bruce backward, back through the placenta barrier. Which closed once more around him.

PADDYWHACK

Back into his own dimension.

Visually, it was like witnessing an after-image imprinted on one's retina rather than the event itself. Suddenly, and for less time than a camera flash illuminates a darkened room, Jack could see Bruce again, and it was his penetration *into* this world played backward. The barrier "healed" itself instantaneously then, and there was a further impression of the dog image receding rapidly, almost as if its head were some sort of macabre ball on an elastic string, caught at the precise moment at which it had spent all its forward momentum... and had begun its inevitable fall backward.

These are the things that Jack *saw* in that fraction of a second. They were enough in themselves to leech away both his newly regained confidence and his courage with all the resistless speed of water drawn through a sieve. "Fortitudinal diarrhea," as it were.

But there was something else too. Something of the tactile rather than the visual realm. Something that so filled him with terror—a mind-freezing, body-numbing, doomed-in-hell kind of terror—that he would have run screaming from the room, run from it at all costs, had he been able, had his feet not been rooted to the floor.

Bruce had *touched* him. He had felt, unmistakably, the physical presence of something at his throat.

The not quite needle sharpness of animal teeth. Dog's teeth...

And the wetness of saliva...

There had been only the beginnings of pressure, certainly not enough to leave marks, and then it had gone away. It had gone away in the same instant that he could actually see Bruce again, the barrier reclosing round the ghost-dog, the hate-twisted face pulling back. *Pulled* back.

Jack stood rooted to the floor. His hand crept

slowly to his throat. But even before it reached its goal, he knew what he would find there: Wetness. Spittle. Saliva.

A vast feeling of hopelessness and *helplessness* enveloped him then... and his mind fastened on a single word. In his head and in his soul it echoed over and over again, like a death sentence pronounced on him by God Himself, absolute and immutable.

It was a simple word. Almost innocuous.

Invisible.

Till one considered the dread possibilities inherent in it.

Bruce was back, he was undead, he had substance ... and he was *invisible*.

"Daddy! Daddyyyy!"

Rachel was standing in exactly the spot she'd been in when he'd entered the room. Before the attack. Only now the eerie, almost trancelike calm and detachedness with which she had announced Bruce's presence ("He's still *maaaaaad* at youuuu.") was gone, and she seemed nothing more, or less, than a badly frightened little girl.

His daughter.

"*Daddy!*" she cried again. "He's still mad! He wants to kill you!" She ran to him as she had when she was three and the lion they'd been watching in Central Park Zoo had stared right at them and roared...

And he recoiled from her. Still in shock, still caught up in the horror of what had just transpired, he recoiled from her, backed away. *She had been part of it!*

She stopped a foot away from him, unsure, still very much frightened. "Daddy?" There was a confused, supplicatory tone in her voice that reached partway through the shock. But only partway.

"How...did...you...know?" Each word was a

separate entity, a harsh accusation choked from a fear-constricted throat. His hands reached out as if they had a will of their own and grabbed her by the arms, frightening her more. "How did you *know*?"

She began crying, softly. "I don't know; I just *know*! He *tells* me!"

His hands clamped down harder. "You mean he talks to you?"

She simply shook her head mutely and cried the harder, helpless to say more. Afraid, for the moment, to say more. And for the first time that fear, *her* fear, penetrated his own, and he knew that she was not part of it, not in the collusive way he'd imagined. He let go, and, no longer kept at arm's length, she rushed at him, hugged his legs.

After a few moments he had his answer: "Not words. I just know. I just *feel* what he's thinking when...when..." She looked up at him, and her tear-filled eyes reflected both incomprehension and an awkward, almost apologetic hesitancy. "...when he's *close*."

He stared back, not having to ask what "close" meant. He knew. And how the hell did you discuss with a six-year-old the concept of another dimension, anyway? Or, under the circumstances, the subtle distinction between "living"...and "dead"?

Close. Suddenly the thought struck him that it might not be over. Still staring down at Rachel, he had to reach deep inside himself for the control to keep his face from twisting into something panic-stricken that might set her off again. His voice shook, but only a little, as he said, "Honey...is he coming back? Is he...'close' now"?

She shook her head. Again the fleeting look of hesitancy that was half uncertainty, half a peculiar mix of apology and embarrassment. Like the way she had looked just the other day, when her mother had asked what she wanted "Santa" to bring her for Christmas this year.

Christmas. Could it really be that time of year? After all that had happened? Even as he waited, with his blood frozen, for an answer to a question no person outside a bad dream should even have to ask, he was seized by an incredible yearning for the mindless, vacuously happy spirit of "cozy" that had always in the past pervaded that season. Bad things didn't happen at Christmastime. No evil could reach—

"No," Rachel said finally, still shaking her head. "He can't *stay* close. He gets too tired, and then he gets..." She wrinkled her brow, groping for the word she wanted. "...weaker. And then they pull him back."

Jack felt a quick and powerful surge of relief. And something else. Hope. Yes, hope. If only she knew. If only she really knew...

"Who are 'they'?"

The brow knit again, stayed knit for a long time. He had seen that expression before; she was trying hard, trying hard for her daddy. It usually ended with a look of triumph, the blinking ON of an invisible light behind the eye. This time she came up empty, though. If anything, her eyes gradually assumed that peculiar, almost reproachful expression of one who has just been addressed, rather urgently, in a foreign language. *(Where are our suitcases? Where are our clothes? El GARMENTOS! El SUITCASIO! Comprende?)* She lifted her shoulders high, held them there in a frozen shrug.

The bright flame of hope dwindled from the size of a bonfire to that of a pilot light all in the span of a moment. She probably didn't know. How could she know... about any of it? And, with the dwindling, a return of what one might call "controlled panic."

They had to get out of that room—that was first.

Judy was standing on the bottom step, looking up at them questioningly. She didn't look particularly worried, and the thought struck home with something akin to sick amazement that he hadn't even cried out through the whole thing. This was a soundless terror, one that robbed you of even the release of a primal scream.

And then, seeing her look up at him that way, another thought hit him, one that left him weak in the knees again: What if this were also a *private* terror? One that only he could see. *Feel.* Something he couldn't share, something they couldn't face together...

And, close upon its heels and equally frightening, though in a different way: What if it *weren't?*

"What's the matter, pumpkin? Bad dream?" The question was directed at Rachel, but Judy's eyes kept flicking back and forth between the two of them. Each time they met his, they held for a little longer. Now they did look worried.

He guided Rachel down the steps like one might a sleepwalker, a hand on each shoulder. She didn't answer her mother, and he didn't, either, until they were all the way down. Then he said, quite simply, with very little emotion, "He's back. I saw him, and Rachel...'sensed' him. She'll have to sleep with us tonight."

Then a surprising thing happened. Out of nowhere, nature called. Urgently. No, *violently.* He felt quite suddenly as if a giant hot-water balloon were expanding somewhere in the region between his bowels and his bladder and that if he didn't make it to the bathroom quickly, say within the next five seconds, his wife and his child were going to witness something neither of them should have to see—the "man" in their life soiling himself as a result of the most virulent, most explosive case of fear-induced diarrhea that ever existed. He gave Rachel a none-to-gentle shove toward her mother and bolted for the bathroom.

And as he slammed shut the door, he could hear Judy's voice, shouting after him, *"Who's* back? Not that dog—that dog is *dead!* Things don't come back from the dead!" Then a pause. "They *don't!*"

She knew. She knew and he was *glad* she knew, because fear, like misery, loves company. And along with everything else, he felt ashamed.

"I...just don't know," Judy said to her husband, who was also sitting up in bed, though not quite next to her. "I don't know *what* to think." She spoke in a quiet, careful voice.

"But when I went into the bathroom..." Jack also spoke in a hushed half-whisper. Rachel lay between them, sleeping. They had waited until she'd drifted off to have this discussion, and every time either of them forgot and used their whole voice, she stirred fitfully, frowned, and murmured in her sleep.

"I know, I know. Maybe we're *both* crazy."

Jack looked at her sharply. "Both," he said in a voice that was a study in neutrality.

"Honeyyy...you know what I mean. It's just that it's all so..." She groped for the right word. "All I can think of is 'fantastic.' But in the bad sense." She paused. "I mean, if we accept this..."

Jack watched her struggle with the concept anew. He'd told her everything: Bruce's sudden appearance above the pillow in Blanche's room; the chewed rat toy in the bathroom; what had happened tonight, including everything Rachel had said... And she in turn had admitted to a powerful sense of the animal's presence on several occasions during the last two days—one that till now she had refused to acknowledge on a fully conscious level. He watched her face cloud over, her brows knit together, relax, then knit again. And then, gradually, her eyes widened. Not a lot. Just a little. Just enough to give her the look of, say, a college freshman who has just begun to realize, half an increasingly desperate hour into the test, that this is the final exam for Psych 103, *not* Psych 102...and that she is hopelessly late for the exam she *should* be taking. The kind of look and feeling that leaves you frozen inside, unable to think through what you should do next, so that all that runs through your mind is something completely vacuous, like, *Oh shit, oh shit, oh shit, oh*—

Only this, Jack knew, was a far more serious dislocation. Wrong class be damned. Wrong universe, wrong reality! *(The misplaced test taker finally lays down her pencil on the slanted desktop. It rolls. Uphill. The girl at the desk in front of her, distracted by the sound, brushes the hair from the back of her neck and watches. Watches with the single eye located where her fifth cervical vertebrae should be...)*

("*Things don't come back from the dead! They DON'T!*")

He reached across Rachel's sleeping form and held Judy's hand. They sat there holding hands.

"I don't know. I don't think I can accept it," she said finally. "I don't want to accept it." Then she turned and looked at him. "And I don't want you to either." There was both stubbornness and supplication in her voice, and in the way her bottom lip protruded, quivered just a little.

"Accept?" he said. "There's a difference between 'accept' and 'believe.' In *my* mind. I can't accept it; it's unacceptable. But I believe it happened." He paused. "You don't?"

She frowned, looked frightened all over again, then looked away. "I don't know what to believe."

"You think I imagined it?"

"No."

"Well, then..."
"I believe you saw... something."
Silence.
"Oh."
And suddenly she was reaching for him, clinging to him across Rachel. "Jack, I'm scared. Whatever you saw, I would've seen too; I know that and I'm scared."

He swallowed back a great lump of emotion that had materialized almost instantaneously just below his larnyx. Relief? An enormous upwelling of protective love? All he knew was that he couldn't face this thing alone, and that in this case the fear she felt was a prudent emotion. They held each other.

"What do we do?" she asked after a long while. "If it happens again? If it keeps happening?"

He thought about the question. And his mind kept slipping off of it as if it were something wet and covered with slime moss, the way it always did when he was forced to confront what seemed, basically, like an insoluble problem. "I don't know. It's not exactly the kind of thing you can call the police on, is it?" Abruptly, almost savagely, he snatched an imaginary phone to his ear. "Hello, police? This is Jack Lerille at 115 Romeo Road, and we've got this dog that died a week ago..." His voice drifted off. But the scenario played on in his mind: *"He's come back. He's real, he has substance, and he's come back for me. For US!! And he's fucking invisible! And he's going to tear out my throat, and I won't even know he's there till it's too late! Mine or my wife's or my daughter's...!"*

Again he felt an involuntary loosening of his bowels. But there was nothing left there; the first shock earlier that night had emptied him completely.

"Jack?"

She had pulled away from him during his phone act, and as he looked over at her, it was obvious he was frightening her more. "There's not much we can do," he said. "Except wait. Maybe it won't happen again." (Somehow he knew that wasn't true.) "If it does... we'll move." He reached over and gave her leg a squeeze beneath the covers. "Let's get some sleep now."

Reluctantly, very slowly, Judy slid beneath the covers. She made no move to turn off the small endtable lamp on her side, and that was fine by him. He watched the way she tucked the comforter high up under her *(throat)* chin, first doing the same for Rachel. Protection. From more than the cold.

He thought about that final precaution. And its implications...

Anytime. He could come anytime. And Jack couldn't think of a thing he could do to stop him. All he could think was, *Oh shit, oh shit, oh shit, oh—*

XXI

IT WAS SATURDAY, "SLEEP-IN" DAY FOR MOST FOLKS IN Granger, but somehow Henry just couldn't get the hang of it. Old habits die hard, and weekend or no, he was up every morning by seven. Which was still two hours past the five A.M. he'd been used to for most of his life. But then these days there were no chores to be done, no fifty or sixty lowing Holsteins with their udders painfully distended, waiting to be milked. ("Fifty big-bosomed girlies," his father had once said in an uncharacteristically ribald moment when Henry was young, "all a-moanin' for the touch of a man's hand you-know where." Henry could still hardly believe that *that* taciturn, wholly restrained man had said it; it was one of his fondest, most "human" memories of his father.)

It was Saturday, and it was just past eight now, and it had begun to snow—the first full-fledged snow of the season—as Henry trudged out to his "baby," his Ford pickup. He was on his way to Birch's, a small coffee-donuts-and-burgers restaurant out at the intersection of Main and I-94. There he would meet with other retired and nearly retired farmers from the area, some of whom knew him well enough and long enough to call him the "Dozer." They would discuss ... "whatever" over coffee, and he would feel as if he belonged again, "important" ... for a while. It was a regular, once-a-week affair for all of them, and he was late.

Still, he paused, one hand on the Ford's door handle, and watched the cat as it cut a diagonal across the Lerille backyard as if it owned the place. It was the momma of the three kits that miserable excuse for a dog had destroyed, and he had a kind of soft spot for her despite the hiss-and-spit way she'd acted out by where he'd buried her babies. She'd been gone about a week after that, and when she'd come back, she'd been her usual gentle, placid self. Almost too placid. "Spiritless" might have been a better word, as if she wasn't much interested in life anymore, and it did his heart good to see her walking now with quiet confidence where she'd never dared walk when Squashface the Dog was still alive. It reminded him somehow of the custom among certain Amazonian tribes of urinating on the doorstep of a feared yet vanquished enemy. (*Piss on you, bug-eyed killer of my babies. It is I who have the last laugh.*)

The smile that played on Henry's lips at the thought

remained frozen there through the duration of what happened next. Not that it was in any way amusing; it simply happened so quickly, so unexpectedly, that shock and frozen immobility were the only reactions possible.

Something hit Momma. Hit and pinned her to the ground by the neck as if she were a mouse caught in a trap.

Something visible for less than the blink of an eye, but there, definitely *there* . . . for longer.

And then that something was gone.

There was no time for any major damage to be done, though in retrospect Henry sensed a power, and a viciousness that certainly didn't preclude it. The cat let out a single caterwauling wail unlike anything, in its piteously despairing notes, that Henry had ever heard before. Then she was gone as well, a low-to-the-ground projectile vacating the premises post haste.

No real damage done. Except to the spirit. And not just the cat's.

The frozen smile slowly melted, thus unlocking Henry's lips. Enough for him to mutter, "God in *glory*." Then: "*Jesus*." He suddenly felt not at all like rehashing old and not-so-old times with friends who still called him Dozer; he felt very little like the brash, afraid-of-nothing young man who had won and worn that appellation. He felt, instead, old, more than a little vulnerable, and . . . not so smart.

Because . . . what could he say to them?

("Hey, Dozer, you look pale. You see a ghost or somethin'?")

How did you tell the kind of people who were gathered at Birch's that, yes, you guessed you had? Seen and *not* seen.

How did you tell them about the impression that was still etched beneath your eyelids—of a face, an ugly, evil face belonging to a creature dead and buried a week ago, alive again and pushing through God knows what kind of barrier? About jaws dissolved to invisibility... yet still producing very tangible, visible, and violent results in this *real* world?

You didn't, not if you ever wanted to feel truly welcome among them again.

And then another scenario, equally disturbing in light of what he'd just witnessed, superseded the first on the private viewing screen that was his mind's eye: an angry Henry Mallory, lashing out at a still very much alive Bruce with a booted foot, and with a loathing in his heart beyond any rational explanation, each and every time the dog had trod his property unaccompanied by Blanche Lerille. The foot connecting solidly on one occasion, lifting the animal—who *had not cried out,* had taken the blow silently, except for a single explosive grunt as the air was driven from its lungs—in an arc that had carried it all the way back into its own yard. The look, the steady, hate-filled gaze the creature had fixed on him after it had landed and scrambled to its feet... A look that had gripped his heart coldly and forced him to look away.

He had seen that look often in the weeks and months that followed the incident, though the beast had kept its distance. And always it was the same: steady, undiluted, un*dying* hatred. Henry let go the truck's door handle, about-faced abruptly and headed back in the direction of the house. Suddenly he wanted nothing so much as to crawl into bed and to hold in his arms the woman he loved. And who loved him.

Between the hours of eight and eleven the sky, which had been a steady slate-gray all morning, dumped four and a half inches of wet, slushy snow on Granger, the kind that packs itself quite readily, with only a mini-

PADDYWHACK

mal amount of shaping from juvenile hands, into missiles roughly the size, shape, and hardness of croquet balls. The kind that finds elementary principals, teachers on recess duty, and noon aides muttering silent (*always* silent) curses under their breath as they strive in vain to enforce the no-snowballs rule... and as they usher the wounded back inside to see the school nurse.

But this was Saturday, and knots on little foreheads, the swollen eyes and other bumps and contusions, never happened. And at precisely 11:01 the snow stopped. The sun forced its way between a rift in the gray a few moments later, widened the gap steadily, and by eleven-fifteen had once again proved the old adage regarding Michigan's climate: "If you don't like the weather, stick around a few minutes. It'll change."

That is when Judy and Rachel came out their front door, tired, anxious, in need of some cheering up after a relatively sleepless night spent huddled, three to a bed, listening for ghosts. Or one ghost in particular. Judy was determined to do everything in her power to combat the mood, and some good old-fashioned mother-daughter horseplay in the winter's first snow seemed just the thing.

Eleven-fifteen. Jack had gone in to open up the library despite everything, and wouldn't be home till later. Life goes on.

Their front yard, in fact all the front yards along the urban few blocks of Romeo Road, looked beautiful. In the last several minutes before the snow had stopped altogether, it had been mixing with freezing rain, just enough to cover everything—tree limbs, bushes, houses, the snow itself—with a reflective glaze. And then the sun had come out. Even through troubled eyes the effect was... beautiful.

By 11:16 Rachel, who had immediately siezed the

spirit of things, had managed to slip a handful of snow down her mother's neck as the latter knelt to tuck pant legs into boots, and now the two of them were busy "splashing" great globs and clusters of the white stuff at each other as if they were two bathers frolicking in the surf.

And by 11:18 a tight-lipped Judy was carrying her daughter—because the child could not walk fast enough on her own—away from the yard, away from the house, more frightened than she had ever been before and determined to never be left alone there again. If she had ever even in a small way doubted the reality of her husband's experience in Rachel's room the night before, those doubts were gone. Bruce was, in truth, back.

They had quickly tired of "snow splashing" and decided to make a snowman instead. She would roll the base, Judy proclaimed, while Rachel could do the head and make a start on the middle. It proved to be not such a good idea. Despite the snow's easy packing by hand, *rolling* a ball of any size on the ground was next to impossible because of the thin crust of ice that topped everything. The only area free of the ice coating was a strip right up against the house, and Judy sent Rachel to work there, reasoning that the weight of the larger ball, which was her own responsibility, would eventually break through the crust once she got it started.

That, too, proved to be not such a good idea.

She heard Rachel cry out, "Mommeee!" There was genuine terror in her voice. Then, again, "Mom-m*eeeee*!"

She knew what it was—that it was Bruce—even before she reached Rachel's side. Not some stranger bent upon abduction; or an older child beating up on her daughter for some unknown reason; or anything

PADDYWHACK

else that was part of a sane world's repertoire of things-parents-fear-most for their child. It was a ghost dog. Something dead eight days now, but come back. Somehow... come back.

Even the knowing did not prepare her for the sight of him.

Rachel stood beneath the picture window, the window they had replaced a week ago today, staring up at it, transfixed. She was whimpering now, incoherent. Judy followed her gaze.

He was there again, hung from the shattered glass.

She hadn't even heard it shatter.

He was there again, and his head was nearly severed again, and the blood ran in rivulets on both sides of the shards of glass that held him, impaled, suspended. It had mixed and diluted to a watery pink along the bottom of the window, where it had met and melted the thin edging of ice that formed there. Which seemed, to the portion of Judy's mind that had already retreated, stepped back, and was now viewing proceedings as a detached spectator, a nice touch, a most effective assurance that this was real and not some kind of hysterical flashback to a week ago... even as the rest of her mind was consumed with a mad horror-revulsion that kept her rooted to the spot.

His head moved. Only his head. The body, which she could only see vaguely now through the blood-smeared glass, hung limp on the other side of the shattered window, straight down. The last time

(How many MORE times?)

he had fought, scrabbled, and clawed to pull himself off the glass. Jack had told her. But this time only the head moved.

It swiveled, rotated impossibly far, releasing a fresh gout of blood from the slashed neck. It was almost turned sideways now, and Bruce's half-closed, half-smiling gimlet eyes focused on her own.

They smiled and smiled.

Then one of them closed in a very human, very conspiratorial wink.

"*Guhhh!*" she said. "*Guhh...God!*" And at that point Judy somehow, miraculously, was given back control of her body, and she grabbed Rachel and ran. Later she would tell herself that it was not so unusual for an animal to die with one eye open and the other closed. And that it didn't matter anyway because it had really only been some kind of super-realistic illusion *(hadn't it?)*, because when they had returned, much later, with Jack, the window was still intact. Unbroken, unsmeared, unmarked in any way...

Which all gave her absolutely no comfort, because, if that were the case, why had she and Rachel shared the same illusion?

And why were there, even now, little spatterings of blood, minuscule pieces of glass stuck to the fleece collar of her daughter's coat?

They lay next to each other, still three to a bed, again that second night. The only difference was that Rachel was no longer between them but to Jack's left, cradled in that arm. With his right arm he held Judy; or rather they held each other, because he most certainly needed her there, pressed up against him, as much as she needed him.

In the past, holding her that way had fostered at least the illusion of towering strength, invincibility. It was as if the life-giving warmth of her body completed some vital circuit inside himself, a kind of "kryptonite in reverse," as it were, that made him feel capable, for the moment,

(With thee at my side...)

of handling anything.

But tonight it was different; tonight holding her that way worked only a fraction of its usual magic. He felt fortified but not invulnerable, sensed that she felt the same, and that fact heaped a sadness, a certain blue nostalgia, on top of the fear for self and family, the helplessness he was already feeling. And the beginnings of something else: Anger. Hot, bitter resentment that it should be this way.

WHY?

"We should have gone to a motel," he said, and the bitterness was there, in his voice.

Judy lifted her head from his shoulder so that she could see his face. "Should we...give up that easily?"

Jack didn't answer for a while. Instead he contemplated the sleeping face of his daughter, who, in typical six-year-old fashion, had been desperately afraid of what the night might bring one moment...and the next had been peaceably ensconced in slumber. Nothing more had happened since the incident at the window, but he was sure that wasn't the end of it. Then again, one couldn't be sure of anything. He'd felt (why, he didn't know) reasonably sure that the visions or visitations, or whatever the hell they were, were meant primarily for him, were for his *(ha)* benefit; and then the picture-window thing had happened when he wasn't even around. Somehow that fact frightened him as much as anything. "We wouldn't be giving up," he said finally. "How about you going and visiting your folks for a while, then? It's not that far away. You and Rachel. Maybe after a while..."

His voice drifted off, and all the while his eyes kept moving, searching the room, seeking the spot where *he* might come at them next.

Christ.

A drawn-out silence, then: "Oh, Jack..." There was so much hopelessness and just plain fear in her voice, almost a whimper, that he temporarily ceased his searching and glanced down at her. She was watching him, *had* been watching him as his eyes darted about the room—not exactly something to inspire confidence...

"I wish..." she began again. "I wish we could just..." And when she was sure he was watching, she cast her eyes downward and made a semicircular, down-scooping motion with her cupped hands, almost as if she were diving. *"Ttssheww,"* she said.

The motion was aimed at the junction of her thighs.

"Ttssheww," she said again, repeating the scooping motion, and this time the cant of her head, the way her eyes fastened on Rachel then followed her hands, indicated clearly that she meant to include her daughter in whatever process or act it was the pantomime represented.

"Ttssheww." This time it was Jack who was pulled into the process by her eyes, and he smiled, a little ruefully, a lot wistfully. Because he knew exactly what it was she was trying to say, what it all meant. She had first made that rather unusual down-scooping motion with her hands, that sound, in the first year of their marraige when, once, during the preliminaries of lovemaking and with a strange mix of passion and frustration, he had told her that what he really wanted to do was for the both of them to be able to "just crawl all the way up in there, forever, and be done with the rest of the world." Back to the womb. She had smiled brightly then and done her little pantomime for the first time, sitting there naked on the bed, and somehow the realization that she would do that for him, albeit symbolically, had driven home like nothing else save the birth of their daughter the wondrous, loving depths of their intimacy....

And from that had always come courage, the ability to cope, same as when he held her, only much stronger...

(With thee at my side...)

Only now... Only now...

She had repeated that little pantomime any number of times in the intervening years (though not always in the buff), sometimes for Jack's benefit alone and sometimes to indicate that both of them needed insulating from the world. And each time they had laughed, joking that it would be some trick if she could pull it off, and that everybody would be wanting to do it. (He could see it now, Jack had kidded. A chain reaction. A kind of "Freudian fusion" rather than the nuclear type. Each generation successively pulled back into the womb of the previous one. History collapsing back in on itself until mankind ceased to exist. A non-coper's version of Armageddon.)

The laughs had varied, depending upon the degree of worldly problems that had prompted her little pantomime. But one thing had not varied; it had always, *always* reaffirmed their unity, and in so doing, made the problem seem somehow within their grasp.

Until now. Until now.

And the bitter truth of that fact made Jack hate this devil-dog who would not stay dead. Truly hate it. Which, perhaps, was the first step toward fighting back.

XXII

THE TRUCK, SO DIFFERENT FROM THEIR OWN MILD-mannered Renault, seemed to reach out and pull the road to it, hauling in mile after mile of blacktop, with just enough grumble from its oversized engine to make conversation a raised-voice proposition. And for that Jack was grateful; Judy was not a raised-voice kind of person.

It wasn't that he didn't want to talk with his wife, it's just that there really wasn't much more to say. She didn't want him to stay alone at the house, and he was determined to do just that—while she and Rachel spent the week with her parents, Bob and Sylvia Ross, just outside of Chalmers, the next township over. First the retreat from New York to Granger, and now this. He would *not* be driven from his "home" again; at least not without a fight. But there was no reason for Judy and Rachel to be exposed along with him; and if Bruce was a "spirit," a "ghost," wouldn't he, like other ghosts, stick close to the habitat he'd known in life? It made sense that they would be safer in Chalmers, and the "discussion" had ended with his asking, "What's best for Rachel?" And that one had been pretty much unarguable because, despite the fact that the night had passed without incident, she had awakened screaming. Twice. Moreover, she was not comfortable enough with Judy's parents yet to be left alone there.

Besides, the lack of conversation gave him time to think, and what he was thinking right now was that their being "chauffeured" to the Ross place in Henry's truck was more than a happy coincidence. It had almost been as if the older man had been lying in wait for them. They hadn't even covered the distance between the side steps and their car, which sat in the driveway on the same side of the house, when Henry had come chugging around the back corner and said with, it seemed to Jack, forced casualness, *"Jack, where you headed?"*

He'd told him, not explaining the why of it, and it wasn't until he'd mentioned he wouldn't be staying with his wife and daughter, that he'd be coming back, that Henry had suddenly—almost too suddenly—announced that he was heading out "Chalmers-way" himself and offered them a ride. Why hadn't he reacted at least in some small way more immediately when told they were going? For most people, spontaneous and immediate comment on even so minor a coincidence would have been reflexive.

At any rate, he had accepted, despite Judy's strained but polite protests. Not that he hadn't felt guilty in doing so, but he was on a roll as far as getting his own way was concerned, and it was best to keep his momentum. Besides, there was less chance of further argument with Henry along. And so here they were, riding along, none of them speaking, insulated from each other by more than the grumble of the engine; and occasionally he would catch, out of the corner of his eye, Judy giving him a bleak yet puzzled stare.

Finally, just outside Chalmers, she surreptitiously placed a hand on his thigh. Not for long; just long enough to say, in a language as clear to Jack as if she had said it aloud, "I love you. I still think you're wrong, I'm still pissed...but I still love you." And for that, too, Jack was grateful.

The town of Chalmers, when they reached it, managed to convey none of the sense of temporal abandonment—of having died unbeknown to itself, somewhere back in the fifties—that Granger did. It was situated on the elevated, unusually steep north bank of the St. Joseph River, climbed all up and down that slope, in fact, in such a way that one never had to travel more than a hundred feet or so on any street to catch a glimpse of the water. And the water here, the river, was, well..."sprightly," in the expanded-brook way it bubbled and rippled its path across beds of rock and lesser boulders. Sprightly was as good a word as any, Jack decided when it came to describing the town too. It bubbled with the same kind of animation as the stream, and the sun tracked equally the movements of dozens of after-church shoppers, the tinsel and ribbon of Christmas decorations, and the wavelets themselves. Plus, one got the feeling they would more likely find display posters of Bruce Willis holding up a bottle of Seagram's Golden Wine Cooler than you-know-who hoisting Hostess cupcakes and pies in the local grocer's windows.

They drove on through town because Judy's folks lived a mile north of it on Chalmers Road, which was also Main Street...which was also M-47; and Jack couldn't help thinking that Bob and Sylvia Ross belonged near a town like Chalmers. He wouldn't have been surprised, although they were both in their sixties, to find them out building a snowman in the front yard or something equally buoyant as they drove up. As it turned out, Bob was watching Sunday-morning cartoons, and "Sylvie" (no one called her Sylvia) was in the kitchen making eggnog "with a bite to it" in the blender to offer them as a welcoming drink.

They were both genuinely disappointed to hear that

Jack wouldn't be staying too. They liked him, the feeling was mutual, and it pained him to fabricate so elaborate a lie about a "complete changeover in the library's filing system," which would require so much of his time that he wouldn't even be able to drive out in the evenings and spend the nights. It also didn't help that Henry sat waiting for him outside in the pickup, which seemed a little odd since it bordered on impoliteness and was definitely antisocial, and he knew Henry was neither of those things. Normally.

As he finished his eggnog and moved to set the glass down, stating that he should be on his way, Sylvie—a short, barrel-torsoed woman with skinny arms, skinny legs, and thick-lensed glasses which so magnified her eyes that it seemed she was in a perpetual state of wide-eyed wonder—intercepted him, took the glass with one hand, his wrist with the other, and stared up with those enormous dark pools. "You be good to yourself," she said. "Dad and I know how hard it is for you these past months, and..." She squeezed the wrist, gave it a pat with the other hand. "Just... be good to yourself. Don't let that library rule your life."

And the thing was, they did know. They knew far better than his own parents, simply because of the kind of people they were. Jack nodded, moved; and from across the room Judy's father gave him the thumbs-up sign.

"I second the motion," Judy said, moving in against him, snuggling under his arm. "Be good to yourself. *Especially* good."

Substitute the word careful for "good."

That was it, other than a promise extracted from him by Sylvie that he would "commute" to their place for the nights once he got things under control at the library—a promise he would have loved to have kept.

Then Judy was kissing him good-bye, whispering, "I love you dearly" into his neck.

"I love you too."

"Change your mind."

"Can't."

A pause. Then a soft, guttural sound that may or may not have been a whimper. Probably not; probably more like a subdued groan, he told himself. Then she was moving him farther out of earshot, out into the breezeway. "Then be careful. And if he comes at you *one more time*, get out. For good!"

They kissed one last time, and he left for the waiting pickup.

Neither he nor Henry said a word until they'd put a bend in the road and a hill between them and the Ross place. Then his neighbor said, "I been wonderin' what to say if you was to ask what my business was in Chalmers."

Jack digested that much for a moment. "And what did you come up with?"

Henry shrugged his thick-set shoulders, squinted out at the road. "Sometimes old men just like to go for drives. And sometimes they just *know*, ahead of time, which way they'll be goin'."

He said it with the hint of a question mark, almost as if he were trying it on for size, and Jack was sure that tone had intentionally been made obvious. He laughed. "Boy, you *are* old if that's the best you can come up with."

Henry didn't join him in the laughter, not even a little, and for a few tight seconds Jack thought that maybe he'd assumed too much. "I am that, and I've been feelin' a lot older since yesterday. Yesterday morning."

Still thinking maybe he'd screwed up, Jack said, very solicitously, "How so?"

Henry took a deep breath, braked down real slow,

so they were barely rolling, before he answered. "I seen Bruce yesterday. Out in your backyard." The truck was stopped now. "I been waitin' a whole day, wondering *if* and *how* and *when* I should tell you."

Somehow the news didn't surprise Jack. It affected him though—in much the same way as a man who is facing a life-threatening operation the next day but is distracted from his fear and worry by a visitor he is fond of, is affected by a phone call from his lawyer concerning last minute changes in his will: *BaBOOM* goes the heart. Not from surprise but from its having been so suddenly refilled with all the tension, the anxiety he had wanted so desperately to escape. *Ba-BOOM*, the terrible reality is confirmed. The *inevitable* reality...

He waited a long time before he said anything. Then he surprised himself, said something completely out of character: "So... what's new?"

Henry looked at him, quicklike, and Jack thought his face had remained pretty much expressionless, but Henry *knew*, immediately, and he said, "Thank God. I think. I never really thought I was crazy. Maybe I did. Not really, though. I'd like to think the reason I told you was 'cause you needed warning. You seen him, too, huh? How many times?"

"Twice. And Judy and Rachel one other time. And even before that, I—"

And that's when it really hit him. The

(REAL)

(happening to YOU)

(we have confirmation on that, Mission Control)

fucking weirdness of it all. Here they were, two grown men, at least one of them wise with practical earth-wisdom, comparing notes on ghost-dog sightings. He began to panic all over again. A different kind of panic, though, than immediately after the attack in Rachel's room—less visceral, more cerebral

—but panic nevertheless. He sat for how long—seconds? minutes?—wrestling desperately with this new piece of information, the fact that Henry had seen Bruce, too, as if it were the key to some life-or-death equation, his mouth hanging partway open and unable to finish his sentence, before the older man broke the spell by grabbing his shoulder, saying, "Jesus, Jack, whyn't you tell me? This has been goin' on for how long—three, four days now? You shoulda told me. That's what friends are for." And he felt so damned grateful for those words. Tears of gratitude (or was it self-pity?) welled in his eyes, almost but not quite spilling over, and he looked out the passenger-side window till they receded some, and spoke to the glass.

"It was crazy. Too farfetched. I—"

"Not to me, it ain't. Tell me now." And when Jack still hesitated: "Like the neighbor girl used to say, out behind the corncrib, 'You show me yours and I'll show you mine.'"

Jack smiled at that, and it eased the tightness in his throat a little, so he told him, everything, starting with Rachel's, "If Bruce *has* to come back" supper prayer, and progressing from there.

Henry sat very still, simply listening through most of it, but his hand rose involuntarily toward his throat at the point where Jack described how he'd actually felt the teeth, the wet spittle on his neck, and Jack didn't like seeing that; he would have preferred Henry be an absolute rock. Despite that, he concentrated on the finishing, on getting it right, and when he was done, the older man made up for it anyway, because his only comment was, "That bastard! That little *piss*-ant!" spoken through clenched teeth.

A rock. The kind of
(hero)
man Jack himself needed to be to get through this

thing. Just telling another human being made him feel better, and with Henry he felt a little like he had John Wayne on his side.

Henry Mallory proceeded, then, to tell him about his own experience; and the similarities, the *way* Bruce had appeared, the placenta barrier (Henry eloquently described it as "a sheet of snot stretched thin"), the visible/*in*visible phenomenon, only succeeded in instigating another attack of controlled panic. Jack wondered if he would ever be able to accept the reality of it all.

When he was done with his story, there was a heavy silence between them, which Jack broke after a good thirty seconds by saying, "So . . . what do we do now?"

"Don't know."

So much for John Wayne. Jack looked at him askance, but Henry didn't seem to notice.

A hard December wind rocked the truck just then, as it sat idling on the deserted stretch of road.

"When I was little I seen a movie once," Henry said at length, "where a skeleton comes alive. It scared the bejesus out of me. 'Cause how could you fight that? How could you stop somethin' that's already dead?"

He paused briefly, as if Jack wouldn't immediately see the connection.

"I spent a lot of God-awful nights after that, pretty much sure that the door to the attic, which was a walk-in job opening onto *my* room, was gonna creak open soon as I looked away for long enough, and in would walk Mr. Bones."

Another pause.

"Then, one night when I'd had just about as much as I could take, a thought struck me: Mr. Bones couldn't be killed, but he could be stopped. Because bones can be broken, they can be *crushed*." At that point Henry raised one oversized hand from the

Ford's steering wheel and clenched it so violently that Jack could hear the knuckles pop. Lyle Alzado couldn't have done a better job of conveying a sense of invulnerable power....

"If somethin' from the other side enters this, the physical world, then it can be dealt with in physical ways. What the hell difference did it make if the thing was the walking dead or not? If I took a hammer and knocked the damned bones apart, pounded them to powder, how was they still gonna hurt me? From that point on I wasn't nearly so scared. It was the *idea* as much as the actual physical threat that had me worried. Once I got used to that..."

He shrugged, as if the rest were a piece of cake, and Jack had to admit there was at least some logic to his reasoning. He felt a small, inane glimmer of hope. "So you're saying deal with Bruce the same way?"

"Why not? If he comes through again, clobber him! Chop him up in little pieces, if you have to! Hell, Jack, he's only a quart-sized dog. We gotta keep that in mind."

It wasn't much, but it was *something*. And Jack needed something.

Henry was putting the truck back in gear now, starting to roll again. "I mean, which would you rather have jumpin' out at you, a live nine-thousand-pound tiger or a dead twenty-pound dog?"

Jack had to smile at that, not so much because the concept behind the analogy was any comfort—he would have preferred neither—but because he caught himself wondering if Henry really believed tigers went some nine *thousand* pounds.

"Anyway," the other man continued, "we're in this together, and that's better than facing it alone, and that's somethin', isn't it?"

And that, indeed, was the "something" that Jack needed most.

Maybe not John Wayne, but then again, there were similarities: the imposing physical presence, the rough-and-ready down-home pluck and wisdom...

He pushed from his mind a small voice that reminded him there were some things even John Wayne hadn't been able to beat, that John Wayne was dead...

XXIII

JACK LAY SUBMERGED TO THE NECK IN BATHWATER drawn as hot as he could stand it and willed his muscles to relax. Sweat rolled down his forehead, dripped steadily from the end of his nose in almost-perfect sync with the larger-volume droplets making the plunge, one by one, from the tub's faucet.

Spoink. Spoink. Spoink.

It was the only sound in an otherwise voiceless house.

A lonely house.

A pitiless house.

The cramped position necessary for near-total submersion—knees drawn up, neck and back hunched—was a little uncomfortable, but not so uncomfortable as what he'd been feeling prior to entering the hot bath. Because he hurt. He hurt all over, and hurt especially in his shoulders, back, and hips. It had begun that same day he'd first seen Bruce, or Bruce's ghost, in Blanche's bedroom, and had steadily grown worse, till now it took a determined act of will to move at all. At first he had ignored it, but that seemed no longer possible.

Fibrositis. That was what he had. He was sure of it. Pain, aching burning pain in the muscles and muscle attachments at certain predictable sites—the same sites at which he was experiencing it. Pain of unknown origin. Pain from otherwise healthy tissue, but linked now to severe depression, emotional upheaval, or both. His mother had had it, for about a year following a mastectomy and the death of her own mother, all within the same month, or Jack would not have even been aware that such a thing existed. He tried to take comfort in the fact that it was not physically damaging and almost always went away, eventually, as soon as the underlying depression or stress was resolved.

As soon as...

Right.

If he hadn't been feeling so defeated, so hopeless, he would have snorted. Derisively. But derision presumed a certain rebelliousness of spirit, a certain confidence, and Jack was emptied of both. Instead he thought about what it would be like to simply relax his bent knees and slip the rest of the way beneath the water... and not come up for air. Ever. God, such an idea had never seemed so tempting, so inviting...

"No!" he shouted aloud. "I can move! I can still fight back! Fuck the pain!" Because he actually *had* been slipping lower in the water, half inch by half inch, as if one part of himself didn't want the other part to notice.

He forced himself to leave the imperfect womb of the tub then, and as he was drying himself off, he kept up his monologue—because he found he much preferred the sound of his voice, even talking to him*self*, to the soulful drip, drip of the faucet. Or to the silence between drops, which it underscored.

"What's a little pain? It's not like I'm in agony. Can I still move fast if I have to? Yeah. Can I still handle a twenty-pound dog, invisible or not? Rip out his eyes? Fucking *strangle* him? Yeah. Yeah. And then I'll get better."

He liked what the words did for him—they were like minuscule shots of morphine against the pain—and he groped for more of them.

"Bane Bruce—"

Whoops. Bad choice. They were an acknowledgment of the ghost dog's power, and he tried to get beyond them. But he couldn't.

Bane Bruce. Henry had called him that just before he'd pulled in the driveway after the return trip from the Rosses'. "You know," he'd said, "I'm of Scotch-Irish descent, and I can't help thinkin' bout Robert the Bruce when I think of that devil-dog." He'd paused, then, to rub the ever-present stubble on his chin, the way he always did when he was trying to say something that couldn't be said in a sentence or two. He looked bemused. "Don't know why; the man's a hero over to Scotland. My grandmother, who came from there in 'ninety-three, used to tell us stories 'bout how he fought the English, *terrorized* them to the point they thought he wasn't even human. Thought they'd *killed* him once..." Again the pause, but this time he kept his hands on the wheel. "But he kept comin' back. They took to callin' him 'Bane Bruce' when he actually invaded England, cause to them he was just that: a bane, a fearful burden... the scourge of the Earth."

In the silence that followed, Jack thought he was finished, but just about the time he started to say something in reply, Henry went on again.

"There's a statue of the man, of Robert the Bruce, over in Scotland. I seen a picture of it once in the *World Book*. Seen it less than two years ago, but I remembered my grandmother's stories, remembered how they made me feel...uneasy. 'Cause the picture made me feel the same way."

Again the silence, but this time Jack knew better than to interrupt, knew it was all part of the way Henry told his stories.

"He's sittin' atop this horse, and he's in armor, and the damn *horse* is in armor too... And all you can see of either of 'em is the eyes, the fierce, glaring eyes..."

He'd snorted then, in the very derisive way in which Jack could not.

"Bane Bruce. They all of them had the same eyes. The horse, the man... and our hellbound friend."

Just then the phone rang in the kitchen, startling Jack from his thoughts, and he went to answer it, wrapping a towel around his middle as he went, thinking it must be Judy.

It wasn't; it was the man whose words he'd just been pondering.

"Jack?" his neighbor said. "Henry here. Is everything all right?"

"Yeah, I guess. As much as it could be."

"Good. Listen, Jack, I'm gonna be callin' you every once in a while about this'n that. Only what I'll really be askin' is, 'Is he there? Do you need me?' You get my drift? I just don't want the Missus to know."

"Yeah," Jack answered. "Got you. Thanks." He felt, in a different way, the same upwelling of gratitude and affection he'd felt when Judy had placed an affirming hand on his shoulder as he'd sat facing his father in Exman's office prior to the reading of the will.

"She's upstairs right now, out of earshot, but I'll make this short anyhow. You *call*. Call anytime you even think you got a problem, all right?"

"All right. Thanks. Thanks again."

"Hell, no thanks necessary. Talk to you later, Jack. G'bye."

" 'Bye."

He had all of about two seconds to feel some measure of relief, to feel less alone and less like a man removed from this world and replanted in a sister dimension where the very air you breathed was made from molecules of fear. Then Bruce came at him again. Came at him before he'd even replaced the phone on its hook.

And this time he came from floor level, up *under* the towel.

"Oh *God!*" he screamed. "Oh Jesus, *no!*" He clamped his legs together, and it all happened so fast he wasn't even sure whether the words were a prelude to the worst of it or part of the aftershock.

He wasn't even sure he *saw* Bruce. All he knew was that he felt him, that his legs caught and held on something round and fur-covered and alive. With teeth. And that those teeth bit his inner thigh several times as the living orb they were lodged in twisted and struggled to push its way up farther, to where they could inflict the most damage. The *worst* damage possible in any male child's nightmares. . . .

Then, before it could reach its goal, the demonhead dissolved. It melted to nothingness between the grasp of his thighs in much the same way as a fistful of sugar might evanesce if that fist were swept suddenly through a pool of water. He could feel it collapse in on itself, and he was left with nothing but the coarseness of his own breathing, punctuated intermittently with small guttural sounds.

"Uh-ungh-uh-uh."

They, like the gasps for air, came from himself, from *inside* himself, but from a deep, animal place he was unfamiliar with. A place that can only be opened up by the most primal of emotions, goaded, magnified to their ultimate power: rage. And terror. Jack felt them both.

Blood, a single bright red rivulet of it, ran down the flesh channel made by his pressed-together thighs. Jack stared down at it, and he began to shake. *Nothing is safe,* he thought. *Nothing! He almost had my—*

The two emotions built, became the insanity glimpsed in the eyes of a wounded, cornered animal; and if a man can growl, can snarl—not figuratively but literally—the way a dog snarls, then Jack did just that. Two words:

"Keep AWAY!"

If anyone had looked in on Jack later that night, they would have been convinced they'd stumbled into the lair of a madman.

For openers, not too many people still in touch with reality wear a catcher's mask to bed. Or wrap their throat in layers of foam rubber, held in place with a knotted winter scarf.

And had they looked beneath the bedcovers... jeans, baggy sweat pants over those, and *more* layers of foam stuffed inside the sweats at the crotch.

But the clincher would have been the giant hedge-shears, blades two feet long and gleaming sharp, held at ready with gloved hands above his chest. That and his wide-staring eyes...

But the mind behind those eyes was not crazy. Not yet. It was busy playing through a thousand scenarios, a thousand possible ways to deal with an invisible dog named Bruce—*Bane* Bruce—come back from the dead to kill him.

NOT crazy, he told himself. *Not—*

So far the garden shears seemed like the best idea.

("If I took a hammer and knocked the damned bones apart...")

He'd wait till Bruce had hold of him, then he'd snip the fucker's head off, invisible or not. Then he'd soak it in gasoline and set it on fire. Bruce deserved fire; it was where he belonged.

He focused on that thought, that image, and it carried him to a little past midnight when, without warning, a still, small voice inside his head asked the question, "What if his head won't burn?"

Another voice chimed in: "What if he doesn't even *need* his head attached to his body? What if none of the laws of physics apply?" And he listened to that voice because, for Christ's sake, where did coming back from the dead and invisibility fit with the goddamned laws of physics in the first place?

He held fast to the shears, though, even tightened his grip. But his mind began to vacillate between wide-eyed, fear-induced vigilance and sudden mad excursions into...fantasy. His own situation's escapist equivalent to the man freezing to death who imagines he's feeling warm again, even fancies himself in a cozy bed with the fireplace going...

Jack's version was a little more creative, though. *His* fantasy featured the Ghostbusters. He imagined them come to save him, *wished* them right there into the room. And standing in the forefront, all wisecracks and sleepy-eyed grins, would be Bill Murray. He'd tell Big Bill all about Bruce, and Bill would say something cavalier like, "No prob-o-leeemo." Then he'd flip to ON that wonderful machine of his, the "ghost sucker-upper," and suck Bruce, squealing *(Oh, he hoped Bruce squealed. Good and loud!),* right out of the air and into some sort of spirit prison, some cosmic bell jar for phantoms....

Not crazy. Not—
No Ghostbusters.
No Bill Murray.
No joke. That was the way to madness and not-so-

sweet surrender. He had himself. He had Judy. And he had Henry. And because the first of those three was a little bit shaky right now, and the second he wanted to shield from as much of this as possible, he thought about Henry. Henry was his rock. Henry was a hero while he was not.

He'd called him right after the attack, just as soon as he'd stopped his leg from bleeding and gotten some clothes on. All he'd needed to say was, "That dog's creative when it comes to doin' the most with what he's got," and Henry had been there almost as soon as he'd hung up the phone. His tone must have said the rest.

"Makes sittin' on the throne to take a crap a whole new adventure, don't it?" he'd remarked after Jack had told him the circumstances of this latest attack. *"Gawd!"*

Jack had looked at him more than a little askance. "Thanks. That makes me feel lots better."

"Sorry. I mean... had you thought of that? I meant it as a warning. Shit."

He'd walked over to where Jack was sitting slouched in a living room chair and let both hands fall, heavy, enormous, on Jack's shoulders. That was when Jack started to cry. Nothing major or out of control, just a covering of his face with one hand, a welling of tears. "I can't handle this," he moaned through clenched teeth. "I can't... *deal* with something that goes for the balls!"

The hands kneaded Jack's trapezius, then his shoulders. They were powerful, but gentle. "Yes, you can. You've got to. I won't think much of you if you can't; plus which, you'll be dead."

He looked up at Henry, stricken, to see if he really meant what he'd just said, and there was not a hint of the harshness inherent in those words contained in the other man's eyes. Only pain and concern.

PADDYWHACK

"I'm sayin' this cause it's just about all I have to offer: courage. Not mine; hell, I'm not brave, just big. Though I get the feelin' you think I am." He lifted his hand a good foot off Jack's shoulders and let it come back down again, heavily. "Courage. Your own courage."

He stepped back away from Jack then, and sat down facing him on the edge of an old padded rocker, which tilted forward at a precarious angle in response to his bulk and threatened to dump him on the floor. Resting his forearms on his knees and leaning into the discourse, he went on: "The other night you told me you wanted to be a hero. What's a hero, Jack? By my calculation it's someone who's afraid, or hurt, or tired, or just plain thinks, *I can't*... that keeps chuggin' on through anyway. The 'I can't' is at the very heart of it. You got to be a hero, Jack."

There must have still been a hint of something wounded in Jack's eyes, something that craved sympathy more than truth, because after leaning back in the chair, thus eliciting a composite creak and groan from its individual wooden parts, Henry added, "And if you want to call me chickenshit or a stone-for-heart fool for sayin' these things when it's not me going through it all, go ahead. I'll understand. 'Cause you're right, I can't possibly know how bad it is, and I'd probably fold like a pansy if it was me."

Somewhere in the middle of the speech, Jack got a more complete grip on himself and glimpsed a mental picture of what he must look like to the other man. He had to fix that picture. Or taint something special between the two of them that he needed far more than a shoulder to cry on. "How 'bout 'candyass football player'?" he said in a voice thick with feigned sullenness. "Can I call you that?"

Henry did a slow blink. Then his neck reddened and the color suffused upward.

"I'm kidding, Henry. Just... kidding."

Another blink, followed by a careful, considered swallow, the kind a man makes when he's downing something whose taste he isn't entirely sure of. "I knew that," he said. Another swallow, then a nod of ...what? Reproach? Approval? It was hard to tell; his face was a mask. Finally a grin broke its surface and Jack knew it was the latter. "And you're a real turkey, Jack Lerille. You had me goin'."

"You just said you knew."

"I lied."

"So did I." And suddenly Jack was dead serious again. " 'Cause I don't want to call you anything else but 'friend.' "

In the silence that followed, Jack felt the bond between them grow. He'd get through this simply because Henry was one more reason, along with Judy and Rachel, why he couldn't fold.

"You know I'll do anything I can," Henry said after a while. "Don't you?"

Jack nodded.

"How 'bout I wait the night with you?"

He shook his head. "I have a feeling he'd just wait till you're gone. Besides, it happens so quick, I don't know what another person could do."

Henry shrugged, winced, then looked away. "Help if you're bad hurt, maybe?"

Jack snorted. "Mr. Sunshine and Roses. I got some ideas on how to prevent that."

He told Henry about the foam rubber—an idea that had sprung full-blown into his head just then. It was Henry himself who, a bit later, added the finishing touch, the hedge-shears, to what a best-dressed victim wears to bed.

And just before the older man left, the phone had rung again, which made them both jump. It turned out to be Judy, and Henry had nodded his approval when

Jack had answered the obvious question, carried cross the lines from out Chalmers-way, with nothing more than, "So far, so good."

He finally drifted off to sleep, still holding the shears, repeating that same phrase over and over again: "So far, so good." Which, Ghostbusters aside, was simply another form of fantasy.

XXIV

"IT'S GOT TO BE TIED UP WITH THAT *OH*-CULT BUSINESS she was messin' with," Henry said. He was leaning on Jack's desk in the library with both hands, looming over him, in fact, and the way he said *occult*, with the accent on the first syllable, might have rendered the word less ominous, something even to be smiled at inwardly, two weeks ago. Not now, though.

Jack stared up at him, wondering where the man got his vitality. His own stores were down to nada, and even getting out of bed this morning, after having survived the night, it felt as if he were struggling against at least three gravities.

After having survived the night... His first reaction upon awakening had not been one of thanksgiving or joy, but a barely stifled moan of despair, a need to cry that he had to wake at all to a reality

(A dream, please God, just a bad DREAM!)

so totally unacceptable and out of control. The kind of reaction a man might have the morning after the day he is struck blind, when first he opens his eyes...

"We gotta track those people *down*."

This time the emphasis was on the word down, and with an effort Jack focused on what it was Henry was saying. *People? What*— "You mean the ones that stayed—"

"Out at the converted church, yeah. I didn't mention it before, but she mostly took Bruce with her when she went to see them. Especially toward the end, when they picked her up in their 'Batmobile.' "

Jack glanced past Henry's shoulder at the clock on the far wall. Eight-fifty on a Monday morning. The library wasn't even officially open yet, which was good because Henry wasn't exactly speaking in hushed tones. "How? You know where they are now?"

"Nope. But I know who might: your 'friend,' Bob Michaels."

Jack's brows arched in surprise. "Michaels? I thought he was the one that asked the drug cop from Detroit to check them out."

"He was. But let me ask you somethin'. If a certain 'looker' of a young lady was to show up in town and, real quicklike, establish a reputation for 'peanut-butter legs,' who would be the first one to condemn her publicly and be sniffin' at her bedroom door privately? And what if that door just happened to be part of a certain little fixed-over church that set on some property of mine?"

Jack opened his mouth to respond, but Henry waved him off.

"I know, I know...I said there was two *couples* that rented the place. But I don't think the word meant the same to them as it does to you and me. At least not to this one."

Jack shook his head. "I wouldn't think even Michaels'd be that dumb—from a political standpoint."

Henry snorted. "You wouldn't think a lot of 'politicians' would pull the dumb moves they do. He's that dumb allright. He got a lock on 'dumb' about twenty years ago and has been edgin' on toward 'moron' ever since."

That brought the first heartfelt smile to Jack's face he'd had in days. *Down-home wisdom,* he thought. *I love it.*

"Dumb enough," Henry went on, "to get hisself seen by me comin' out the front door of the place with his arm around the girl and her wearin' nothing but a extra-long T-shirt."

"How'd that happen?"

"The fields on both sides was in corn at the time. Tall corn. There's not two, three cars comes down that road a day. I guess he figured he'd hear any in plenty of time to duck back inside. What he didn't figure on was a man walkin' *through* the corn rows checkin' on his crop. I'd parked at the other end of the field, probably when they was still real 'busy' inside, and took a good long while to get that far." He chuckled. "Boy, was he surprised when I come strollin' outa one of those rows. So was I."

"What'd he do?"

"Took his hand off where it shouldn't be real fast, jammed the both of them in his pockets and just stood there. I didn't know what to do myself, so I goes, 'Evening, Bob. Just out here checkin' my corn.' I think it woulda been left at that, except the girl kinda giggle-laughs then like I'd told the world's funniest joke. I think if it hadn't been for that, we both woulda just made like she wasn't there. So then he says, 'You're not gonna make a big deal outa this, are you, Henry?' smooth as snot. And I say, 'Outa what? Your Elizabeth's a good woman. I wouldn't hurt her for the world,' and turn back down the next row and keep walkin'."

Jack ran it all through his mind a second time before he said, "He's an arrogant prick, isn't he? You think he kept seeing her after that?"

Henry nodded. "I think so. Right up until they left town. I seen his car there just a few days before that. That's why I'd almost bet on his knowin' where they are now. Or at least where *she* is."

There was a long silence then, except for a creak from Jack's desk as Henry pushed himself straight from where he'd been leaning on it. When he finally did go on, it was almost as if he'd been reading Jack's mind: "I'll do the askin', seein' as how you still have to work for the man. He doesn't have to know why."

Jack didn't even try to hide his relief; he felt too weak, too defeated to deal with Michaels right now. "Thanks," he said.

"I'd do it right now if I hadn't promised to drive the Missus over to her sister's in Ann Arbor. I'll do it tonight, though." He half turned then, as if to go, hesitated, studied Jack's face as if he were noticing the downcast of it for the first time, and reached out, quicklike, to give the younger man's hand a rough double pat where it rested on the desk. *Thump-thump*. "Chin up, Jackie-boy. At least we're doin' something. And I got a hunch it's gonna help."

Then he raised his eyes.

"Brucer... we're gonna get you! *Some*how."

It didn't take much, these days, to choke Jack with emotion. Close his throat right off. And for that reason he didn't say thanks again, didn't tell Henry, before he left, how grateful he was to have him in his corner. He also didn't tell him he was like a father to him and one helluva man. He wished he had.

The St. Joseph River also runs close to Granger, about a mile and a half due east of the town; but it is an entirely different river there than in Chalmers. Nothing about it would ever bring to mind the word sprightly. It is a somber river, sluggish, deep, and, on a December seventeenth, very, very cold.

As Henry drove east and in the direction of the St. Joseph, on his way to deliver his wife to her sister's house in Ann Arbor, his heart was as cheerless as the river itself. Despite the way he'd behaved at the library, the things he'd said, he felt helpless. As helpless as a younger version of himself had felt some thirty years ago when his own son, then a twelve-year-old, had temporarily lost his sight due to a head injury sustained in a bike-car accident. What had he been able to do to make things right again? Nothing. All he'd really had to offer was some hope, maybe, by way of his own rather pitiful show of bravado. It hadn't been the kind of thing you could wrap your hands around and fight.

And that was probably the best he could do now. He could *be* there for Jack. Which was the reason he was making this drive in the first place.

It hadn't been easy convincing Dolores to visit her sister, who was always asking her to do just that. Or to stay there for a couple of days without him. In the last several years, as the aging process had laid an increasingly heavy hand upon them, she had become more and more reluctant to spend time away from him. He'd finally had to make up a lie about wanting to go north with Walt Simms for some ice fishing, and had then had to corroborate that lie with a second one told to Walt himself about disliking his sister-in-law and needing an alibied excuse for not staying with Dolores after they'd both been invited. He felt badly about the lie; he could count on the fingers of one hand the number of times he'd told a major lie to his wife during their entire forty-one years of marriage. But he also felt, strongly, that she should be protected from all this, and he wasn't sure he could do that and be there for Jack too.

"How do I know you and Walt aren't meeting some women up there and having yourselves a good ol' time?"

The question, out of the blue and while he was so firmly entrenched in his own dark thoughts, caught Henry off guard, and he glanced at his wife to make sure she was only kidding.

She was only ninety-percent kidding.

"We tried that. Last year," he answered laconically. "But each and every one of 'em I asked had heard what a woman you was and begged off. Said you was too tough an act to follow. 'Course, I had to agree with 'em."

She smiled; he could always make her smile, and that, since he lost football, was his greatest gift.

"They *all* said that?"

"Prit near. I guess a few said somethin', too, about my bein' too dumb and ugly."

She was quiet a moment, then said, "Now I know you're lying."

He feigned surprise. "Huh? How you figure that?"

"Because no woman would call you ugly."

He reached an arm around her and pulled her to his side, pressing his mouth against the sweet, familiar perfume of her hair. "What about the 'dumb'?" he growled.

"Let's leave well enough alone."

They drove on in comfortable silence, broken only once, when she murmured, "I wish you were staying too."

He didn't answer, just held her a little tighter.

And he was still holding her that way when Bruce came at them, came right *through* the windshield as if it had suddenly melted to something viscous and less clear.

But then he let go. He let go to fight the wheel, which he'd yanked hard to the left in a purely reflexive response to Bruce's snarling, demonic face looming suddenly in front of him. And as they slid sideways down the road and into the left lane, his Dolores, who had removed her seat belt to be closer to him, did a slow slide of her own, until she came up short against the passenger-side door.

Bruce pulled back then, passing from invisible to visible to invisible again as the placenta barrier-cum-windshield closed around him. But he had chosen his time and place well. They hit the left guardrail of the bridge spanning the St. Joseph with enough undercutting force to tip them onto their passenger side. From there they continued their sideways slide a good sixty feet more, balanced *on top of* the barrier... before skidding off and into the frigid mid-stream waters of the river.

Those final sixty feet cost them their passenger-side window, Dolores's window—and something more, much more: time. Instead of hitting the water upright and then sinking slowly as the almost-airtight cabin filled from underneath, they hit with the punched-out window facing down; the icy waters rushed in and the vehicle went under almost immediately.

Cold. Life-
(Guh-Goddd!)
sucking cold. Cold so virulent it drove all the breath from him, hit him with a physical force like a jolt of electricity. Henry was paralyzed by the shock of it. The truck's cabin was filled and they were submerged before his mind could function at all.

And when it did function, all he could think of was Dolores. His mind screamed her name, *wailed* it, over and over again. His dear-heart, his companion, his one-he-couldn't-live-without. Visions of her as the girl he'd married, as a mother holding *their* children, of the way she'd smiled just moments ago, flashed in his mind, all in the instant it began functioning again but before the cold/shock allowed his limbs to move. He had to save—

Then he was reaching for her, groping in the lightless, gelid tomb that was the truck's cabin lying on its side in a dozen feet of water...and he couldn't find her. Couldn't...*find* her!

He undid his seat belt, working by feel alone—and even that was fading into numbness, fast. He followed the bench seat down, deeper down, all the way to the passenger-side door, which by now was embedded six inches deep in river-bottom mud. Nothing. How could he not find her in a total space not much bigger than a broom closet? What kind of a cruel joke was God playing on him?

Then he found her, pressed up against the windshield, still alive—still moving weakly, he thought—but by now he had no feeling all the way to his elbows, making it hard to tell. By now the frigid temperatures were making even the smallest motion a supreme act of will, as if his arms and legs were congealing slowly to immovable stone. It must be the same for—

Get her out. Open the...(what?) the...

Why couldn't he think clearly?

Door! *(Where was it?)*

Disoriented, his thinking at right angles to what it should be, what it needed to be, it took him precious seconds to realize it was above him now and that he would have to stand on the passenger-side door and push up with one hand while working the handle with the other.

He couldn't *feel* the door handle.

Oh please, god. Dolores—

And all the while his mind was growing fuzzy, fuzzier...

And his limbs were the limbs of the Tin Man, gone to rust.

PADDYWHACK

No air. No oxygen. No good, he'd have to...?
Please Lord. For her sake. Think!
Windshield! Push out the windshield! With his legs!
He maneuvered his Dolores out of the way in the liquid ice. Somehow. No movement there, and he wondered if
(No!)
it was already too late. Then he braced his back against the back of the cabin...
It was next to impossible to bend his frozen knees and hips to the degree necessary to plant his feet against the glass, but somehow he accomplished it. But he had nothing left. He willed his legs to push, and they responded with something so feeble that it was as if they were someplace else and he was directing them from a distance.
Air! Need air! Lungs-on-fire-so-dizzy—
He pushed again, strained, and something thumped and turned over in his chest. No pain, but he felt immediately as if he were falling; falling down an endless tunnel that was his consciousness. Except that he sensed Dolores there, too, a little ahead of him, just ...out of reach. Understanding filled him with a muted, detached kind of fear, and he tried pushing one final time. But only with his mind, because his legs—as stiff as if they'd been frozen solid for days—would not move at all. And the windshield was a thousand miles away.
He felt an enormous sense of failure then, of having let his Dolores down, and with a last *supreme* act of will he reached out to her with his mind, caught up with her and mentally held her in his arms, told her he was there for her, wherever they were going...
Then he died.
A man who in his prime could swing a hundred-pound sack of wheat to his shoulder with one hand and, still one-handed, press it overhead ten times.

A sensitive man who could agonize over the fate of one kitten, love one woman forever, and be a friend when you needed one.

People would miss Henry Mallory. The Dozer.

They would miss Dolores, too, a woman as loving and giving as the day is long.

Jack would miss them. Especially Henry. And when he would think about him in the times to come, one word would come to mind. It was the essence of Henry, or at least the keyword by which that essence could be conjured up. The word was MAN.

One *helluva* ...

XXV

JACK WASN'T ALLOWED TIME TO GRIEVE PROPERLY.

Part of the reason was that he didn't find out about Henry's death until halfway through the next morning. No one thought to tell him, simply because no one save Judy knew how close they had become.

The main reason, though, was that Bruce pushed through from the other side shortly after he did find out.

The last words Henry had spoken before leaving the library that Monday morning were, "Brucer... we're gonna get you!" and they had been uttered with such confidence that they'd lifted Jack's spirits, if only a little bit. Enough, however, to get him through the rest of the workday, which hadn't seemed at all possible before Henry had walked in.

Ironically, there had been a few bad moments around eleven, when both fire-rescue trucks pulled out simultaneously from the station a half block away, sirens wailing. The sound, with its cogent reminder that we as humans are never completely free from the shadow of tragedy, affected Jack the same way as the sound of quiet sobbing heard late at night. He had no way of knowing, of course, that it was in response to Henry's accident, which a motorist who'd been trailing the pickup by a hundred yards had witnessed and reported. It never even occurred to him that Henry could be vulnerable too.

That afternoon was his "elementary" bookmobile day, so he was considerably less in contact with any adults who might have mentioned the accident offhandedly than if he'd remained at the library the entire afternoon. It wasn't until seven or eight that evening, in fact, that he began to feel any unease at all regarding his friend.

At first it was simple disappointment that his

(*rock. my rock*)

neighbor hadn't returned from Ann Arbor yet.

Then, by nine, it was a feeling that something was not right. Henry would have called, checked on him by now, even if by long distance.

By bedtime he was in a state of near panic again, and as he donned his protective gear—the catcher's mask, the foam, even the hedge shears didn't seem so bizarre this second night; they seemed a normal precautionary measure, like wearing a hat in the sun, in a whole *world* turned nightmare—he thought he'd never felt so alone. A man cast back in time to the Mesozoic would feel this separated, this alone...

He regretted having lied again tonight when Judy had called around six. (*"No. I'm fine. Give me a few more nights."*) But he'd thought Henry would be there and that Henry would be enough.

Along with the loneliness and fear came a sense of betrayal.

He fought them all till he slept.

"... killed yesterday, at approximately eleven o'clock, when their vehicle plunged out of control and into the St. Joseph River east of Granger. Mr. and Mrs. Mallory were traveling east on Woerner Road, sheriff's deputies said, when the accident ..."

It was the first thing he heard the next morning when he switched on the kitchen radio, already tuned to WCXI out of Chalmers, and it froze him to his breakfast chair as effectively as if an intruder had just placed a loaded gun to his temple.

There was no first stage in the process of grieving, no "period of denial"; he knew immediately that it was true, knew instinctively that it was Bruce's doing. There was only an empty feeling, a giving up inside ... and a numbness.

Henry...

Dolores...

And he was next.

He should be crying right now. Or raging or wailing or *something*. Instead he felt listless, drained, completely drained of all energy and emotion. Instead he sat with his head bowed and stared into his perennial bowl of bran flakes.

He couldn't finish them, not now. He couldn't finish this life either. His appetite for both ventures was gone. Like a slow puppet he rose to dump the cereal in the sink. Then he remembered it had no disposal. He dumped it anyway. What did it matter if it clogged the drain? What did anything matter?

He stumbled to the bathroom next in case he might be sick—he felt like he *should* be sick—and it was as if each of his limbs had a fifty-pound weight attached to it. It was an effort to move them, and they burned with acid fatigue commensurate with having just swum to exhaustion.

This time Bruce came at him from the medicine cabinet.

One minute it was just a medicine cabinet—something to stare into stupidly with the faithless hope that it might hold some ally in pill form to help get him through this... and a less disturbing focal point than his own haunted image reflected in the mirror which comprised its door—and the next it was a window on hell, sealed not with glass but with a wet, thin placenta barrier stretched tight against the demon-dog's snarling face.

The barrier tore and Bruce came through, became invisible. And this time the fiend marked him.

Later he would try to tell himself that it was because he was already numb with the shock of Henry's death, slowed by it and the fibrositis, and that under more ordinary (?) circumstances he would have been able to fight him off. But the truth was that Bruce's penetration was for longer, that he had more time to get around Jack's defenses (which were not all that effective anyway, considering the fact that he was trying to ward off something invisible) before he was yanked back through to the other side.

For the ten full seconds he was there, Bruce was all over him. Jack's hands were bitten twice before the dead animal slipped unseen beneath them and got hold of his chin. That was the worst bite in terms of depth and damage done—the rest were nips and slashes preemptory to seeking a more lethal hold—but not the worst in terms of damage to Jack's morale. The worst was the track of a single canine tooth that just barely broke the surface less than an inch below Jack's left eye....

The attack, as always, was a silent one on Bruce's part. Even during the brief, horror-filled moments when Jack could see his face straining to break through the barrier to this side and invisibility, *see* that he was snarling, there was no sound.

And, other than for a single inarticulate grunt, Jack was silent too. But when it was over, after he had stood there panting for a few moments, he found his voice. "You bastard!" he screamed. "You stinking *bastard!* You couldn't come last night... when I was ready for you! 'Cause you were too *tired!* From killing *Henry!*"

Then he cried, for himself and for his more-than-friend; and it was a long time before he was again capable of articulating his despair, his loss, in anything but sobs. Finally, though, the sounds became intelligible again. They went something like:

"Dad. You were my... *dad.* You *can't* be... How can I...? Oh, God, Henry, I...

"Dad!"

As Judy Lerille swung the big Buick Electra off of Main and onto Romeo Road, the sense of foreboding she'd carried with her all the way from her parents' house suddenly came alive and crawled up from its place in the pit of her stomach to stare her in the face. She, of course, could see right *through* its fearful eyes, as if they were her own, to the house itself. The third house on the right,

(didn't a crazy woman live there once?)

past the IGA. But it was there just the same. The house, in fact, was inside the animate foreboding, inside its skull, and as she drove toward it, she entered there too. She *was* the foreboding; it and she locked animas.

It had been less than an hour ago—they'd been clearing the dishes after a late breakfast—when her father walked back into the kitchen with a pained look on his face and said, "Your neighbors've been killed.

Yesterday. In a car accident. Maybe you better call Jack."

She didn't have to ask which neighbors; she knew immediately. And after she'd tried both the library and the house, letting it ring twenty or thirty times at each location, there'd been nothing left but to borrow her dad's car, ask them to watch Rachel, and head back toward Granger. Her and Mr. Foreboding. And his alter ego, Mr. Panic.

Somehow she knew it was a waste of time stopping at the library. If he'd been *there*, he would have picked up the phone. Why hadn't he answered at home, though? And why hadn't he told her about Henry and Dolores? Why had he lied to her last night about everything being all right? Mr. Foreboding whispered these and a hundred other ominous questions to her, intimately, as she carried him with her up the front walk. But nothing he said in any way prepared her for the way Jack looked when she stepped inside.

The door was unlocked. She turned right, into the living room. He was there, in an overstuffed chair, facing across the room, toward the kitchen. From where she stood she could only see him in profile, and so her attention was drawn first to the most obvious signposts marking his departure into the Twilight Zone: the catcher's mask, the hedge shears held straight up at white-knuckled readiness...

"Jack?" she said. But she said it the way one speaks when they're unsure the person they are addressing is sleeping or awake.

He didn't move and he didn't answer. She circled around so that she was in front of him, afraid, for the first time, not just for him, but *of* him. The atmosphere in the room was fairly alive with... *something*. Insanity? Despair? The supernatural? More like a combination of all those things. It wouldn't have surprised Judy at all if there had been a mist, an actual fog of the stuff sifting and rolling in the air. If this had been a movie instead of a real live nightmare, there would have been.

"Jack?" she said again, her heart trip-hammering its way up from her chest and attempting to force itself into the passageway of her throat. And that's when she saw his eyes, the—

"Hello, Judy. You shouldn't be here, y'know. 'S dangerous."

—horrors-I've-seen, concentration camp look of spiritual exhaustion and worse there. She was no longer afraid of him. She was at his side, pulling off the catcher's mask, cradling his head against her cheek and throat, murmuring, "Oh, Jack! Oh, baby! I should've never left you alone! I should've been—"

She stopped in mid-sentence. Blood was smearing at the crook of her arm, where it curved around his chin as she cradled him. The mask had hidden the bite, judging by the way a huge torn scab hung there by the tiniest piece of itself now.

"Oh God, Jack, I'm sorry! I didn't know you were hurt. I—"

"'S *dangerous*. You shouldn't be..." His eyes stared straight ahead.

"We'll get it fixed," she said, knowing he wasn't talking about the bite at all, but pretending he was because she didn't like what it said about his state of mind if he wasn't. "Clean it out with hydrogen peroxide and—"

"...killed Henry, y'know. And Dolores. 'S my fault."

"Jack, stop it," she said with all the composure she could muster. "Stop talking *at* me and talk *to* me." Her eyes scanned the other marks—the red furrow beneath his eye, his hands... "It's not your fault. They were in an accident."

"... worst part... going to the bathroom. Henry saw that right away."

Something fluttered in her stomach. "Jack, stop it! Stop talking in tangents," she said with more urgency.

He giggled then, a short, chopped-off giggle. "You know Bill Murray, any chance? Ghostbusters?"

This time she came around in front of him, pushing the giant shears, which he still held at absolute ready, aside. She grabbed both his shoulders, forcing him to look at *her*, focus on *her*. Her voice broke with emotion. But there was something else there as well—a sense of the "right words," almost as if they'd been handed to her, placed there in her head. "Jack," she said, "stop talking like you're crazy. You're *not* crazy. You've got to deal with this, and... and I won't think much of you if you can't. Plus which, you'll be—"

Jack's eyes widened. He sat up straight, stared at her, and she stopped. Not just because of what she saw in those eyes—which, thank God, let her know that he was back again, *connected*—but because her own choice of words took her so completely by surprise. It was not at all what she would have imagined herself saying.

"... dead," she finished quietly, in a puzzled tone.

"That's what *he* said!" Jack exclaimed. *"Exactly!"* Then his agitation died, faded as quickly as it had come, and he was somber again. "He was like a father to me, Judy. Do you believe that? Someone I knew for such a short time?"

"I know. I know," she soothed. But she didn't know. Not the part about it being Henry's precise words. And she didn't want to know. She was too grateful at having her husband back again, and there was too much of the eldritch they had to deal with already. It didn't seem that important. Not compared to the fact that Jack sat right in front of her, bleeding from a bite wound delivered by an animal dead almost two weeks now. "Don't talk. Not now. First we've got to get away from here. Then we'll talk about Henry."

XXVI

QUESTIONS. SO MANY QUESTIONS IN HIS MIND.

His life, it seemed to Jack, had been dissolved into an endless series of questions, most of them life-critical, all of them insane. There was an ebb and flow of them, dependent upon how well his rational mind controlled the aching, soul-deep yearning to simply drift away from reality. His... *damned* reality.

When Judy had walked in on him late Tuesday morning, he'd had little, if any, control. He'd been out to sea. The fact that she'd been able to haul him back in again, plus the uncanny coincidence (if it had been a coincidence) of the words she had used to do it, was testament to the fact that not all things preternatural were of the evil domain. There could be "good" miracles. The power of love, whether for one's wife or for a departed friend, was one of them. He would keep that in mind, use it as an anchor against the current of insanity inherent in dealing with... the Questions.

The Questions.

Do ghost dogs carry germs? Are the bugs that cause rabies, infection, and God knows what else, resurrected too? And if they are, are they like Bruce—

already dead once, yet living again, somehow? Dear God, what antibiotic could stop them?

Could this spirit-made-flesh version of Bruce be stopped? Or at least hurt? What would happen, for example, if he were actually able to "snip" off its head with the hedge shears the next time it came at him? Would that end it (he thought not), or would it simply grow another for the next time after that?

Could they escape him by moving away from the house or, if need be, away from Granger entirely? Most ghosts were bound to a specific location, an inseparable part of the place they haunted. Was it that way with Bruce? Was he even a ghost? No ghost he'd read about had nearly the physical solidity Bruce had, nor did they "appear" in quite the same way, through a placenta barrier.

If not a ghost, then what? What enabled him to come back? Did the answer lie, as Henry'd believed, in what had gone on between Blanche and the four "suspect" occupants of the abandoned church he'd owned?

And what if there were no answers, if the attacks kept occurring no matter where they moved or what he did to stop them? What kind of life would he have? What kind of life would his family have? He tried to imagine continuing to function as a father, a husband, as any kind of human being at all while forever keeping covered all the more vulnerable parts of his anatomy because to do otherwise was to run the risk of being castrated, torn at the throat, or blinded by something demonic and invisible. *Insanity.* Even if he could survive, somehow, all the lesser bites which, undoubtedly, would take their own cumulative toll... insanity.

Then there were the more practical considerations, the ones rooted in *(ha-ha)* normality...

Like his job; what about his job? Funny how the world went right on, business as usual, while your own private world was collapsing around you: Wife dying-by-inches, from cancer? *Sorry, but we've simply got to have those figures by Friday or we lose the client.* Twelve-year-old daughter paralyzed from the neck down because *you* ran that stop sign yesterday? *Take a few days off, but remember, sales are down in your department...* Family pet won't stay dead? Wants to kill you too? *But tomorrow's bookmobile day at the middle school. Can't disappoint those middle school kids...*

And how would he explain his "protective" clothing when he did come back in? The padded groin could, he believed, be replaced by a steel cup (did they really make them from steel these days, rather than from hard plastic? He hoped so) like the ones baseball catchers and (he presumed) hockey goalies wore. And the wrappings at the throat? At least he'd been thinking there, had the foresight to work that in with his short-term excuse for missing work. Neck injury. Whiplash. Parking lot over at the new mall. They even made special padded collars (braces?) for that, didn't they? But the catcher's mask...? Never. And what about his hands? They were likely to be bitten a lot...

All those questions would, of course, be meaningless if one of the really big ones, the life-critical questions, turned out to have the wrong answer: *Could Bruce get at him other places besides the house itself?* If the answer was yes, he wouldn't have a job, at least not for long. And conjecture on his unusual clothing would be secondary to other, more damning considerations once the public caught a glimpse of him thrashing about, attempting to fight off something invisible! And if he was right about the real reason Henry had died, he thought he already had the answer to that question.

XXVII

HENRY AND DOLORES'S DOUBLE FUNERAL WAS ON Thursday at ten A.M., and by that time Jack had an answer to at least some of his questions.

There was no infection. The wounds were healing nicely, or, with regard to his scoured hands, would have been healing nicely if Bruce had allowed them to. If there were bugs, resurrected or otherwise, they were every bit as susceptible to the killing effects of hydrogen peroxide and Neosporin as more normally acquired germs.

Would relocating put a stop to the attacks? Jack had stopped believing in that one the moment he'd heard about Henry, and for that reason had refused to go back to the Rosses', where Rachel was. Instead they stayed at a Days Inn (Judy would not leave his side, which was both a comfort and a worry) six exits east of Granger on I-94, and Bruce hit him again just after they stepped into the room on Tuesday night. It wasn't so bad, in terms of physical damage, because he hadn't removed his winter coat yet and had, by then, purchased a steel cup, held firmly in place by an extra tight-fitting jockstrap. He'd simply wrapped his arms around his head and face and let Bruce fire at will. But it was extremely hard on Judy, who, until that moment, had never been hit with the full-force reality of the nightmare; in much the same way as a child, upon being told that his or her pet has been killed on the highway, doesn't truly grasp the significance of those words until they see for themselves the flattened, mangled remains of what had once been their puppy. She cried, and they were bitter, bitter tears.

The second attack was far worse. It occurred around four on Wednesday afternoon in the motel room's bathroom. He'd just stepped from the shower, and if he hadn't had the presence of mind to paste himself, face first, legs clamped together, against the tiled bathroom wall, it could have been very bad indeed. As it was, he was bitten about the hands, shoulders, back of neck, and buttocks. But it was the *idea* that made it the worst one yet, the

(He knows when you've been sleeping...
He knows when you're awake...
He knows when you've been bad or good...)

certainty, now, that the demon-dog knew exactly what it was doing, that it was watching, and knew when he was most vulnerable. Tuesday's less physically punishing assault had simply been Bane Bruce's way of not allowing them even a few moments of hope that relocation might save them.

But Jack wasn't thinking about any of those things right now. Not the pain of the multitude of bites which, unclothed, made his flesh look like a battleground. Not the other, more debilitating pain/stiffness of his fibrositis, which made him feel thirty years advanced in age. Not even the seeming hopelessness of his ever being able to put an end to it all. This was Henry's time, and as he and Judy were ushered inside Bordine's Funeral Home, all he could think about was what he and the rest of the world had lost irretrievably.

The room, which was really two rooms with a dividing wall folded back to accommodate the larger number of mourners, since this was a double funeral, was filled to capacity. With strangers. That was the first shock. All those rawboned, mitt-handed, blunt-fingered farmers and their salt-of-the-earth wives who had known Henry their entire lives and shared so much through common experience. In the subdued murmur of a hundred whispered conversations, he heard the words "the Dozer" spoken any number of times, always, it seemed to him, with reverence and awe. What right did he have to be here? How could his presence do anything but diminish the combined tribute of a community bonded by time? And yet he was the reason Henry had died.

The second jolt was when they stepped up to the casket to view Henry's body. He didn't look dead. Not the way other people he'd known for longer, but perhaps less well in terms of feeling a real bond with them, had appeared dead at their funerals. Henry was right there, beneath the exterior of what was his face in repose. The only difference, the only "oddity," in fact, that hinted at a change in Henry's status and in their relationship, was his position: Jack had never seen him lying down before. Or with his eyes closed. It altered his larger-than-life perception of the man in much the same way as seeing his fifth-grade teacher asleep on the next cot when that good man had chaperoned the boys' cabin at fifth-grade camp had forever changed his view of teachers, rendered them all more human and vulnerable. His heart leapt. It was all a mistake! No, a ruse! Henry was not dead; he was just pretending to be dead as part of some elaborate plan to fool Bruce! He even knew that Jack was there now, standing over him, and was—yes!—telepathing him a message: *Can't look away right now—got to play my role. But we'll talk. Later.*

Then he saw Henry's hands... and his hands were unquestionably the hands of a dead man. For a moment the room, the casket, the people standing in his

peripheral vision, canted sideways and began to spin.
All he could focus on was the folded hands, and if he
didn't tear his eyes away from their flattened, latex-
gloves-masquerading-as-flesh image, he was going to
pass out right there on the coffin. God*damn* death! It
took away the best parts of you! The *essence* of
Henry was his hands! They *were* Henry, and if they
were dead, then—

Judy took him by the arm and led him away from
the casket. A soft groan caught in his throat, but only
Judy was close enough to hear it, and her grip tightened on his arm. She was looking up at him with a
great deal of concern. Had she noticed the hands too?

He concentrated hard on the inane sound their feet
made on the carpet. Sounded like corduroy. His feet
seemed to be dragging more than they should be—
better draggy feet than dead latex hands...

Stop at Dolores's next. Her eternal nap couch. No,
her coffin. Every part of her looked dead, and that, of
course, was his fault too.

Swish-swish. Feet on carpet. Don't get sick on the
carpet. On the corduroy carpet. Back to some extra
wooden chairs that had been set up along the back
wall. Was he leaning too much on Judy? God, he
hoped he wasn't making a spectacle of himself. What
if Bruce came at him again now? Then he would really
make—

Back wall. That's all he deserved; he didn't even
deserve that. And yet Henry and Dolores had died for
him...

They sat down on the wooden chairs (along the
back wall) and waited for the actual service to begin.

He was still waiting, more or less, when it was
over. He had settled into a timeless haze of grief,
guilt, and a peculiar numbness through which an occasional word like "gone," "departed," and "irretrievably lost" filtered maybe once every decade. The

particulars of the eulogy were beyond him. Except for a few frozen moments when the minister said something like "...you, Andrew, and you, Ronald, who knew him as a father, a kind, loving father..." and had indicated the persons he was speaking to with a nod in the direction of two stolid-looking full-grown men in the front row. *Full-grown men.* That fact impinged itself on his consciousness with almost the visceral impact of staring at Henry's dead-folded hands. They were around Jack's own age, yet sons, *Henry's* sons! The envy he felt, the bitter longing for what-might-have-been, redefined his grief in ways he was not proud of, turned it into an exercise in self-pity... and he would not have that. He had blanked his mind again, and when he refocused, the service was over.

The ordered, processional way they were ushered out made it impossible to avoid the line of relatives waiting to thank everyone for coming and receive condolences, though he would have liked to. It had always seemed a grotesque tradition (was it really a tradition?) which only underscored the fact that there was nothing any mere human could say or do to

(Can you bring him back again? No? Then please don't prolong this.)

ease the family's pain, and at the same time forced those family members to hold up their grief for public scrutiny one last time. There were representatives of both Dolores's and Henry's families, and, together with Judy, he worked his way down the entire line as best he could, mumbling something about being neighbors with the deceased and admiring them both —which was the truth, and heartfelt, but such a futile, pathetic understatement that again he felt as if he were diminishing Henry in some way. Still, things went fairly smoothly, if not altogether comfortably, even with Ronald and Andrew (who did not look or speak at all like a younger version of Henry, thank

God—that would have been especially hard), until the end of the line. At the end of the line stood Henry's mother.

She was a small, even diminutive women—barely more than five feet—which might have explained why he hadn't noticed her during the service, surrounded as she must have been by much larger people. Because he most certainly *would* have noticed, had his eyes rested on her for even a moment. There was something compelling about her, a radiance, a beauty that had only a little to do with the eighty-eight-year-old but remarkably vital countenance it shone out from. It had as its base a loving disposition—a gentleness, a kindness, an empathy—combined with incredible strength of character. He saw all that in her eyes even before she spoke. And he saw Henry there as well.

"Mrs. Mallory," he said, absolutely sure of who she was without being told, "I...lived next door to Henry, and...I'm *so* sorry he's gone."

She regarded him for a moment with those gentle eyes, eyes you wanted to please and shield from suffering as much as you'd wanted anything in your life. Then she said, "Thank you," in a voice very much like Katharine Hepburn's; there was, in fact, much about her that reminded him of Katharine Hepburn. Only kinder, more loving..."You must be Jack, then. He spoke of you often. We talked on the telephone almost every day, and he seemed delighted, in these last few weeks, to have found a—how did he put it?—a 'kindred spirit.'"

Something caught in his throat then, and he couldn't reply immediately. When he could, he said, "That's...the greatest honor I could...I mean, considering the source..."

She nodded, smiling faintly and gazing not just at

him but through him. "He was a good boy...a *wonderful* son."

Visions of a thirteen-year-old Henry, seated at this dear woman's bedside, begging her to get well, promising her anything, confessing all his little-boy sins if only she would not die, blurred Jack's eyes with tears then. His throat closed even more, but somehow the words got past the obstruction, unbidden, and they were good words, words with a power all their own: "A good boy, a good *man*. Because of you. It was obvious from the way he spoke of you." He paused. "His place in heaven is assured because of you."

The farseeing, wistful eyes appeared startled, then focused on Jack's again. "Thank you. Thank you for helping immeasurably to make an old woman's grief more bearable."

He didn't say anything else. He couldn't. He simply bent down—a little stiffly, due to the neck brace he still wore—and kissed her aged cheek. And he didn't feel at all ill at ease or presumptuous in doing so. Now he understood why there was a line of family members down which the rest of the mourners must pass: their coming together that way was the first, the preliminary stitches to close and someday heal the awful wound.

They went home again after the funeral because staying at the motel seemed pointless. Glancing over at Henry's quiet, empty house strained Jack's metaphorical stitches some, and there was more than a little pain. But it wasn't until after they had eaten a mostly silent lunch that he felt them tear. How badly, only time would tell. It was the damn radio again—the same one that had informed him of Henry's death. Judy had turned it on to drown out the silence, and the first thing they heard was Lou Rawls singing his soulful version of "Wind Beneath My Wings"—the song whose first line asks the lyrical question: *Did you ever know you were my hero?*" He wouldn't have made it through those moments at all if she hadn't been there to hold him.

PART III

Heroes

*The hero is not fed on sweets,
Daily his own heart he eats.*
 —Ralph Waldo Emerson

XXVIII

THE CAT, WHICH HENRY MALLORY HAD NAMED Momma back when its kittens were still alive, had no way of knowing that its caretakers had both been buried just this morning. Or that in the house next door a man and a woman sat waiting, dressed in what the man called their "protective clothing," for the thing both he and the cat feared most. Waiting and ready. Too ready, as it turned out, for the feline's own good. All she knew was that, after five days of hiding in the garage, she was finally more hungry than afraid. And that a plaintive meow at the back door of the house she now approached usually brought food.

Today it brought death. Death at the jaws of an invisible monster.

She had meowed only once when the air just in front of the door began to quiver and take on substance. Her ears laid back flat. She hissed and backed away, her little cat heart pounding at an incredible rate. Then she wheeled and ran, but she hadn't covered even a dozen feet when she was bowled over, pinned by her throat to the driveway by those same awful, *invisible* jaws that had gripped her five days ago. They crushed her windpipe before she could let out a single terrified squall, and even if it had ended then, she would have choked to death soon enough. But it did not end, and she was not dead yet, so she fought back, raking her front claws repeatedly over the bony skull she could feel but could not see. Whereupon she was shaken like a dishrag, whipped back and forth so violently by the hold on her neck that the vertebrae separated and her body went limp.

And still it did not end. The shaking, the whipping back and forth, continued until Momma's flesh tore and there was not enough left connecting head to body to afford much of a hold for decent leverage. By then more than *two whole minutes* had elapsed since the attack began, and a spray of cat blood had outlined an almost perfect half circle on the cement of the Mallorys' driveway. If it had continued much longer, the head and the body would have gone their separate ways, but as it was, they dropped, quite suddenly, to the ground. One moment the cat's front quarters were suspended, seemingly in midair, limp forepaws inches from the ground, as if they and she were levitating. The next, she was a dead heap upon the cement. Bane Bruce, also deceased, but with just a "pimple" of an evil man's soul to keep him going, had been pulled back through to the other side....

XXIX

THE CITY MUNICIPAL BUILDING WAS A SINGLE-STORY, brick and glass structure just north of town that, in its chaste, strictly utilitarian design, reminded Jack of a hundred post offices he'd seen. He'd never been there before, never been in Bob Michaels's office. The latter smelled, overpoweringly, of Old Spice after-shave as Jack stood just inside the door, waiting for the source of that smell to finish arguing with someone on the phone about the cost of new sidewalk on Main. Finally Michaels was done and hung up.

"Nobody wants to do an honest day's work for an honest price anymore," he grumbled, half to Jack and half to himself. "This job used to be fun." Then he focused on Jack completely, taking in the neck brace and dismissing it all in one glance. "What about you? You ready to get back to the book business now?"

Jack didn't like the way he said it, what his tone of voice implied: that his absence had been a childish, whimsical thing, the equivalent of an eight-year-old running away from home because he has to clean his room... then returning again, hangdog fashion, for supper. "That's... what I'd like to talk to you about, actually." He forced himself to meet Michaels's stare straight on. The other man was first to blink.

"And that's not what I like to hear. You already missed three days. How bad can a neck injury be? It's not broke, is it?"

"No. It's not broke." Irritation and the beginning of resentment spilled over into his voice. He loathed having to explain anything to this man, having to lie...

"Then what's the problem?"

"No problem. I just need more time to heal. The ligaments are strained."

Michaels eyed him suspiciously. His gaze traveled down to Jack's gloved hands, but he didn't comment. "Are you in pain?"

"Yes."

"Lots of pain?"

"A fair amount."

He seemed to be giving the last fact a great deal of thought, tenting his fingers in front of his face and hunching forward just a little so that he could rest his chin on the outstretched thumbs. Suddenly he said, "Jack, I want you to look out that window and tell me what you see."

Jack did as he was asked. Across an open field from them was Granger High School. Tomorrow was Friday—he thought he knew where Michaels was heading. "I see the high school," he said in a tight, begrudging voice.

"So do I. But I also see a man who just turned his head, *not his whole body,* to look out the window. Jack... I'm not *stupid,* y'know."

At first he was so completely taken by surprise that he only stood there, gaping at the other man's fat, smug face. Then came humiliation, which, he realized, was exactly what Michaels was hoping for—great leverage tool, humiliation. And that realization, in turn, brought anger, waves of it that manifested themselves physically, as they washed over him, as a series of hot flashes running up his cheeks and into his hairline. He weathered them and was left, finally, with a deadly calm.

"Yes, you are," he said quietly. "Maybe not in IQ points—I don't know—but in the way you deal with people...? Yes. Definitely." He paused, watched the other man's smug expression change to something more narrow-eyed and ugly... and was hit with sudden inspiration. He closed the door separating Michaels's office from that of his secretary's, sealing them off. "But hey, that's okay. *You're* stupid? *I'm* stupid. I didn't even know what game we were playing. Here I thought it was You Be Nice I'll Be Nice, and all along it's been I Got You by the Balls! Now that I know—"

"Jack, I think you'd better—"

Jack ignored the interruption, ignored Michaels's beet-red face. "Now that I know, here's my move—yours, by the way, was the look-out-the-window bit,

PADDYWHACK

calling me on something you don't know *shit* about, acting as judge and jury on how much I'm hurting! Here's mine: you and the cult girl. The one Henry saw you with out by the abandoned church he owned. Maybe the town council would like to know. Maybe your *wife*. That's my Got You!"

The color had slowly drained from Michaels's face. Several times he started to say something then appeared to think better of it. His eyes kept roving from Jack's face to the closed door. Finally he said, rather hoarsely, "And you think they're gonna believe you? *You,* a big-city boy? An *actor*...? Where's your proof?"

Jack never even changed gears. He was amazed at how easily the lie unfolded. "My aunt's diary. Everybody in Granger knows she was tight with them. It's all there in black and white—in handwriting so distinctively hers there's no way I could forge it. Interesting reading. It's almost like they wanted her to know. *Everything*."

Michaels was defeated; Jack knew it, could see it in the other man's eyes even before he said, "You *prick*! *Have* your days off! Hell, it's gonna be closed Monday and Tuesday anyway. For Christmas. But that doesn't mean there's any truth to what's in that diary. It just means, truth or not, it could be damaging tryin' to fight it."

The question now was, how far could you push a wounded bully?

"That's only half of what I want. The other half is where those people are now. Henry said you'd probably know. You'd *better* know...'cause I need that even more than I need the time off."

There was a long silence, during which it felt to Jack as if everything inside, all his internal organs, were settling toward his bowels. All his hopes were riding on getting an answer to that one question. If he didn't get one... Or if there wasn't one...

"I don't know," Michaels said finally.

The words drained all the fight from Jack, like a punch caught squarely on the nose. He felt very nearly like fainting. Instead, he set his lips in a grim line and said, "I think I'll call your wife first."

He forced himself to turn around then, put a hand on the doorknob... and had the satisfaction, no, the absolute last-minute-stay-of-execution *relief* of hearing the man say, "How do I know that won't just make things worse?" He turned back, knowing he'd won not just the first set, but the whole damned match.

"If you're 'innocent,' it can't. If, on the other hand, what I get from them helps me—which, by the way, has nothing whatsoever to do with you, but has *lots* to do with my 'neck problem'—I promise you I'll be the best goddamned librarian you could ever hope to have, and there'll be no more mention of your 'extracurricular activities.' Provided I'm treated fairly." He paused, shook his head with a feigned sadness that was not so much strictly part of his act as he wished it could be. "If it *doesn't* help... I'll probably quit my job. And why would I want to break Mrs. Michaels's heart when there's nothing else in it for me?"

There was another long silence, even longer than before. Then Michaels growled, "Ann Arbor, 4113 Amherst Street. No phone. And you can think whatever the damn hell you want! I don't care!"

Jack again turned to go. Suddenly he needed very badly to just get away from there. Speaking to his back, Michaels went on: "I shoulda never hired anyone from New York, y'know! You're all alike: hard-nosed, pushy little pricks that don't care *who* you step on!"

Jack half turned back, too drained to even begin to

appreciate the irony there. "Did you go to Henry's funeral?" he asked.

No answer, just a malevolent glare.

"I didn't think so."

XXX

HE CAN'T STAY CLOSE. HE GETS TOO TIRED, AND THEN he gets... weaker. And then they pull him back. It seemed as if he'd suffered through a thousand lifetimes since Rachel had spoken those words in her bedroom after Bane Bruce's first attack. He kept repeating them now as he snail-paced his car toward Ann Arbor, never exceeding thirty miles an hour. They were his primary rationale for attempting the trip, despite the fact that he was emotionally and physically exhausted after the funeral that morning and his confrontation with Michaels that afternoon— Rachel's words... and how they related to what he'd found lying far up in his neighbor's driveway upon his return from the City Municipal Building.

The mutilated cat hadn't been there when he and Judy came home after the funeral; of that much Jack was sure. He couldn't have missed it, the way his eyes had been drawn first to the Mallorys' house, then to the driveway, where he'd half expected Henry's wide-tired pickup—an extension of the man himself—to still be sitting. Whether it was there when he'd left for Michaels's office was another question, because he'd purposely not allowed himself to glance next door again. It could have been; he remembered how uncannily silent the attacks—all of them—had been. But it didn't matter, really. All that mattered was that it had happened *today*... and that trying to assign a specific time to it had started him thinking. About patterns. About Rachel's words...

The minimum amount of time, it seemed, between each of Bruce's forays into this world was something on the order of twelve hours. *(He gets too tired, and then he gets...weaker.)* The only exception was the brief, three-hour interval between the *first* time he'd gone for the cat, with Henry as witness, and Rachel and Judy's seeing him later that same morning hanging, half decapitated, from the living room window. But they had only *seen* him, which it was quite possible to do without his actually coming through the barrier to this side; once he came through, he was invisible. Which meant that that particular incident was really not an exception at all...

Twelve hours. He was sure the dead cat, lying in its perfect half circle of blood, was Bruce's work. And that meant that he couldn't be hit today because the cat had been. Not the most solid of theories, but in desperate times men took desperate chances. (Was he really even a man anymore? He felt like something less than that, inching his way toward Ann Arbor, still wearing his neck brace, wincing every time a passing cloud altered the amount of light coming through the windshield because he thought he pretty much knew the way things had gone down with Henry.) So he kept driving, kept replaying Rachel's words, which had been spoken with the kind of conviction only children and heroes (like Henry) possessed.

Twelve hours. It was, at best, the same kind of transitory, unsettling, untrustworthy relief one feels briefly between mad dashes for the bathroom during an especially virulent case of stomach flu.

* * *

4113 Amherst Street. Judy was waiting for him back in Granger. Maybe he should just turn around, go collect her, then get Rachel from Bob and Sylvie's and make a run for New York, hoping distance would—

Right. Remember Henry? his common sense told him.

He sat parked in front of 4113 Amherst, staring at the house in much the same fashion as a man with cancer might stare at a hospital's linear-accelerator machine immediately before undergoing his first session of radiation therapy: trying to read some special significance into its appearance, into the shape, texture, and form of the thing which very likely held, within itself, the ultimate answers to some life-and-death questions. . . .

He got nothing from his scrutiny. No sense of doom or malignancy. And certainly nothing that might foster hope either. It was just a house, an unremarkable, single-story, smallish house—vintage 1940, he estimated—that sat in a gone-to-seed neighborhood not too far from the railroad tracks. He got out of the car.

There were a few long moments after he'd rung the door bell a second time when he thought they were gone. Not just out shopping for groceries, but . . . gone. Moved away. Disappeared. And that sudden feeling made him physically ill. There were, after all, no cars in the driveway and no lights that he could see inside the house; and because today was December twentieth, one day away from the shortest day of the year (was there some special significance in *that?*), it was already nearing twilight at five o'clock. Then he caught movement out of the corner of his eye—a curtain being drawn aside just an inch or two at the window to his right, he thought—and a few seconds after that the door swung open.

The woman who stood framed in the opening

looked like a twenty-two-year-old version of Barbara
Feldon from the old *Get Smart* series. She wore her
dark, very nearly black hair in a straight-banged Cleopatra cut that, along with the amazing resemblance,
made it seem as if he had stepped back in time to the
late sixties or early seventies.

"Yes?" she said in a clear, patient voice. Like most
people, she diverted her eyes from the neck brace as
soon as she touched upon it.

He realized he was staring. She was dressed in
some sort of lavender body stocking, and the effect
wasn't so very different from what might have prevailed had her nude form simply been spray painted.
Those things were designed to be worn with appropriate underclothing, but apparently no one had told
her that. "I, uh... my name is Jack Lerille. From
Granger, west of here. And I was wondering, did you
ever live—"

"Come inside," she interrupted. "You're letting the
cold in."

He did so, and for a moment it was a toss-up as to
which had his heart pounding more: the sudden conviction that this was not one of the four people he was
looking for—she couldn't be; she looked too...
clean—or a painful awareness of the visible changes
the blast of cold air had made beneath the braless
contours of her body stocking. Plus, her face was extremely pretty. No, it was beautiful. Before he could
repeat his question, she said, "Are... you here to do
business?"

He reflected on that a moment, on what it might
mean. Then said, "In Ann Arbor, you mean?"

"No. *Here*." She looked at him as if she were trying
to communicate something with nothing but her eyes,
and if the one flaw in an otherwise perfect face had
been just a hint of hardness there, it disappeared
when he failed to get the message. "Guess not. Good.

PADDYWHACK 235

I wouldn't want to be responsible for what it might do to your neck."

Then it hit him—the words, the way she was dressed—and he felt like an idiot. *"Oh,"* he said too loudly, shouldn't have said at all. Still, he followed it up with a softer, "Oh, you're..."

She waited for him to finish, amused. When he simply shrugged, she said, "Yes? What am I?"

Still he didn't answer. He felt embarrassed, disappointed, and hopeful all at the same time, if that were possible.

"How about 'gynecological engineer'? If you get caught this way again, ask the girl if she's a 'gynecological engineer.' It means nothing... and everything. And it takes both of you off the hook as far as admitting too much to the wrong person." She was smiling now, a warm smile, and he knew he was being teased. "And do you know what *you* are?"

Still embarrassed, he said, "I... thought I did. Before I walked in here."

"You're a 'sweet-shy.' I like sweet-shies... because they're a pleasure *not* to do business with." She extended her hand. "Hi, I'm Elizabeth."

He took it, liking, even attracted to this... call girl (he was loath to use the word prostitute) who spoke in circles, but also despairing, on a deeper level, because she didn't fit at all the cruel-edged image of a Devil worshiper. Then all of that changed.

"Oh!" she said a half second after their hands had clasped. "Oh, *no*...!" Abruptly she let go.

"What?" His heart was pounding again.

"I could *feel* it!" She backed away a step and her hands flew to her breastbone. "All the... *suffering!*"

The hairs on the back of Jack's neck prickled despite the fact that the supernatural was almost an everyday occurrence now. For *him,* not for strangers. They stood facing each other, both of them staring openly, not unlike two people who have, in each other, just come face to face with an identical twin they never knew they had. "Are you...from Granger?" he said finally.

"Yes."

"One of four people who rented an old abandoned church there?"

"I'm not proud of it...but yes." She was still staring at him that way.

"Then we have to talk."

"I can see that. *Feel* it." She gave his face one last, searching look, as if it were familiar somehow and she was struggling to place it. Then she said, "Let's sit. In the living room."

He followed her down a short hallway then into a room where everything was old—the furniture, the wallpaper, an overhead chandelier—except the carpeting, which was new, plush, and a deep, rich earth tone. It all blended amazingly well.

"I'll be right back," she said, and ducked into the hallway again. He could hear her shoeless feet padding toward the rear of the house as he sat in one of two armchairs facing the room's focal point—a tall-backed, possibly Victorian (he wasn't sure) couch. Visions of the church's interior, as described by Henry, painted wholly in black, seemed at odds with what lay before him....

Wait a minute...had Henry actually described its insides...or had he just envisioned it now? Before he had time to decide, she was back. She had put on a terry-cloth bathrobe over the body stocking, and she made reference to it by brushing the backs of her fingers down the lapels. "I was doing yoga when you rang the bell. This is better. For talking..."

She was, without a doubt, correct on that count. But even in the midst of his mission's deadly urgency,

Jack felt some disappointment, a desire for one last look. At least he didn't blush again, merely nodded.

"So..." she said, sitting on the couch and curling her legs underneath her, "it comes back on me. Finally."

Jack didn't know quite how to respond to that. In a way, the statement was reassuring. At least, once the story was told, this woman might not immediately dismiss it, and him, as crazy. Still, he should proceed slowly.

"You... know my aunt Blanche, then?"

Surprise came then disappeared again somewhere deep in her eyes, barely perceptible. "Jack... *Lerille*. I should have guessed."

A short, uncomfortable pause. "She's dead."

"I know. And I'm sorry. I came to visit her at the hospital, you know. It couldn't have been more than three weeks ago—when she broke her leg. She never mentioned you then. Were you... around? In Granger?"

"We'd moved in just a week and a half before. I'm the one who found her after she fell."

She considered that a moment. "Oh. Well... she was pretty heavily sedated."

A question rose up then, unsummoned in his mind, and he almost didn't ask it, because he didn't think he really wanted to know: "How... did you know she died?"

"Someone told me. Someone from Granger."

There it was. The answer to something his subconscious had been tripping over since the moment he'd seen how desireable she was. This was the girl. Not just one of the two female members of the cult group, but *the* girl. The one Henry had actually *seen* with Michaels. *Stop it*, he told himself. *Cut the crap. You don't know that. And even if you did, business is business, and she's a*—

He cut himself off, and the old fear, its terrible urgency, got him back on track. But he decided then and there that he didn't need to tread so lightly from here on in. "Did you know," he said, "that her dog died too? That same day?"

Something registered in her face. Again it was barely perceptible, guarded, but it might have been fear. "No. But I'm not surprised."

Suddenly Jack felt angry. Angry at the girl for being so... appealing... and outwardly good... and at the same time as much as admitting being involved in something ugly. Angry at his situation and the knowledge that she and her friends must be partly to blame.

"Would it surprise you to know," he said bitterly, "that he still comes to visit me? Or that he killed my friend... more than a week after he, himself, had died?"

Yeah, it had been fear all right. In her eyes... It was easy to read now. And there was something else there too: guilt, a haunted brand of guilt. Then she was no longer looking at him, was pressing the fingertips of both hands to her temples and staring into her lap. *"No!* I mean... oh, God, I didn't think it would come to *that*! I just knew it was wrong. That the whole thing just didn't feel... *right*."

"What thing?" he asked calmly. The fact that there was no denial, no challenging the truth of the statement—which in essence informed her that the dead walked—didn't even rock him. It all seemed part of some nightmarish, preordained script.

She looked up at him, and the fear was mostly gone now. Or under control. She looked, simply... resigned. "The ceremony."

He didn't ask her to explain what that meant; his stare did the asking, because he no longer felt "sweet" or "shy" in her presence, and part of the reason for the change was that he already knew. Not the particulars... but he knew.

"Look," she went on, "not that it matters... or can change anything... but before I explain, I want you to know I'm no longer part of that group. And that if I could take back what we did, what we *were*... I would, Oh *God*, I would!"

He nodded, and said: "The ceremony."

A wounded look flickered across her face like the shadow of a bird in flight, then she was explaining: "She wanted to be with him forever. With 'Bruce.' Cam—he was the unofficial leader—said that it could be arranged... but that it would cost her..." She looked away from Jack again, swallowed with a click that was perfectly audible against the deathly silence of the room. "Five hundred dollar plus her soul."

She paused. It was almost as if she were waiting for some kind of censure. When it didn't come, because so far things weren't much different from the way his gut feeling told him they would be, she continued: "And that's what the ceremony was about: her trading her soul for eternal union with... with *Bruce*. And I know that's an unforgivable thing, but hold onto your hat because it gets worse. Because your aunt was crazy. Or at least terribly, terribly confused. She had —*during the ceremony*—Bruce-the-dog mixed up with Bruce-the-*man*!" Finally she turned back to face him. "You know about Bruce-the-*man*?"

Jack shook his head. This was where the waking-dream script and he parted company. Ahead was uncharted territory.

"Bruce Holmes was his name. A real prize she lived with, I think, during the early fifties. She used to talk about him quite a bit once she was coming out to the church on a regular basis. And we were all good listeners... because Cam said the easiest way to win people over, get them to accept you, is to be a good listener." She paused, apparently lost in her own thoughts for a while; and, judging by the pained, faraway look in her eyes, they were not pleasant ones. "Anyway," she went on, "he died a long time ago, in the mid-fifties, and it was pretty obvious from the way she talked that she was obsessed with that. With losing him, with finding him again..." She smiled a grim caricature of a smile. "With being reunited, 'forever and always,' with her long-lost love."

A slow chill ran up and down Jack's spine. An image of his aunt, after she'd caught him teasing Bruce with the rat toy, saying, *"He's more than you can see, so...much...more,"* fluttered across his mind. He blanked it out. "And...you think she thought Bruce-the-dog was this...Bruce Holmes *reincarnated*?"

"In a way, yes. But not completely. All I really know is that she was confused. And that if she had the man and the dog mixed up during the ceremony, there's no telling what the end result of that pact might be! I think you're being *visited* by the end result!"

Pact. Jack's mind was stuck on that one word. Hung up on it. Couldn't get around it. *Kind of like Bruce had been hung up on the shattered window, still WAS up there,* he thought.

Pact. Pact with the *Devil*. This beautiful girl sitting in front of him...his aunt Blanche...and the dog, the demon-dog...! The more he tried to get a grasp on it, move beyond it, the more it sucked him in. And down. Down an ever more dizzying spiral of disgusting, despairing, horrifying images resembling something from Dante's *Inferno*.

"...—be you should tell me exactly what's been happening. Maybe then at least we'd know."

Know what? He tried to focus on what she was saying. But it was like trying to make sense of what the nurse is telling you while she draws your blood. In his mind's eye the images continued to whirl and twirl. Still, he told her. In a monotone, and with very little facial expression, he told her everything there was to know about Bane Bruce, the Incredibly Invisible and Animate Dead Dog.

By the time Jack had completed his story, it was dark out. The girl who looked like Barbara Feldon sat across from him as silent and expressionless as a mannequin. Only her lips moved—barely—as if she were carrying on some internal dialogue in mental whispers. Then she said aloud, "He's not just a dog. Dead or otherwise. I'm sure of that now. He's too calculating, too malicious. Only *people* are that way." She looked at Jack now. "He's...just what I suspected him of being while he was still alive. After the ceremony. *Because* of the ceremony. I just didn't know it would stay that way after he died."

A lapse into silence then, during which her eyes never left his face and seemed to be looking for absolution there. Finally he nudged her on by asking, "What way? Obviously you have a theory...?"

She swallowed—there was that audible click again—and said in a voice that matched her eyes, "I do. It's something I've thought about a lot. Even before you came to me. And I want you to know up front... it's the reason I left the group."

Again she stopped, but this time it took nothing more than a nod to urge her on.

"Bruce," she said, "is a dog...with the soul, or *part* of the soul, of a man. A *damned* soul. She had the man and the dog all mixed up, all twisted together, when she made her pledge. And"—she chuckled softly, but there was no humor to it; it was a laugh of futility—"like Cam used to say, 'When you bargain with the Devil, you'd better have your head on straight.'" A form of wonder, of wounded surprise, replaced the apology in her eyes, "You know...I could feel it the moment the ceremony was over: he wasn't just a dog anymore. And when he looked at you...Didn't he ever look at you that way? Like he ...knew more than a dog should know?"

Jack remembered the first night he'd heard his aunt talking and had crept downstairs, looked through the open doorway of her bedroom. The expression on his face must have been answer enough. She went on:

"That's when I knew that Satan was real...and that the whole 'cult' thing was more than just a game." She paused. "I *should* have known when he asked me to...*whore* for him...as a way to make money for the 'cause.'"

That same expression—wounded, reproachful surprise, like a toddler who's just had his butt smacked for the first time for not minding—was all over her face now, and Jack almost felt sorry for her. But a desperate need to know, to have something to fight Bruce with—and a mounting fear—overrode the feeling. "So how do I stop him?" he said. "Can he be killed? Can the ceremony be reversed?"

The expression died, and she was all business again. Terse. "I don't know. Here's the rest of my... 'theory,' based on what you've told me. Blanche Lerille made a deal. To be with 'Bruce' forever. When she made it, she had Bruce Holmes and Bruce-the-dog mixed up. Bruce *Holmes* is in Hell; I've no doubt about that. While Bruce-the-*dog* is just that: a dog. And dogs have no souls. So the Devil, in order to keep his end of the deal—thus acquiring Blanche's soul too—mixed the two of them together the same way *she* had them mixed up when she made it. The end result, now that both she and the dog are dead— and I don't think it's just coincidence that he died right after she did; that's *his* work—is that she's in

Hell with *most* of Bruce Holmes's soul, because that's who she primarily had in mind when she made her pledge... And the dog is in some kind of netherworld close to Hell—an anteroom to Hell—still alive, in a sense, only because it has a little piece of Bruce Holmes's soul tacked onto it. Souls, you see, are immortal, good *or* bad. And only people have souls..."

She paused for a moment, considering what she'd said so far.

"I think it's a great joke from the Devil's point of view. It's just the way he *would* twist things up. Not only does he have Blanche and Bruce Holmes, but a way, through honoring the bargain *exactly as struck*, of spreading more suffering in *this* world." Her eyes, which had been staring past him or through him, refocused on his face. "He knows the kind of hate a dog would feel for the person who kept it from its dying master...."

Jack felt numb. It was a choice between shutting down his emotions entirely or possibly screaming, and he couldn't afford to scream just yet. Not before he knew everything he needed to know. "I repeat," he said calmly, evenly. "How do I stop him?"

There was a hint of the same mute apology in her eyes that Jack had seen earlier. Or was it pity? It lingered there long enough, before she answered, to start his heart pounding again.

"The ceremony itself can't be reversed. That's strictly between your aunt Blanche and the Devil, and it's ironclad, and there's nothing we can do... directly. But the dog... I'm thinking that maybe the dog... if we got rid of the *man*..."

And suddenly Jack was a step ahead of her and his mind was reeling again. Horror and excitement... Hope mixed with unspeakable dread... "You mean ... an exorcism. Exorcise the man from the dog, like the dog was possessed."

She nodded. "He *is* possessed, Jack! From the moment of the ceremony. I could feel it. And from what you've told me, you could too. The only way he's kept alive is through that piece of Bruce Holmes. I'm positive. Or else things like this would happen all the time."

For a moment the hope, and the excitement it fostered, took precedence. Then the doubts came roaring back in. "But... how could I do it? I'm not a priest; I don't even *know* any priests."

"You don't have to. You believe in God, don't you?"

He frowned. Good question. He had, at one time, had a very strong faith. But now...? It seemed now, after all of this, that if he believed at all, it was not a healthy belief but rather a desperate, selfish clinging —to something he was simply too afraid to let go of completely, because then he couldn't even *pretend* there was hope. God was his adult version of a night-light, and he was past the age where he could truly believe such a light had magical powers.

"Yes," he said. And it was a wondrous revelation, because he said it with conviction.

"And in Jesus?"

Another surprise: "Yes."

"Then you have as much as a priest has. And believe me, if Satan is real, they're *just* as real. Besides, from what I've read, it's not as hard to... 'cast out demons' from an animal as it is from a human being."

Cast out demons. The words brought him back down, had an effect similar to that generated earlier by the word "pact." They gave an air of unreality to their little talk. It was the same kind of feeling he might have had if they had been sitting there rationally discussing Martians....

"And," she went on, "we're not talking about the Devil himself. Or even any of his major-league demons. All we're talking about is a tiny part of an evil man's soul..." She stood up, walked over to a small bookcase he hadn't noticed when he'd first entered the room. From it she withdrew a single book, brought it back, and handed it to him. "Here," she said. "Take it with you. It'll give you a better idea of how to go about it than I could."

Jack glanced down at the title. *Exorcism: Past and Present,* by Martin Ebon. She made no move to return to her place on the couch. Instead she stood there, directly in front of his chair. And surprised him by saying, "It's...past six-thirty now. And by seven I've got to be dressed and made up to look *exactly* like some guy's wife. He's a regular since...since she died of leukemia eleven months ago...."

He stood up, confused. And for a moment she didn't look twenty-two anymore. She looked...much older than that, aged with the sadness and hardness of time. Then she was walking him to the door and an alarm was going off somewhere inside his head. There was so much he needed to know...and this was the only person he knew who might have some answers!

"I...need more," he said when they got as far as the door, trying not to sound so desperate it would frighten her. "More to go on. I can't perform—"

"There *is* no more," she cut him off. "If there were more, don't you think I'd tell you? Anything I know, I got from the book." She laughed her short, unhappy little laugh. "Our...'field of expertise' was kinda from the opposite end, you know."

Yeah, he thought, *I know.* But the concept couldn't generate the same kind of anger it had earlier. Just a generalized, unfocused bitterness. "What about the others?" he said. "This...'Cam'?"

"Moved. All of them. They could be anywhere by now. Their plan was to simply head west. Read the book, Jack. Plus anything else you can get hold of.

Then call me—Bob Michaels is wrong; I have a phone now...747, like the airplane, then L-O-V-E. It's easier to remember that way." She'd opened the door for him, and when he didn't step into the night, she touched his face...the way Judy sometimes touched his face. "Really, Jack, all your staying now could accomplish is to destroy this...regular's illusion. And he wouldn't be able to handle that yet, though, believe me, we're working on it. I mean, we're talking about a guy—a good-looking guy, still in his prime—who's given *me* all his wife's clothes! Because I *look* like her! He spends most of his time just...crying. In my arms. And saying her name..." She let her hand fall back to her side, and her eyes turned wistful. "Jenny." Then her eyes refocused on him. "And that, Jack, is almost as sad as what you're going through. Except in his case I didn't help create the thing that's eating *him* alive..."

He should have gone then. He knew that. But there was one more question, something he had to know. Especially now, after the things she'd just said. It was the age-old question, and someone in her line of work must have heard it a thousand times: *"Why?"*

Even so, at first she misinterpreted it. "Because I didn't know it was real. I didn't really *believe* there was a Devil. Not really. So it all seemed perfectly safe...and innocent. And if...if you could have seen Cam through my eyes..."

Again, there was that look: "wounded surprise" only approximately described it; it was the look of someone who had been betrayed in a deeply fundamental way....

"No. I mean, why do you still...do *this*?"

Instantly it was as if an invisible wall had gone up between them. Jack could feel it, see it in her eyes. And hear it in her voice. "Maybe I want to write a book." Then she softened just a bit—at least her voice did. "Look, everybody has their own way to self-destruct. We all spend our adult lives committing slow suicide. Someone said that once. I happen to believe it; can we leave it at that?"

"Yeah," Jack said. "I guess we can. For now. But I want you to know you're one helluva cheerleader. I feel positively inspired."

She winced a little, then grinned. "Sorry. How's this, then? You beat this thing and give me a reason to think differently... Save *both* our lives."

"Better. I think."

He stepped outside then, and was about to turn and leave when she said, "Oh! One more thing—while I'm still in the 'cheerleader' mode. You're not the first person this has happened to—I don't *think*. There was a girl back at the turn of the century, in India, and another in the Philippines around 1950. Neither case talks about a dog specifically, but *something* invisible and not too big was biting them, and the British doctor who wrote about the first case does mention the girl's screaming, 'Shiva! Shiva!' over and over again...."

Jack stared at her, stunned. Finally he said, "And...?"

"Shiva, in the very loosest sense, might be considered the Hindu equivalent of Satan. By us, not by them. He's Shiva the Destroyer, god of the dark side, said to occasionally consort with demons. So... there is *that* connection too."

Jack felt his pulse quicken at the prospect that here, finally, might be some answers; but he wouldn't allow the reaction to spread to his brain. "How do you know about them?" he asked cautiously. "The girls."

She shrugged. "I read. Cam encouraged reading. To him, books on the unexplained, the supernatural, and strange phenomenon are all arguments in favor of the Devil."

"Why didn't you say something earlier, then? When I asked if that was all? I mean, maybe there's an answer there, a way of dealing with this that—"

"No," she cut in. "There's not. The attacks stopped on their own in both cases. In less than a day. And never recurred."

Her eyes were asking his forgiveness again, as she said it, but he was fresh out of gallantry. He *had* allowed his hopes to rise, despite himself, and now he felt just a notch weaker, spiritually, than before she'd brought up the two girls. "Like I said," he mumbled, "you make a great cheerleader." Then he turned and walked the short distance to his car.

"Call me," she yelled, just before he climbed inside. "After you read Ebon's book."

She was still there, framed in the doorway and back lit by the glaring brightness of a single bare bulb in the hallway behind her, when he drove away. Through the thin layer of frost on his window, the nimbus of light surrounding her silhouette looked like... well, it looked like a human soul.

XXXI

ON THE DRIVE BACK FROM ANN ARBOR AND ALL THE rest of that evening, Jack wondered if he would have the courage to even attempt such a thing as an exorcism. He even said as much to Judy. Maybe, she offered, they could weather this. Maybe whatever fury that allowed Bruce to break through from the other side would eventually wane.... Then, around eight o'clock the next morning, it was made clear to both of them that it was no longer a question of having enough courage. It was, in fact, no longer a question at all; it was a necessity.

He should have known it would come to this. Especially now. Now that he had reason to believe there was a human element to Bruce. What better, more typically human way, if he couldn't harm Jack directly, than to come at him through his family? Why hadn't it occurred to him earlier? After Henry? After the cat? *Because,* he told himself, *even in this life he had clearly hated both of them; while he'd been indifferent to Judy, and had actually seemed to like Rachel.*

That is what he told himself, but deep down he knew that he was to blame. He'd simply been too wrapped up in his own suffering to make the connection. Like any coward.

He'd known, from the moment he'd picked up the phone on Friday morning, heard the way his father-in-law said his name, that something was wrong. "Yeah, Bob?" he'd answered cautiously. "What is it?"

A short silence, then: "Jack...I don't know exactly what, but...something's happened."

Jack struggled to keep his voice calm. "To who? Oh, jeez, not to Rachel! Is she—"

"She's all right, near as I can tell. Just a few... bites or somethin'. Whatever they are, they didn't break the skin; but...god*damn*, Jack, I can't figure..."

Bites! All the strength went from his legs, and he slumped into the chair next to the phone. "You sure she's all right?" he said between heartbeats. "Where're the bites?"

"On her hands, just...on her hands. But she's real shook up. It's that I'm worried about. She's sayin' some pretty crazy stuff... about it bein' that rat terrier of your aunt's, come back to get her, but it's really you it wants, and... stuff like that."

Oh, God! he thought. *Oh, Jesus, no! Please don't let this be happening to my baby! Do it to ME, if you have to! But not my BABY!* Then he went cold... as he realized he was addressing the wrong end of the hierarchy. "Bullterrier," he said tonelessly. "Bruce is a *bull*terrier. And you got to remember the way he died. It was all pretty traumatic for a six-year-old. She has dreams..."

Why was he doing this? Why didn't he just tell him the truth?

"That's what I thought too," Bob Ross said, "because when we came in the room nothing was there ...and she was strugglin' as if there was, like in a dream. But the bites..."

There was a prolonged silence, and Jack used it to answer his own question. *Because what good would it do to tell him? People thinking I'm crazy would only get in the way...*

"Say..." Bob Ross said finally. "You don't think ...Sylvie and me saw something on TEE-vee once. It was on *60 Minutes*, I think, or some such show... Anyway, it had to do with how much power the mind has over the body. You know, stuff like a guy bein' hypnotized into thinking he's burned and his skin raises up in blisters? You don't suppose that's what's happened with Rachel? 'Cuz, Jack, she really *believes* it was that Bruce-dog..."

TEE-vee. No, it would be best not to tell him. Out loud, he said, "I, uh... don't know what to think, Bob. It could be. All I know is that it's been hard on her—the way her aunt Blanche, then the dog died..."

"It's gotta be something like that. Jack, there's *no*

way even a squirrel coulda got in that room, let alone a dog! It's as tight as a drum."

With his mind whirling and twirling, Jack took more time than he should have before he answered. "I'm sure it is. I think you're right. Some kind of dream. I guess she just wasn't ready to stay overnight someplace else. I'm sorry, we should've—"

"*You're* sorry. Jack, *I'm* sorry. I know this is a rough time for you, and I hesitated to call at all . . . but maybe that's it; maybe after three days she just needs her mom and dad."

Was there just a hint of reproach there? Jack wasn't sure, and it didn't really matter that much anyway, on top of everything else that was happening. He told his father-in-law they would be out to pick up Rachel by nine-thirty (no way was he going to risk sending Judy out alone, not now, no matter how recently Bruce had "expended" himself). Somehow he remembered to say something about having to get right back to open up the library, so that he would have an excuse for not staying and possibly getting tripped up by something Rachel might say. But that was the last clear thinking he did for quite a while. Telling Judy, then calming her down afterward . . . even the seemingly endless ride out there, was something he would remember later only as a vague nightmare within a nightmare. . . .

The crux of what had happened out at the Rosses', Jack gathered, was that both Bob and Sylvie had been awakened a little before seven A.M. by Rachel's screams, coming from the next bedroom. Interspersed with the screams was the phrase *Tell Daddy! Tell Daddy!* shouted over and over again in a terrified, pleading voice. When they burst into her bedroom, they found their granddaughter pressed up against the bed's headboard, with all her blankets bundled in front of and around her neck and head. She was still thrashing about, twisting from side to side with her hands and forearms shielding her blanketed face in the way one might move if he were trying to avoid being slapped.

But all of that stopped at about the same time they reached her, although it took more than a minute of holding and soothing and comforting before she would allow the covers to be removed from her face, and at least another minute before she could say anything beyond the two-word phrase she'd already been repeating. In the meantime they had noticed the marks on her hands, which looked, unmistakably, like bite marks that had stopped just short of breaking the skin, and it was in reference to these that she was finally able to speak in a coherent, if not altogether rational, manner. "He can bite harder," she said. "He can bite all the way *through*. Tell Daddy; *he* knows." She looked frightened and miserable, but definitely not glassy-eyed like a child experiencing a waking dream, and when they asked her who "he" was, she told them what Bob Ross had already related to Jack over the phone: that it was her aunt Blanche's dog Bruce, and that he really wanted not her but her daddy.

And that's *all* she said. She had refused to talk about it beyond that statement, and for that Jack was grateful. He had not worn the neck brace when they went in to pick her up, and with his gloves on, his coat buttoned high, and the smallest bandage possible over the gouge on his chin, he looked like nothing more ominous than the victim of a shaving accident. He hoped. At any rate, they managed to get out without arousing any noticeable suspicion, and with only the promise that if these "nightmares" continued, they would take Rachel to see a doctor. It was almost as if, in her refusal to discuss what had happened, at least in her grandparents' presence, Rachel had *known* that

PADDYWHACK 253

it would only make things worse. He thought he saw that in her eyes when her mother—right in front of Bob and Sylvie, because it seemed as if they were expecting her to do so—had asked the obligatory question: "What happened, pumpkin? Tell Momma." And though he had been relieved when she hadn't answered, had climbed into her mother's arms instead, the look she'd given both of them had been... disturbing. It was too knowing a look for a six-year-old, too old... and despite the fact that they were by definition wholly inaccurate, inappropriate, two words had come immediately to mind in reference to that stare: *carnal knowledge*.

Now he had to weather that stare on the way home. And, on a much subtler plane, Judy's as well. Not that it was intentional on either's part; and had he even suggested to his wife that deep down she blamed him, or at least wondered if he hadn't done something terribly wrong—made some crucial error to precipitate this vendetta—she would have been appalled. But it was there, *something* was there, and it showed just a little in her eyes and in the way she involuntarily tightened her arms around Rachel, whom she held on her lap, when he reached across the car seat to stroke his daughter's hair. It was, he thought, the same kind of feelings that must eventually surface when one half of a married couple has a wasting, crippling disease. Any number of perceptive, articulate, but critically ill, people had chronicled just such circumstances... and they had almost always made mention of the quiet desperation, even martyrdom, in their spouse's eyes.... The disease set them apart, isolated its victim with a loneliness and a form of guilt no well person could possibly understand. *Bruce* was a disease, one that *he* had contracted... and now the disease was dragging his family down.

Then he remembered something else, how one of

those chroniclers of slow death had spoken candidly of his options: If he were to go through with a very painful, highly improbable new mode of treatment for his disease... and be cured, or partially cured... he would be a hero. If, on the other hand, he were to give in to his incredibly powerful yearnings for release—in the form of suicide, because he knew he was a terrible burden to his family, though they would never admit it—he would be remembered as a coward and a disgrace. And if he made neither of those two choices, simply hung on, no matter how bravely, until the disease eventually claimed him, he would be, simply, a burden....

With those *kinds* of thoughts turning round and round in his head, Jack reached across the seat again, an idea, some kind of resolve as yet unclear to him, forming in his mind. This time he squeezed Rachel's leg through her wool slacks. "Is there anything we can do, honey?" he asked gently. "Anything Bruce... 'told' you that would help make him go away?"

She burrowed her face into her mother's breast. "Jack, don't," Judy scolded. "She's had enough."

Jack ignored her. "Honey...?"

"He doesn't talk," Rachel said. With difficulty. She was puff-panting now, breathing in short little gasps, the way she always did before she began to cry in earnest. "I *told* you that. But I *know*... He lets me know." Little hitch-sobs mixed with the puff-pants. "Either I get... bited up or... or I lose my *daddyyy!*" Then she was bawling outright, twisting and squirming in her mother's lap, affected physically by the intensity of her despair, and Judy was giving him an icy stare.

He opened up his mouth to say something—he didn't know what—then closed it again, afraid that he might cry too. Not for himself, but for the anguish in his daughter's voice.

"I don't *want* to be bited! And I don't want my daddy dead *either*!" This, muffled but still intelligible, as she strained for maximum contact with her mother.

"You... won't be," he said, struggling for mastery of his voice. He found that he could only say a few words at a time between involuntary closings of his throat. "And *I*... won't be... either! Because I'm... going in... after him!"

Option number one, he thought to himself. *No hero, but... what other choice do I have?*

They drove the rest of the way home in silence.

XXXII

SAYING IT OUT LOUD THE WAY HE HAD, ALMOST IN the form of a promise to his daughter, was the first time Jack had allowed himself to think about what he had to do in terms of going *in* after Bruce. Until then his mind had veered away each and every time he'd attempted to visualize the specifics of just how he might perform an exorcism on something from some other "living-dead" dimension that was only in this world for brief, unpredictable periods of time and was both violent and invisible when it *was* here. He could understand why: the idea terrified him. What had the woman, Elizabeth, called the place where Bruce was? An "anteroom to hell"? Still, it made sense, as much as anything about this putrescent nightmare made sense. An exorcism, as he understood it, took time. And there was no way he had that much time while

Bruce was on this side. Nor, he was almost positive, could he keep Bruce here for longer. There was something irresistibly powerful about the force that pulled him back through the placenta barrier. No one needed to tell him that; he could sense it the same way he could sense the power beneath the clutch of the 427 'Vette a friend used to let him drive on occasion, back when they were both in college. The question was, *could* he follow Bruce through? For some reason, he was sure he could, that passage in *that* direction, for those who desired it, would be made easy. And the thought made him ill.

He spent the rest of the day reading. And when he had finished the book that Elizabeth had given him, the three of them—Rachel, Judy, and himself—bundled up, talking care to wrap their throats especially well in heavy scarves, made a brief excursion to the library. There he found that the only book of any additional help was volume seven of Cavendish's *Man, Myth & Magic: An Illustrated Encyclopedia of the Supernatural.*

They arrived home again before dark, whereupon he turned down the heat and instructed Rachel and Judy to stay dressed for the outdoors, even insisting that his daughter wear his catcher's mask as well. He himself removed his coat, gloves, outer shirt, and neck brace, with heart pounding. But not the steel cup; he couldn't quite force himself to go that far, despite the fact that his goal, now, was to make himself as vulnerable, as tempting a piece of bait for Bruce, as possible. He had a plan, and there were portions of it that needed testing before he could go through with it in its entirety. According to his theory on the frequency of Bruce's attacks, the way would be open any time after seven P.M. As he lay down on the bed in Blanche's room—the way a condemned man must take his seat in the electric chair—he

PADDYWHACK

marked the day in his mind. Friday, December twenty-first. It would stand as either the day he first took control of his situation . . . or the one on which he took the initial steps toward the forfeiture of his soul.

Bruce came for him at just past eleven-thirty. The temperature inside had by that time fallen to fifty-five degrees, and although it was enough incentive for even a six-year-old to stay bundled up, Jack, dressed as bait, was freezing. Which was probably good, because at least the cold had kept him alert during the six-hour wait, and had he not been alert, he would most likely have had his throat torn out.

The demon-dog came at him from the side, silent as always, and this time there was not even the fractional warning provided by Jack's being able to *see* the demon-face for a split second before it actually broke through the placenta barrier. That event must have occurred just beyond his peripheral vision. Or perhaps below the level of the bed, as he lay in its very middle. Because first knowledge of the ghost animal's presence came with the feel of its teeth, its hot breath which smelled of decay, high on the right side of his neck.

He shrugged reflexively, and his shoulder must have gotten in the way of any vital hold before it could be secured, because he felt the teeth scrape upward and just catch the bottom one third of his ear. They closed, piercing it all the way through—he didn't need his vision to tell him that—and the pain was ten times greater than he would have imagined it could be. Then they tore away, there was an even worse, burning sensation, and a far corner of his mind that had managed to stay calm even now said, very clearly, *It's gone. Don't worry about it now.*

It may have been that same portion that allowed him to do what he did next.

There were two pillows on the bed: one on which his profusely bleeding head still rested, and another he had purposely kept draped across the bend in his left arm the whole time he'd lain there waiting, so that even a reflexive move to cover his face would automatically place it where it would do the most good. He made such a move now, and it was purely that: reflexive. And it worked! His face and throat were covered for as long as he was able to keep the pillow tightly in place! But that was not the end of it. His hands, arms, and shoulders were still being bitten mercilessly, and to put into effect the second part of his plan required the presence of mind, the deliberate thinking, that only that single, far corner seemed still capable of.

He forced himself to let go of the pillow with his left hand and groped along that side of the bed. Bruce immediately was at the weak spot in his defense; Jack could feel him trying to force his way between the pillow and his face. And he was succeeding! *God, he was strong!* Then he found what he was looking for—a metal crucifix about eight inches long that had belonged to Judy since before they were married. He'd kept it hidden, until a few seconds ago, beneath the same pillow that now shielded his face. And as he grasped it now, pressed it with all his strength against Bruce's invisible side, he said a prayer...

The effect was immediate, though nowhere nearly as dramatic as the same means of defense administered in any of the numerous vampire movies he'd seen: no searing of the flesh, no banshee wail... Bruce simply withdrew. Silently.

And tried once again before Jack could even appreciate the enormity of what had taken place, this time from the opposite side, sinking his invisible fangs into Jack's right shoulder.

But when he reached across and applied the crucifix a second time, Bruce was pulled back through to the other side! His snarling, demonic face became visible for the half instant it took the placenta barrier to close around him, just before he receded into nothingness, as proof positive that he was gone.

All of it, from start to finish, had occurred within the span of a dozen seconds.

When Judy, carrying their sleeping daughter in her arms, finally got to the doorway after having heard the sounds of Jack's struggles, she found him staring at the polished steel cross in his hand as if it were an alien weapon with which he had, quite by accident, just disintegrated an entire mountain. Slowly he turned his eyes to meet hers. There was a strange, almost fanatical light in them. "Now I know," he said in an awed voice. "There's a power of Heaven and a power of Hell." He looked back down at the cross. "They're both real. As real as Bruce is."

XXXIII

SATURDAY MORNING, DECEMBER TWENTY-SECOND. Jack hurt like hell. The ear—or at least the bottom third of it—was not gone, as he'd believed. But it was torn, and torn badly. Completely through, so that, had he chosen to, he could have folded each of its two sections in opposite directions—something that probably would have had him passed out on the floor, judging by the amount of pain generated by the simple act of turning his head or by movements of his jaw.

But it hadn't been the pain that had finally decided him, last night, that a trip to Chalmers Community Hospital was necessary, it had been the bleeding. They simply had been unable to get it stopped. No matter what they did, it had continued. Not in the voluminous, gushing amounts associated with a cut artery, but in a slow, continuous welling that still would have had him on "empty" by morning.

The first thing the doctor in attendance had said was the fact that the ear was bleeding equally from both sections was a good sign. The parts could be stitched together with every confidence they would heal nicely. His second remark was in the form of a question about the circumstances under which Jack had been bitten. Jack was ready for it, because he'd known from the beginning that a doctor would instantly recognize the wounds as coming from an animal's teeth. He gave him a preplanned story about how he'd been carrying the family dog when he'd tripped and fallen against the wall, half squashing the animal between it and his shoulder in the process. Being high-strung, Bruce (why not call him by his name; it made it easier to lie) had simply reacted, wasn't usually vicious, and had not been outside where he could have come into contact with any skunks, raccoons, or any other rabid animal since October. And the doctor had accepted that, agreeing that Boston bulls were indeed high-strung, simply advising them to make doubly sure by keeping the dog confined and under close observation for the next week or so. Fifteen minutes later they had been on the way home again, the ear cleaned, stitched, and bandaged, and the bleeding stopped, by what means Jack had never thought to ask.

But that was last night, and this morning, whatever nerve deadener they'd injected the ear with before sewing it, had worn off. And he couldn't afford to risk taking the Percodan tablets he'd also been given for fear they would make him less alert. He hurt; his whole body hurt as he descended the stairs and walked into the kitchen for some breakfast. He felt like he'd gone a few rounds with Mike Tyson last night instead of a twenty-pound dog. Make that *dead* dog...

He supposed that was the fibrositis talking to him, which surprised him just a little because that was supposed to be a depression-anxiety thing, and he felt less depressed this morning than he had felt in weeks despite the pain.

Because it had *worked*, the cross had worked!

Which, by itself, meant only that he had another piece of armament along with his neck brace and steel cup, not a cure. But it was a clear indication that Bruce was exactly what Elizabeth had said he was—a product of the Devil—and that as a defense against Satan, the power of God was not just protection in theory, but as real, as substantive a defense, as a loaded gun against bear.

And *that,* in turn, told him that the kind of exorcism Elizabeth recommended just *might* be a cure....

The exorcism. It was a sobering thought, more sobering than the pain. Was he ready? He'd read the book, his faith in some sort of divine power was as strong as it had ever been, after last night, but...

With a new level of respect for any additional thinking she might have done on the subject, he reached for the phone and dialed Elizabeth's number. She answered on the second ring.

"Hello?"

"Hi. This is Jack, Jack... Lerille." He'd considered saying Jack *Sweet-shy*, but decided against it.

A momentary silence on the other end, then: "Hi, Jack Lerille. What's up?"

"My spirits, a little. He ... came again, last night. And I used a cross to drive him away."

"Really? *Really, Jack?* That's great! Did—"

"But I have some questions, some things I have to know before I ... go the rest of the way, go through with the exorcism."

Another short silence, then: "Did you read the book?"

"Yeah. I did. Plus some others. But none of them gives anything like a step-by-step plan of the ceremony. Is there such a thing? I keep running into partial quotes from something called the *Ritulae Romanum*. Do you think—"

"I don't know. If you've read *several* books you probably know more than I do. I've heard of the *Ritulae*. It's a book. From the sixteenth or seventeenth century, I think. But it has to do with priests, ceremonies that *priests* perform...."

He sensed there was more. She seemed hesitant. "And?"

"And you're not a priest. But I don't think it matters. You're a Christian, you believe in *Jesus'* God ... and as long as that's who you're calling on for help, I think ritual is ... is secondary to what's in your heart. I think the New Testament makes that pretty clear. But I repeat, *I don't know.* And I don't think you should use me as your final authority."

The incongruity of who and *what* she was, and the things she was explaining, gave him pause for a moment, as it had the night he'd met her, when she'd asked him if he believed in God. In some ways it was like having the Ayatollah Khomeini advise you on brotherhood.

No ... it wasn't.

"Why not?" he asked finally. "Seems like you've put me on the right track so far."

"Because the stakes are too high! You risk your

PADDYWHACK

soul when you do an exorcism! They're dangerous, Jack! And I don't want that responsibility. I've hurt you enough just by being part of what we did with your aunt. And with Bruce."

Jack was quiet for a moment. He was well aware of the risks. Everything he had read had returned again and again to that same idea. And the rest, the part about responsibility and blame, he chose to ignore. Or maybe it was that with blame *came* responsibility...

After a long pause he said, "It's not like I have a year to research the topic. He went after my daughter yesterday morning, my *six-year-old* daughter. She's all right, but—"

"Oh *no*, Jack!" she gasped. "I'm *sorry!*"

"Don't be. Just give me the help I need—answer my questions."

Silence. Jack took it as a form of consent and went on.

"First...why is he pulled back? *What* pulls him back?"

He thought he detected a sigh. Then she was saying, "My opinion? It's Hell's claim on him. On the Bruce Holmes part. The Devil's never been one to give up a soul that's rightfully his. Or even part of a soul. And maybe there's a chance that if Bruce is in the land of the living for too long, the... 'doorway back' closes and the Holmes part escapes, *permanently*. Satan, of course, would never allow that; and yet, in order to honor the bargain exactly as struck, he has to allow the two of them to continue to be mixed—the way your aunt's confused *mind* had them mixed...."

Jack considered that. It was pretty much the same conclusion he had reached on his own. Despite the fact that it inadvertently helped him, he had never sensed anything even remotely benevolent about the power that pulled Bruce back through. Without comment he went on to his next question:

"Second... where is he pulled back *to*? What's an 'anteroom to Hell'?"

She laughed, but it was a bitter laugh. "I don't know. Someplace the 'bad guy' invented to suit his needs, is my guess. Someplace close to Hell so that Bruce-the-dog—who, remember, is soulless—can be 'with' your Aunt Blanche."

His grip tightened on the phone. *Someplace close to Hell.* He'd assumed that. But hearing someone else say it made everything knot up inside. Plus it brought him, unavoidably, to his next question. The biggy. The one whose every answer seemed as if it had to be just another variation on the same theme: his doom.

"Do you... think I can go there? Follow Bruce in?"

She inhaled sharply. "*No!* Not without risk of being sucked into Hell! *You* have a soul, Jack!"

The knot inside tightened. "But... what if I have to? And you know that I do. There's no way I can perform an exorcism while he's on this side. While he's invisible... It takes everything I've got just to protect myself."

"No! There's got to be another way!"

"Then name it, damnit! Just... name it! Liz, I can *see* him when he's on the other side... Until he falls away from the barrier, anyway."

She was silent. It dragged on for long enough this time that he began to wonder if she was still there.

"Elizabeth?"

There was a very quiet, high-pitched, almost little-girlish, "Yeah?"

He spoke more softly now. "What choice do I have? Really. He's not going to quit. Not even if I dress in the Pope's robes and have a thousand crosses. Don't ask me how I know; I just do. And it's just a matter of time before he catches me off guard and rips out my throat. Or, more likely, my wife's or daughter's throat! And that, Elizabeth, is *worse* than Hell."

He paused, and it was then that he realized she was crying. Little, sharp intakes of air, not quite sobs, that he knew she was trying to hide from him. He didn't care. And yet... he did.

"As a matter of fact," he went on, "now that I think about it, it *is* Hell. I mean, we sit... and we wait for him, afraid to go to the bathroom, afraid to make love... because that's just what he's—"

"All *right*!" she gasped. "You're right, it's probably the only way! But Jack, it's *me* that should be going in after him! And I can't, I'm afraid!" Then she gave herself over to crying completely, making no effort at all to hide it.

Jack was stunned. That possibility had never even occurred to him. Or had it? Was that what he'd been secretly hoping for all along?

"No," he said, trying to keep his voice calm. "No, that wouldn't work. The odds on your being able to grab him and get yourself pulled through when it's not even you he's attacking are next to nil." But there was a part of him that welcomed the idea, grabbed hold of it with all the desperate relief of a drowning man to a life preserver. And another part, even further removed, that marveled at the way he was able to discuss it at all, so casually, as if it were merely a technical problem, the prohibitive mechanics involved in an impossible gymnastics stunt.

"I'm afraid that with all I've... done, I'd be sucked right to hell... because I'm destined to go there anyway!" She was still crying, still choking on her words, but not as badly.

Jack swallowed, acutely uncomfortable. "That's ridiculous. And it's also not the point. The point is, *I'm* the one who's got to do it because I'm the one right there when there's an opening. And *your* job—look on it as a form of penance, if you want to—is to have the courage to be straight with me, no matter how heavy that weighs on your conscience. Can you do that?"

When she answered finally with a toneless "Yes," he squeezed his eyes shut. He knew he was right, that it had to be him, but it was a dubious victory. More like drawing straws to see who makes a run through enemy lines to seek help...

"Now," he said brusquely, "here's my plan. You tell me what you think of it." He took a deep breath. "I'm gonna wait through one more time. That is, if it happens today. But not with my guard down; I can't take any more 'chewing on' today. So I'll wear my neck brace, my coat, gloves... the whole works. As will Rachel and Judy. And we'll each have crosses. That way if he comes, it'll tell me last night with the cross did *not* put an end to it—which I think I already know anyway. And it might, just *might*, tell me something else too. Because both Judy and I will have knives, sharp knives... and if he comes—and if things go right—we'll know whether he can be hurt physically, maybe even killed. *Permanently*."

Before he could go on, Elizabeth said, "And if he doesn't come?"

"Does or doesn't, same thing," he answered grimly. "Tomorrow I wait, like I did last night—pretty much stripped—while Rachel and Judy stay bundled to the max. And when he comes for me, I slap the cross against him and ride him through to the other side."

There was silence on the other end of the line, but he thought he could guess what was running through her mind, so he said, "I know it seems bad to wait another night, put my family through another attack maybe, but I'm not ready yet—last night was rough —and I have a feeling that if I go tonight, I won't be strong enough; I'll blow it for sure, and then they'll be *completely* at his mercy." He paused, struck by a sudden, but not foreign, thought. "Which may happen anyway, so I want to be as sure as possible there's no other way..."

His voice drifted off then, and in the deafening silence that continued to emanate from the receiver, he thought he could hear all kinds of uncharitable conclusions being drawn. "Covered up the way I'm gonna make *sure* they're covered, he can't even touch them with his teeth. And if there's any chance the knife—I just thought of the knife last night 'cause the hedge shears're too clumsy, and I won't risk using a gun 'cause I might hit—"

"Jack," she cut in, "no excuses; there's nothing to be excused. You're damned *right* you shouldn't go till you know it's your only choice. And even then, *don't go*." He could hear a small hitch in her breathing, a leftover from her crying. "But it's a good plan. Or at least a logical one..."

He accepted that, wondering why he felt so compelled to justify himself to a woman whom, in truth, he hardly knew. "There's...got to be an end," he said. "One way or another. We can't live our lives this way."

"I know," she said softly. "And you're braver than brave."

A flutter-thrill ran through his body. It was both a physical and a mental thing, like the ghost of an electric current passing through his mind and body at the same time, and it left him fortified.

"No," he said, thoroughly embarrassed. "Just... it's necessary." Then he was groping for a way to change the subject. Before he spoiled the magic.

Whole seconds passed.

"One more question," he said finally. "Why is he invisible?"

More seconds, but the urgency was off of them.

"I don't know," she said. "For the same reason there's cancer and old age and crib death, I guess. Just one of those unexplained, shitty facts of life."

He was quiet for a moment. Then he said, "I'll call you again when it's over." And hung up before she could say anything else, something that might spoil the illusion that he was brave.

XXXIV

IT WAS JUDY WHO DISPROVED HENRY'S KNOCK-THEM-bones-apart theory which, specifically, hypothesized that a skeleton from his boyhood attic would be subject to the same destructive forces as any other ambulatory creature, but in a broader sense would also mean that, yes, you could kill what's already dead. In his own nightmarish corner of reality, however, Jack had always known that those bones, even if more than knocked apart, if pounded into *dust,* would have reassembled themselves and come at Henry again. Just as a six-inch knife blade driven all the way up into Bruce's chest had done nothing to stop or even slow down that hobgoblin...

They had spent most of Saturday morning and part of the afternoon watching cartoons with Rachel, because, what the hell, they had their coats, gloves, and everything else on... and if it happened, it happened.

If he came... he came.

PADDYWHACK

Just your typical small-town, middle-American family—where everyone wears catcher's masks...

Holds crucifixes in their gloved hands...

In their left hands, because, in their right, Mommy and Daddy carry knives.

Jack had finished his phone conversation with the enigmatic Elizabeth by eight-thirty, and by nine the stores were open—Saturday was *the* shopping day in Granger—and since it had been less than twelve hours since the last attack, he had risked a quick, whole-family excursion to Jowett's Hardware, where he picked up the two additional catcher's masks and, amazingly, two more crosses as well, in the form of Christmas tree-top ornaments (the catcher's masks were no surprise simply because it was Christmastime, but the odds on finding a cross in a hardware store were definitely longish, and Jack considered it a good sign).

The knives he already had. One regulation Navy sheath knife from World War II with a black, leather-ringed handle, given him by an uncle on his mother's side... and his favorite, the first and most cherished mail-order item he'd ever sent away for as a kid and then awaited anxiously for the next six weeks: his $1.99 Black Forest hunting knife, as advertised in *Popular Mechanics* magazine.

It was a beauty, the most satisfaction that two dollars, or ten times that amount, had ever bought him. The add said "hunting knife," but its shape was that of a dagger, a medieval dagger. With a silver-colored handle ending in a metal claw curled around a tiny globe. And a wickedly tapered blade so sharp-pointed that its tip would pass through the eye of a needle. Or open a way through flesh for the remaining six inches of blade as effortlessly as skewering a rotted melon—something it finally did, some twenty-odd years after its arrival in the mail. But not by Jack's hand, by his wife's, a person as nonviolent as the day is long. All to no avail.

This time they saw him coming, because Jack had insisted they sit with their backs to the wall. There was a momentary ripple in the sea of air between themselves and the television set, a shimmering not unlike that seen in the distance over a stretch of sun-heated road, only more pronounced. Then *he* appeared, his wicked, leering face made even more demonic by the way it was flattened and distorted as it stretched taut, then broke through the placenta barrier. And winked out of their vision.

Judy said, "Oh, *God*, please—"

Rachel cried, *"Mommyyy!"*

And then he was on them.

Or, more specifically, on Judy.

If he hadn't been so fucking *invisible* . . .

Jack tried to lunge in front of her, but he wasn't fast enough. Or Bruce went around him . . . or maybe over him; it was impossible to tell when you were fighting blind. Then Judy, who had wrapped her coat-sleeved arms around her head exactly as planned, was being knocked and buffeted from side to side with more force and violence than seemed possible from a creature Bruce's size. And she was moaning, a soft, continuous, almost keening sound that he was sure she was unaware of, but that, precisely because of its involuntary nature, tore at Jack's heartstrings as if she were sliding away from him down a steep mountainslope toward the edge of a bottomless ravine, calling his name. . . .

He wanted to kill the bastard dog! No, he wanted to do more than that, he wanted to hack and stab and hack and stab, with his uncle's Navy knife, till there was nothing left but quarter-inch pieces! His grip tightened on its handle until first the knuckles, then the fingers themselves turned white. But the action

PADDYWHACK

was too frenetic, too close, and he was afraid of cutting Judy instead.

And all the while, Rachel was hugging her knees and rocking back and forth next to them, crying—not loudly, but with a lost-soul quality—"Mommyyy! Mommyyy!"

It was then that Judy unwrapped an arm and a hand from around her head and plunged the Black Forest Special—given to her for its superior penetrating power—to the hilt in Bruce's invisible flesh, still keening her song of misery and despair.

Brave girl, *wonderful* girl...

Even in the chaos of the moment Jack knew the courage it must have taken her to perform that single act of violence, and he felt an upwelling of pure emotion—love, pride, savage elation—because he knew, just... *knew* that they had won. How could they not? He had always believed, before adulthood had taken his innocence, that the Black Forest was a blade for slaying dragons. And backed by a heart that was pure, by Judy's heart of hearts, it—

—did next to nothing.

There was a half second when everything stopped. Then she was transformed into the world's most morbidly effective mime.

The knife was wrenched this way and that, twisted, canted... while she struggled with all her might simply to hang on. It would have been obvious, even to the dullest of observers, that its blade was embedded in... something alive.

And then the catcher's mask she wore was knocked slightly askew, and Jack reached out with the cross he held and laid it against flesh he could not see, using the Black Forest as his guide.

Judy cried out, grabbed hold then with both her hands as the handle began to slant from the vertical, forcing her wrists to bend with it until its tip was pointed straight away from her... toward the locus in midair where Bruce had first appeared. For a frozen moment she looked for all the world like a fisherman who has hooked a Great White on a hand-held rod—and the giant shark has dived. Then the knife sprang to the vertical again, as the overwhelming force that had bent it was released.

A fraction of a second later they could see Bruce, his snarling, hate-filled face receding away from them, from beyond the barrier.

In another second he was gone.

Judy remained where she was, frozen, holding the knife almost at arm's length away from her. Then, as if it had suddenly become electric, she dropped it, began wiping her hands frantically on her jeans. Jack felt compelled to pick it up, knowing ahead of time what he would find.

It was wet, the blade especially, but the handle too. And the wetness was familiar—less viscous, more clinging, yet slippery at the same time, it was the wetness he had felt just last night leaking from his torn ear. Only then he'd been able to *see* the blood.

It should have given him satisfaction, but it didn't. Bruce bled but he did not die... And Jack was sure, if he hadn't been before, that the blade had gone all the way in, a wound that would have killed an ordinary dog, even a Great Dane, in far less than a minute. Yet the demon-dog hadn't been affected at all! Until Jack had touched him with the cross...

And if he needed any more convincing that he had to at least attempt the exorcism, and soon, he had merely to look at the paleness in Judy's haunted face. Or at the way Rachel hugged herself and looked at the air with wild eyes...

XXXV

SOON NOW, VERY SOON, HE WOULD DISROBE. THEN HE would walk into his aunt's bedroom—his aunt, who was maybe watching him from Hell—and sit down in a corner and wait.

At least it was Sunday. Barely.

Jack smiled at that. It was the kind of smile that might play upon the lips of a man with a sense for irony just before he faces a firing squad—as the guy tying the blindfold says, "Any last regrets?"

Despite the fact that she was lying with her head on his chest, Judy felt the smile and said, "What?"

"Oh, I don't know...I was just thinking, I guess. About how it all boils down to a gamble on God, the one part of my life I've always been least sure of."

They were lying together on the bed. Rachel lay next to them, sleeping, because it was after one A.M. The attack on Judy had occurred around two in the afternoon—approximately eleven hours ago.

Judy lifted her head so she could see him. *"I'm sure,"* she said, "that you're a good person, that He's on your side...What I'm not sure of is whether that makes a difference, is any kind of protection in *this* life. Maybe it only matters on Judgment Day."

"Judgment Day..." Jack said solemnly. "That point in time at which a decision is made as to whether or not you go to Hell. Which in my case is probably today if—"

"Oh God, Jack, don't *say* that! Don't go through with it!"

He saw the pure misery in her eyes. Wrong thing to say. Downright stupid; she felt bad enough as it was. Then he was verbally backpedaling. "No, wait. You don't see what I'm getting at. I agree, it doesn't seem to matter much whether you're good or bad, as far as who gets cancer and who the drunk hits head-on when he veers into oncoming traffic... but, like you, I think it *does* matter when it comes to who goes to Hell. And so in a twisted sort of way, maybe the fact that what I'm doing will unavoidably 'put my soul at risk' is the one assurance we've got that He'll notice and maybe step in!"

Shaky. But better than nothing. At least an obstacle that the twin armies of doubt and fear marching in her mind had to detour around. In *both* their minds, because he found he was listening to his own arguments. He worked to strengthen his position.

"God would never allow even a semi-good person to go to Hell."

She frowned, still skeptical. "As long as that person wasn't, you know... *testing* him."

"Is that what you think I'm doing? Testing him? I don't think so. Any more than I think a man who shoots and kills another man coming at his family with a knife is a murderer. He doesn't *want* to be put in that position, he's forced into it."

She didn't answer; she just put her head back down on his shoulder.

Maybe ten seconds passed. Then he said, "Besides ... your *mother*."

He half expected her to raise up again, but she didn't. She only asked, "What's that supposed to mean?"

"Isn't she the one who's always saying, 'The Lord helps those who help themselves'?"

She laughed half-heartedly, and he joined her. Not because it was anything close to world-class humor, but because it was a way of relieving tension. Then she raised up on one elbow and said, with a certain amount of wonder in her voice, "Oh, Jack, isn't this whole thing just... *awful?*" And they looked at each other and burst into *real* laughter, hysterical laughter, at the gross inadequacy of the word—like saying that the people who went down on the *Titanic* were having a "bad day."

Then, at some point, the laughter turned into crying. Soft crying, first from Judy, and then, as with the laughter, from Jack as well. And that was okay; in fact it was good, because he'd never felt so close as right now, not even when they were making love. Two people, one emotion. And that emotion was no longer doubt or fear so much as it was a touching of souls—and a grieving that they would soon have to part again.

Finally they stopped and simply lay there. Rachel, who lay next to her mother, mumbled something, whimpered in her sleep, and Judy took her hand. Then she took her husband's hand. The three of them, joined.

"I want you to know," she said, "that it's not your fault. No one's to blame."

He squeezed her hand. "Thanks. That... that helps. More than you can know."

"I haven't been very good about it."

"You've been great. You're still here, aren't you?" And the truth was, he meant it. Maybe part of it was their present intimacy—his love talking. But it also had to do with the way she'd handled Bruce that afternoon. Long ago he'd come to the conclusion that women, mothers especially, were the purest kinds of heroes. Not only did they allow themselves to care on so much deeper a level than most men, they faced what life threw at them—the same adversities men faced—armed for the most part with nothing more formidable than ten-inch biceps and physical powers proportionate to their size. Judy was a case in point, and his overactive imagination kept presenting him with an especially vivid image of the way she had looked while wielding the knife. To the musical accompaniment, within the theater of his mind, of Tammy Wynette singing "Stand by Your Man"...

And suddenly he was ready. As ready as he would ever be.

He rolled onto his side and gave his wife a lingering kiss. Then he sat up, abruptly, and said, "Time to... 'take my walk on the wild side.'"

She offered no protest—at least not a verbal one. But before he could stand, she quickly sat up, put both arms around his shoulders from behind, and silently pressed her cheek to the middle of his back. They sat that way for a long time, then Judy said, "See, the thing is...what if...you can't break back through? What if...you're stuck there?" She said it slowly, deliberately, because her voice was cracking every few words, and he knew what it must be costing her in terms of control.

"If Bruce can break through for hate," he said, as if the *force* of his words could make it so, "I can do it for love."

And then he held her for maybe the last time.

Twenty minutes later Jack sat in a corner of his aunt's bedroom. He sat on the floor because it allowed him to wedge himself into the corner space more tightly, thus making sure that he could see every bit of the empty air from which Bruce might emerge. One experience with having the dead animal come at him from a position beyond the parameters of his vision was enough.

PADDYWHACK

It was cold, though not so cold as the last time he'd lain in wait in this room—he suspected he would need all his physical resources if he were to do what he hoped, and he didn't want to get stiff. Cold enough, though, for a man wearing nothing but MSU gym shorts and a jockstrap. And an eight-inch crucifix taped securely to the underside of his left forearm in such a way that, with his hand resting in his lap, it was hidden (except for the tip ends of the crosspiece, which protruded on either side of his wrist).

He wanted to make himself as inviting a target as possible.

For the first few minutes his eyes moved constantly, but that only served to make him more on edge, more afraid. Each time they shifted to the next object, the next point of reference, it would seem as if the one they'd just left would move just a little. And when his eyes would flick back, it would look... *different*. Either slightly closer or a little farther away. Or changed in some indefinable but sinister way. Finally it got to the point where the pounding of his constantly stimulated heart quite literally "palsied" his vision, and he knew he would have to get a hold on himself to be able to spot the rippling effect, present in the air itself, that was his earliest warning of Bane Bruce's imminent approach. And when the inane but chilling thought struck him, upon focusing on the room's wallpaper (pink eighteenth century ladies carrying pink parasols on a cream-colored background), that it would look particularly bad splashed with *(his)* blood—as if it were raining the stuff—he knew it would be best if he looked at nothing at all, simply stared straight ahead and relied on his peripheral vision.

But that didn't stop his *mind* from working overtime, and the thing it kept skipping back to, like a broken record whose flawed surface always returns the needle to the same damnable line, was the possibility that these might be his last remaining minutes, *seconds* even, in this world. After which he would either be a) dead, b) alive but wandering around in some "dimension of the dead," or c) in Hell.

Worse than when his eyes wandered!

He began hyperventilating, and there was a painful knot in his stomach, as if everything there and below were trying to draw itself up beneath the dubious protection of his ribs and out of harm's way.

He tried thinking of Judy, of their love, but that only made things worse because, more fearful than death alone or even banishment to another dimension, was eternal separation from her. So he thought of Henry, whose memory would always inspire him to be more than he was.

And he thought of, ". . . you're braver than brave."

But none of it, *none of it*, was enough to keep his courage from leaking into his metaphorical boots once he was pulled through to the other side.

Bruce tried to kill him again around three A.M. The air moved, coalesced at one point so that it was more like an ultratransparent curtain. Then it clouded, the way egg white clouds when it is dropped in hot but not yet boiling water. And Bruce pressed his bug-eyed, snarling face to the other side of that curtain, kept pressing till it tore.

He was on Jack in an invisible instant, and rather than try to fend him off, Jack tucked his chin down as far as it would go between his hunched shoulders and embraced him. It was taking a chance because, not wearing his mask, his face was exposed. But with enough fear comes a quickening of one's reflexes, and no sooner had Bruce's teeth grazed his cheek than Jack raked both clawed hands down and in toward his middle, like a blind wide receiver fielding a pass.

PADDYWHACK

They caught hold of the scrabbling, biting animal he couldn't see and pinned it against the lower part of his chest.

There was a moment of triumph, or at least of relief, because what could the demon-teeth grab hold of across the relatively flat plane of his chest? Then he cried out as the invisible, death-cold muzzle burrowed its way into his left armpit and fangs impossibly long for an animal Bruce's size closed down on both sides of his pectoral muscle, up near where it inserts into the arm itself. It felt as if the teeth actually met and that part of his anatomy was being torn apart. And it *would* be—a great, huge mouthful would simply be uprooted, like so much hamburger plucked from the loaf—if Bruce pulled hard enough, if Jack *let* him pull hard enough. But this wasn't hamburger, this was living meat... and so he squeezed the devil-dog even tighter, which brought to play the very set of muscles Bruce was grinding his teeth on, and nothing, *nothing* compares to the pain of using a muscle while it is still impaled....

Then he must have lost it for a second or two, because the next thing he was conscious of was their being "pulled" through the barrier, still locked together, and he very quickly realized three things: First, that in his efforts to hug the animal ever closer, he'd brought the taped-on cross into maximum contact with its dead flesh. Second, that said cross still worked its magic. And last, that, like it or not, he was along for the ride.

Which is exactly what he'd planned and had never doubted the advent of (for reasons he did not fully understand). Except that now he would have gladly traded his grandmother, both his legs, and, God yes, his left pectoral, too, just to be wrong because

(*Nooo!*

God, where are—

Lostforeverlostnooo!)
now he was within reach of the Soulless One. The Torturer. The Devourer of Hope. He could feel *Its* greedy presence. And as soon as they were completely through the wall between this life and Hell's outer limits, the Ancient Evil breathed in and they were sucked toward *Its* planetwide mouth.

He screamed.

Inside his mind, the Devourer laughed.

Another breath and they were drawn closer by a distance measured best on a scale of despair.

Then he tried frantically to separate himself from Bruce, whom he could *see* now, reasoning even in his terror that it was the dog and not himself that served as iron to the magnet of Hell, no longer caring if the Devil's beast took a mouthful of his muscle and blood with him. He let go with both hands, expecting, bracing himself for the tearing of his flesh, but it never came. Instead Bruce loosed his hold, presumably to gain another, more lethal one. But in the same instant he let go, *It* breathed again, and Bruce fell away from Jack, plummeted into the distance the way one sky diver, whose chute has not yet opened, must appear to literally rocket away from his partner, whose chute has. Fell... up? Down? On a horizontal plane? There was no way to tell—no ground, no sun, no sky. No direction. Just movement toward or away from ultimate evil through an atmosphere thick as fog with lesser evil. And as empty of hope and love as the void between stars.

Drifting now toward, still definitely *toward*, damnation. More slowly now, but just as inexorably. Again the Father of Evil touched his mind, this time worse than laughing, whispering, with an obscene intimacy, promises of what *It* would do with him, once *It* had his soul.

Not as sin-stained, as easy to draw as the man-dog,

PADDYWHACK

It told him, but not pure either. NOT PURE, Jack Lerille. And each impurity a weight on your soul. It laughed again. Fall like a feather or fall like a rock, but you will *fall. To ME!*

All conscious hope leaked out of him then, and because God *is* hope, he was less in touch with Him than before, less pure... And so he fell faster.

He wanted to scream again; the beginnings of it clawed at his throat. But he knew that if he did, the last remnants of his sanity would pour out with the sound. It would be the scream of a man falling, not to his death, but to the moment of impact, of *dying*, stretched out over all eternity. Instead he cried out, instinctively—almost as instinctive as the scream— "Lord, help me! Deliver me from evil!" and reached out in the direction opposite toward which he fell.

And had his faith restored. Because God sent him Henry.

We are physical beings. Our noblest emotions, our every perspective, have as their basis the limitations of a flesh-and-blood existence; and though our thoughts may soar at times, they fly out from, and return to, our oft-too-solid bodies. Maybe that is why Jack perceived his answer, his salvation, in terms of a strong, very corporeal arm, reaching out for him through a blazing rictus of light, rather than as something more ethereal in nature. Just the arm; whatever lay beyond it, it was not his destiny to see. Yet. But he knew that arm, that enormously thick, callused hand...just as surely as he knew that Henry was with God now, an *extension* of God! And his heart leapt with joy.

All of this in the split-second marking the end of his prayer and the solid *thwhack* of his friend's hand seizing hold of him halfway up his wrist and abruptly halting his fall. "Catching" him, as if he were off a flying trapeze and Henry was the man who hangs waiting for him upside down...

Then he grasped Henry's wrist, too, so that they were double-clasped, and though the joy and relief of being reunited with The Man reduced his physical speech to an incoherent gibbering, these silent, more articulate words passed between them:

Henry! Oh, God, it's you!

The mental equivalent of an amused chuckle. Then: *You got that right. On both counts.*

Help me! You can—

Stand your ground! You can't fall 'less you think you can fall. The rest is up to you.

I can't!

You got to. Plus which... You know the rest.

Then he was grasping empty air, and because his mind was so filled with this, his second loss of Henry —with the loss, and not with what that meant in terms of his present predicament—he did not fall immediately. That fact slowly seeped into his consciousness, and with it, recollection of Henry's words: "...*'less you think you can fall.*"

All around him the atmosphere of evil, the malevolent cloudbanks whirled and roiled. There were far-off sounds of wailing, then screams. Then nothing at all, nothing but the sighing of an alien wind.

Then the fogs parted, and he could see below him, more clearly than before, the Face of Hell. Again he hovered on the brink of madness.

The Face was made from the torn limbs, severed heads, and eviscerated bodies of ten million souls, each part still alive, each part writhing in its separate agony. Yet they combined somehow, like the separate color dots on a poster, to form a single enormous face. And it was the face of universal hate, suffering, and depravity.

Its face.

The vision hit Jack the way the stench of a dead body hidden in a car trunk several weeks rises up and overwhelms the unfortunate who first opens that makeshift tomb. But that kind of shock is mostly to one's sensibilities...while what Jack now experienced was more akin to what that same person might feel if the rotting corpse were to reach up, grab him by the neck, and pull him down *into* the trunk with it...then close the lid. Terror. Terror and revulsion. The urge to gag, to retch, was strong in him, but even that almost instinctive reaction was frozen before it actually occurred—by the immensity of his fear. He was a bird, mesmerized by the weaving head of the snake. He was a fish, hooked, impaled upon an enormous gant hook, about to be pulled in. He

(*cannot fall 'less I think—Henry said, GOD said...*)

was a *man*...with a will of his own...and would not fall.

He slipped a little, hung motionless again—and did not fall.

That is when the Face bared *Its* teeth and spit Bruce back out at him.

He could see him coming, and it was like sitting on a cloud through which a just-launched rocket is destined to pass. First a speck, then larger, larger... Distance, speed meant nothing in Hell's anteroom. He had no idea whether the Face and Bruce were a thousand feet or a thousand miles away, and even if the latter, he had a feeling he would see...because *It wanted* him to see.

Then the fogs of evil (which he knew now were not so much a physical opacity as they were clouds of malignant, hate-filled thoughts so densely packed they registered visually) closed around him so that, forewarned and filled with sufficient dread, he would have to meet Bruce's attack blind.

It was like being submerged in an ocean of murky waters, bleeding, with a man-eating shark. Waters so murky you couldn't see the killer fish till he was almost on you. Yet you knew, absolutely *knew*, that he was coming for you... But from which direction? Below? In front? Behind? In the spinning, murky waters, you lost all bearings....

Out of the fog Bruce—a *flying* Bruce—appeared then disappeared so quickly that Jack didn't even know he'd been slashed till something hot dripped from his chin and jawline onto his bare chest. He put his hand to his right cheek. Twenty stitches, easy.

"Oh Goddd!" he groaned. "Oh, Je—"

Thhhhwunk. Bane Bruce hit him again, from somewhere south of his feet. It was like being caught with one of those suction-cup darts shot from a kid's toy pistol. Only this particular dart had a head the size of a cantaloupe, a brain filled with concerted hate, and inch-and-a-half, needle-sharp teeth. That buried themselves to the gums in the flesh of his inner thigh, just below the cuff of his gym shorts. From his aim—a little off—it was obvious he'd been hoping Jack would scream for him in soprano before he died, and—

Ha-ha, Bug-eyes, I got a steel jock.

Not funny. His mind was slipping again, from the sheer horror of it all, and, oh God, it hurt, it *hurt*, but he was afraid to pull him off because those teeth were dangerously close to the femoral artery, and if—

Bruce let go and zipped off into the gloom like a wingless bat.

Blood welled, but it did not jet or spray—only the pain did that.

"Oh Lord," Jack groaned again. Then, "*HEN*-ryyy, he's *KILL*ing meee," in a tone and meter gone almost casual, singsongy with (*YOO-hooo. I'm HO-ome*) madness.

sssssWISH. Bruce ripped a furrow from his left eyebrow to his ear, and he hardly saw him at all. Just a blur, here and gone. "God*da*—" he roared, then remembered who his friends were and changed it to "*Shit!*"

The cut wasn't as deep as the right cheek—he didn't think—but he didn't dare check it now. *Got to get my act together*, he told himself. Another part said, *Why? You're already dead and damned.*

He searched the impenetrable fog, straining as much with his mind as with his eyes this time, to catch even a glimpse of the demon-dog before he was on him again. And it worked! With his mind he could penetrate the concentrated evil, just a little, though it was like poking your head into sewer water to get a look at what was on the bottom. And before he "pulled back," gagging and gasping, he "saw" a darker shadow among the shadows coming straight at him like a fastball.

Just enough time to tuck his head down low between his shoulders, not even get his chin tucked tight, before the jaws meant for his throat impacted with the lower half of his face. His head was snapped backward with the force of it, and his eyes knocked out of focus. When they refocused again, a millisecond later, they were staring into Bruce's dead, hate-filled ones from inches away. In that instant, before Bruce bit down, he had time to observe there was a tiny worm of some sort dangling from the lid of the left one. Then the dead orbs rolled backward so that only the whites showed, and, simultaneously, his world exploded with fresh pain.

The pain was both inside and outside his mouth—Bruce had fastened on his chin, but the dog's two upper canines had caught Jack's lower lip, hooked it and pulled it down so it was part of the mouthful, and

Jesus, oh Jesus, he couldn't pull him *off* without shredding—

Then the dead animal, whose phlegm-covered nostrils were less than an inch from Jack's own now, breathed out, and it was the breath of something rotted, the putrid flatulence that distends the belly of run-over possums on country roads. In a panic of horror and revulsion, Jack slammed his fist against the side of Bruce's face.

His *left* fist, though he was right-handed.

It was by sheer luck, or by unprecedented quickness of thought (he could never really be sure which), that he connected in such a way that one end of the crosspiece portion of his taped-on crucifix penetrated the corner of Bruce's mouth.

For the first time since he'd watched the animal die two weeks ago, hung up on the shattered picture window, Jack heard the dog make a sound, and it was the canine equivalent of a scream of rage and pain. A sound so far removed from the *ky-yiing* cry that is a normal dog's first reaction to hurt, as a roar is from a whimper. No momentary lapse into cowardice here. No *fear*...

Nevertheless, Bruce let go.

But Jack did not.

Whether or not the use of the cross had been a conscious thing—the quick thinking of the "man of action" he had always wanted to be—grabbing hold of Bruce now, by his throat, was the deliberate act of a man who sees what is most likely his last chance... and goes for it.

"I rebuke thee! I rebuke thee! I rebuke thee!" he cried out, trembling with the terrible presumptive import of the moment now that it was at hand. "I adjure thee, Bruce Holmes, and summon thee forth in the name of God the Almighty from this animal!"

Time stood still in the anteroom to Hell. All movement stopped. The very fogs that surrounded them ceased in their roiling, became as rooted in their place as clouds in a photograph. All sound was erased too. And Bruce... Bruce was a frozen statue of a dog. It was, in fact, as if everything, everything except Jack himself, had suddenly been made part of some immense, decidedly macabre 3-D picture. And in that moment Jack knew more fear than in all the cumulative terrors of a lifetime—including those moments when he had looked upon the Face of Hell. Fear of God.

Forgive me, Lord, he prayed fervently, frantically, and silently. *I put my trust in You.*

Then whatever needed deciding was decided, and life and death and everything in between was resumed again. Bruce squealed like a stuck pig and struggled against Jack's hands with a strength that was absolutely impossible in an animal his size. Jack felt like a child trying to contain a high-pressure fire hose. He was whipped back and forth at will, and it was all he could do to keep the demon's teeth, which had somehow lengthened so that now they resembled miniature curved knives, from grabbing hold of him again; but still he hung on.

Then, as quickly as it had begun, it ended. Bruce grew motionless again. A crack, then a gaping wound appeared on his bestial throat, just above Jack's stranglehold, in much the same manner as the ground opens in an earthquake. It was an exact duplicate of the damage done by the shattered window, and, forgetting the awful fear of mere moments *(minutes? days?)* ago, which had frightened him into perfect sanity, Jack fought back a hysterical giggle: Bruce was cracking up.

How his mind made the deductive leap from that thought to the sudden conviction that the exorcism must be working was another thing to marvel over later; but it did, and with far less diffidence than before, he shouted, "Again, I adjure thee, Bruce Holmes, in the Lord's name be *gone*! In God the Almighty's name depart from this animal, remove your soul and never enter here again!"

Bruce only shook in his hands. And bled. But it was a feeble shaking compared to what had gone down before.

Then Bruce did something that brought Jack face to face with the fears of his childhood: He huffed, and he puffed. Like the Big Bad Wolf.

Huge breaths, enormous breaths, as if he were trying to pump himself up to something greater than he was; and because the magically reopened gash in his throat cut through his windpipe as well, each exhalation sprayed small amounts of foam-flecked blood and other wet debris directly onto Jack's face. So that, at first, he thought the moaning he heard was from himself, an unconscious expression of the revulsion he felt. Then he realized it came from Bruce. But that was impossible; the beast's whole vocal assembly was in gaping ruins!

Bruce Holmes! he thought, with an equal mix of terror, triumph, and awe. *Dear Lord, he's in there! Just like Elizabeth—*

Without even finishing the thought, and with a voice that shook with emotion, he shouted again, "I summon thee, Bruce Holmes! I *command* thee, in God's name, the God of Abraham and Moses, to depart from this animal at once!"

The groaning became a high-pitched shriek, then a steady, loathsome stream of curses so foul and filled with hate that, along with the fact that they emanated from the slashed throat of a dead dog, they were almost enough to make Jack let go his hold.

"Let me go or join me when you die!" the voice now hissed, ending its cursing abruptly. And it was

the voice a cobra might use, if it could speak. *"Here! In this animal! YOUR soul, ITS savage mind... as it rips your daughter, eats your wife ALIVE!"*

Jack faltered even more, moaned inside. *Not Rachel! Not—*

Then he remembered that this place was home for all lies.

"Be gone, Bruce Holmes," he said in an even voice, forcing himself, *willing* himself, to an absolute faith in the power of good over evil. "In God's name. Remove yourself from this animal and leave us in His peace! Depart! At once!"

This time the scream was the pitch and timbre of a man with both hands caught in a meat grinder: still alive but not, definitely not, wanting to be. The gaping wound in Bane Bruce's throat opened wider, like a second mouth, to let out the scream.

Wider still.

Finally it cracked all the way around, except for a single piece of skin, and Bruce's moon-eyed head flapped backward onto his shoulders in the flip-top box fashion a dreaming Rachel would have been wholly familiar with.

And the body, somehow still animate despite its near decapitation, convulsed then relaxed, convulsed then relaxed. Something... *something* that was less than a solid and more than a gas, was squeezed up from the bloody hole where Bruce's head used to be.

Something...

Something both hideous in its nature and beautiful in its design, in all the things it *could* have been...

And with each convulsion, each spastic heaving of the body, it grew, expanded like some spectral balloon, so that eventually it resembled a second head. A head without features, a formless head, with the shape constancy of an amoeba. A ghost's head... if one believes those restless spirits are, in fact, visual manifestations of dead men's souls.

Jack believed. Believed he was witnessing the eternal soul of Bruce Holmes—or at least part of that soul, if Elizabeth were correct in her theory. He also believed that if he had the courage to stare into its faceless face and order it to Hell, he and his family would be rid of Bane Bruce once and for all. So he stared into its faceless face...

And was caught by its
(EVIL)
grisly beauty. Mesmerized by the sheer depravity there. It took his breath away. His will.

"Be gone," he said, with no real fire at all. "In God's name."

Not until you know what it is you pass judgment on, the whirling, twirling noncolors in its fathomless depths seemed to say. *Touch me.*

Without wanting to, and seemingly in slow motion, he let go of Bruce with one hand, watched that hand pull back then tentatively reach forward, fingers extended, so that it passed through the nonsolid boundaries of Bruce Holmes's soul. It was like watching somebody else's hand, perhaps a hand on a movie screen, as it reaches, inexorably, for the knob of the door it must not open. And all the while he was shaking his head and saying as if it were a chant, "No, no, no, no, *noooo!*"

For a moment nothing happened. Then everything happened. He was falling through evil, *drowning* in evil. He *was* evil. He was everything Bruce Holmes had ever been: wicked, calculatingly cruel... hater of women and children... and he was going to kill himself, remove the cross from his wrist and shove it through his right eye and into his brain because he *(I!)* was BAD,

No, good! GOOD!

and—

(what the—?)

—and the almost-severed head of Bruce-the-dog— still alive, still very much part dog, with a dog's instincts and a dog's memory for enemies—flipped forward again, having spied the extended fingers, and bit at them. And it made not a lick of difference whether those fingers were now governed by the mentations of Bruce Holmes or Jack Lerille, their reflexes were the same: the hand was snatched back from the balloon soul.

But it was not solely the loss of physical contact with Bruce Holmes's anima that made Jack his own man again, it was also the shock, the uncanny, unnerving horror of witnessing the head, severed from anything that could possibly have given it power of movement—every tendon, every muscle, everything it had been anchored to except a tiny strip of skin— still *move*, still flip back into place, like the closing of a suitcase. It cut through whatever spell Holmes had cast on him and twanged on some primitive, superstitious nerve that even the fact of Bruce's flying or that he was two week's dead hadn't touched upon.

For perhaps five seconds he stared in horrified amazement at the thing he now grasped by one hand, which now more than ever appeared to have two viable heads. Stared first and longest at the snarling, teeth-snapping face of Bruce-the-dog. Then, with a sidelong glance—because he was wary of viewing it straight on anymore—at the evil essence of Bruce Holmes, which had been compressed and pushed aside when the dog had "closed its lid."

The Essence said, *"Please?"* inside Jack's mind.

The dog head floated off its moorings just a little, made a muscleless turn sideways and bit at it.

The man, whom the Man would have been proud to call his son, decided he had seen enough blackest magic for a lifetime, and said with perfect faith that he would be obeyed, "GO TO HELL, BRUCE HOLMES! IN GOD'S NAME, LEAVE THIS ANIMAL AND GO TO HELL!"

And, almost simultaneously, no less than four things happened:

The malevolent fogs parted, revealing once again the Face of Hell below.

Bruce's teeth grabbed hold of Bruce Holmes's soul as if, just for him, the phantom being had suddenly been rendered solid flesh.

Bruce Holmes screamed a scream so filled with terror and loss that, for the mere fact of death, it would have been melodrama.

And both heads, spectral and doggy flesh alike, were ripped from the body Jack still held—ripped by the same overwhelming force with which Jack himself had been pulled through the barrier—and sucked, *rocketed*, toward the Face's wide-open mouth.

"Go to Hell..." Jack said again, watching them fall. But this time he said it in an awed, contemplative way, adding almost as an afterthought but still with a certain amount of vindication, "...Bane Bruce."

He turned away then, before the Face received them, and just in time to witness the headless body wink out of existence. Somehow that minor miracle didn't surprise him; instead it raised the inane question: If he were to open Bruce's grave, would the body be with or without its head? And *that*, by its very inconsequence, made him wonder why he was not more elated—he had won! Bruce was gone forever, he knew that with absolute certainty! He—

—felt something watching him. Turning back toward the Face, he was just in time to see *Its* eyes, made from the plucked-out eyes of murderers and half demons, roll with cruel amusement then fix on him again.

Where are you now, Jack Lerille? they said by the way they whirled and twirled. *Between Heaven and Hell? If Heaven is your little girl's arms around your neck, or joining with your wife, then you've damned yourself, because I'll never let you back through!* Then *It* laughed obscenely, and when *It* had finished, *Its* eyes blazed, screamed the word again: *NEVER!*

The cloudbanks whirled and roiled.

The sounds of screaming, wailing; then nothing, nothing but the sighing of an alien wind.

Jack listened, watched. Then he laughed back at *It*, because he knew, he *knew*—

I've got friends, he said with his mind. *As long as I believe*...

—how things worked in this place now. Maybe not the exact means, but at least the end result. He had only to ask.

He asked.

And was, finally, elated. With his answer. *More* than elated. Sweet triumph, fierce joy, proud love coarsed through him in little electric thrills that left goose bumps because—

—the Marines had landed.

—amid the jeers and catcalls of his tormentors, a blinded Samson places a God-powered hand against each of the temple's two main pillars and shoves mightily. And the first groaning cracks stun the multitudes to silence.

—Henry "Dozer" Mallory, the way he must have been forty years ago, before a Jap bullet changed the course of things—the way he *is NOW*—steps through the mists looking unstoppable in his cleats and pads and says, "You ready, Jackie-boy? Coach says up the middle one 'one.' I'll bash a hole for ya—all you got to do is follow me through, smooth as snot, and you're home free."

And Jack is crying as he runs because he's so proud

to be part of Henry's dream, so happy for the way things have turned out for *both* of them...and because the run itself, at least Henry's part of it, is the most beautiful, most perfect, most God-*blessed* inspiring thing he will ever see. And then he was
Home.
Home free!

Epilogue

IT IS THE DAY AFTER. THE FIRST DAY OF THE REST OF Jack Lerille's life. And though he hurts more than he has ever hurt before, and looks like someone whose face exploded then was stitched back together, he knows that both the pain and his facial resemblance to a road map won't last forever. It's how he feels inside that counts. And inside he feels more "healed" than he's felt since an off-Broadway play named *Video* folded in New York four months ago.

There are two things he feels compelled to do, though, that will make the healing process complete. Two things.

The first is as easy to accomplish as picking up the telephone. Dial 747 (like the plane), then L-O-V-E.

She answers on the third ring: "Hello?"

Oddly, he feels shy, even hesitates a few seconds. Then: "I think you should marry him, Elizabeth."

"What? Who—"

"The guy who calls you Jenny. You should marry him. You know it and I know it, and I bet he's even asked. And the only reason you say no is some weird notion you've got that if you keep punishing yourself long enough, things will be made right. Well, I'm here to tell you things *are* right. They're fixed. And you're really ignorant if you keep throwin' it all away."

For the span of a few seconds there was nothing but silence. Then he could hear her breathing. Little "hitch kicks" of emotion that did not quite equal crying. Yet. "Oh...*Jack*," she managed finally. "He's...? Bruce is...?"

"Gone. Exorcised. You were right. About everything. You should take that as a sign."

Another prolonged silence, save for the breathing. Then, in a small, quiet voice: "God bless you, Jack."

He smiled. It hurt his lip. It hurt his cheek. There was, in fact, nothing from the neck up that it didn't hurt. "He has. You too... if you'll let Him." Then he hung up. Because there was still one more thing he had to do.

The marker, which had been purchased for him by his sons, was wider than it was tall, six inches thick and sturdy-looking. Beneath the name and date it went like this:

At the bottom of this stone lies a big, big MAN.

It was chiefly that, those few simple words, taken in paraphrase from Jimmy Dean's decades-old hit recording, "Big Bad John," that took Jack by surprise, closed up his throat so that, for a while, he was unable to say what he'd come here to say. So he just stood there, mute, at the foot of Henry's grave, and thought about how they fit the man so well. And when he *was* able to speak again, he tried to put things just as simply, just as straightforward as the inscription— the way he might have put them had Henry really been there, really been able to hear. Because he was. And he could.

"I, uh... didn't get a chance to say thanks yet," he started out. "And I need to do that."

He paused.

"Thanks. Thanks for... being a friend. And for... showing me what being a hero is all about."

Again he paused, swallowed, and drew a ragged breath.

PADDYWHACK

"It's about you, Henry. You're the hero. And I... just wanted to tell you that in case you—"

But he never finished. Because, at that precise moment, a vision, a miraculously clear, supernaturally real and alive flashback played through his mind with all the perfect replication of a television instant replay. It was like being there, *again*, as Henry leaned forward in his chair the night before he died... hearing him, *again*, as he said with grim earnestness, *What's a hero, Jack? By my calculation it's someone who's afraid or hurt or tired... or just plain thinks 'I can't,' that keeps chuggin' on through anyway. The 'I can't' is at the very heart of it*. Then, in the vision, Henry paused a moment, before he said, *You got to be a hero, Jack*.

And because Jack was like most people, who tend to miss their strengths just as surely as they see right past their weaknesses, he didn't quite grasp the significance of what "Henry" was trying to tell him. Yet. And he simply answered back, "I'll try."

Do You Dare Enter the Crypt of... St. Martin's Horror?

KATE'S HOUSE
Harriet Waugh
_____ 90142-9 $3.50 U.S.

TALES OF THE DARK
Lincoln Child, editor
_____ 90339-1 $3.50 U.S.   _____ 90345-6 $4.50 Can.

TALES OF THE DARK 2
Lincoln Child, editor
_____ 90769-9 $3.50 U.S.   _____ 90770-2 $4.50 Can.

TALES OF THE DARK 3
Lincoln Child, editor
_____ 90539-4 $3.50 U.S.   _____ 90540-8 $4.50 Can.

BLACK ASHES
Noel Scanlon
_____ 90270-0 $2.95 U.S.   _____ 90271-9 $3.95 Can.

THE CRONE
Bill Garnett
_____ 90747-8 $3.50 U.S.

Publishers Book and Audio Mailing Service
P.O. Box 120159, Staten Island, NY 10312-0004

Please send me the book(s) I have checked above. I am enclosing
$ _____ (please add $1.25 for the first book, and $.25 for each
additional book to cover postage and handling. Send check or
money order only—no CODs.)
Name _____
Address _____
City _____ State/Zip _____
Please allow six weeks for delivery. Prices subject to change
without notice.